WILL IN SCARLET

MATTHEW CODY

A YEARLING BOOK

Visit us on the Web! randomhouse.com/kids

Educators and librarians, for a variety of teaching tools, visit us at RHTeachersLibrarians.com

The Library of Congress has cataloged the hardcover edition of this work as follows:
Cody, Matthew.
Will in scarlet / by Matthew Cody.
p. cm.
Summary: In the late 1100s, thirteen-year-old Will, the future Lord of Shackley, is exiled to Sherwood Forest, where he meets Robin Hood and the Merry Men and bands with them to try to retake Shackley Castle.
ISBN 978-0-375-86895-5 (trade) — ISBN 978-0-375-96895-2 (lib. bdg.) —
ISBN 978-0-375-89980-5 (ebook)
[1. Inheritance and succession—Fiction. 2. Robbers and outlaws—Fiction.
3. Robin Hood (Legendary character)—Fiction. 4. Middle Ages—Fiction.
5. Great Britain—History—John, 1199–1216—Fiction.] I. Title.
PZ7.C654Wil 2013 [Fic]—dc23 2012042503

ISBN 978-0-375-87292-1 (pbk.)

Printed in the United States of America
10 9 8 7 6 5 4 3 2 1
First Yearling Edition 2014

For Alisha, Willem, and mischief-makers everywhere

—M.C.

CAST OF CHARACTERS

The Throne of England and its allies

RICHARD I, THE LIONHEART—King of England, sailing back to England after having fought in wars overseas

PRINCE JOHN (LACKLAND)—Younger brother of King Richard, ruling England in Richard's absence

SIR GUY OF GISBORNE, THE HORSE KNIGHT—Mercenary captain in John's employ

HIS MANSERVANT—Sir Guy's Bribes Master

MARK BREWER, THE SHERIFF OF NOTTINGHAM—Prince John's recently appointed sheriff of the county of Nottinghamshire. Longtime friend of the Shackley family.

At Shackley Castle, on the edge of Nottinghamshire

WILL SHACKLEY—Heir to Shackley Manor. Age thirteen

RODRIC SHACKLEY—Will's father and lord of Shackley Manor. Currently traveling with King Richard

LADY KATHERINE—Will's mother

GEOFF SHACKLEY—Will's uncle, brother to Rodric and regent of Shackley Manor while Lord Rodric is away

SIR OSBERT—An old knight, Will's favorite, in service to Shackley House.

HUGO BLUNT—Shackley family steward and chamberlain

MILO—A stableboy, Will's playmate

JENNY—A kitchen maid.

NAN—Will's nurse

Outlaws, bandits, and ne'er-do-wells of Sherwood Forest

MUCH THE MILLER'S SON—Scout and sneak-thief, the youngest member of the outlaw band the Merry Men

GILBERT THE WHITE HAND—Leader of the Merry Men

JOHN LITTLE, ROB, STOUT, AND WAT CRABSTAFF—Members of the Merry Men

TOM CROOKED—Leader of Crooked's Men, a rival gang of bandits

THE PARDONER—A scurrilous churchman

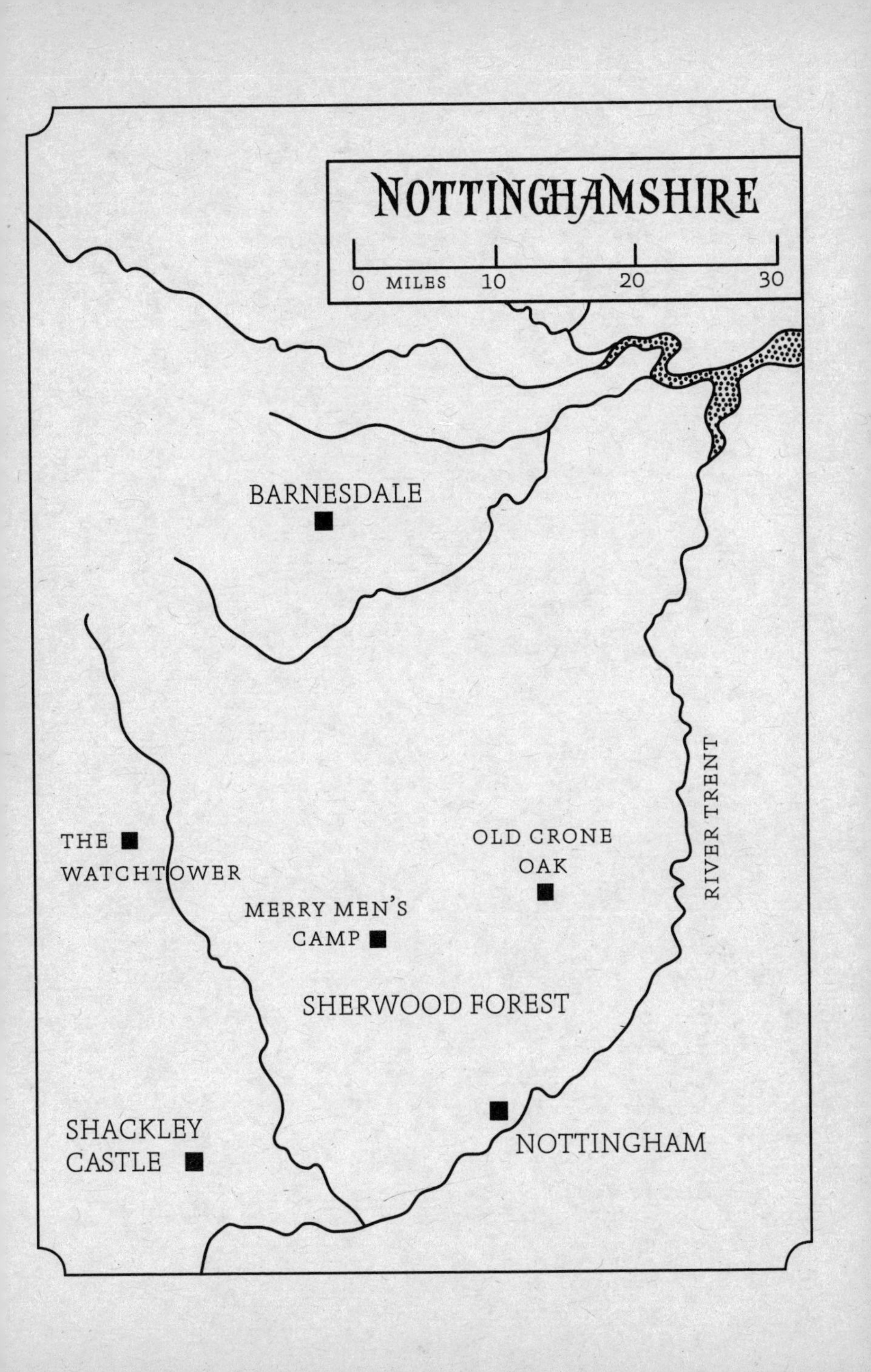
NOTTINGHAMSHIRE
0 MILES 10 20 30
BARNESDALE
RIVER TRENT
THE WATCHTOWER
OLD CRONE OAK
MERRY MEN'S CAMP
SHERWOOD FOREST
SHACKLEY CASTLE
NOTTINGHAM

Part I

The Wolfslayer

ONE

Killing wolves is supposed to teach me to be a great lord of men?
Aren't there any books on the subject?
—William Shackley

In the year 1192, while King Richard the Lionheart was on his way home from fighting in far-off Jerusalem, the lords of Shackley Castle were out hunting wolves by moonlight. Bitter cold, an aching backside, and hours of fruitless searching had made the oldest, Sir Osbert, irritable. Will Shackley, the youngest, listened patiently as the old knight passed the time by trying to scare the britches off the lad.

"It's this bloody weather," said Osbert, beating the crust of frost out of his enormous beard. "Drives them beasts out of Sherwood looking for something, anything, to eat. Bold enough to challenge a man on horseback, even."

He leaned forward in his saddle and winked at Will. "Or a young lord. They wouldn't bother with a tough piece of gristle like me when they can have a juicy young lordling. That's why I'm not riding up there with your uncle. I'm sticking close to you, Wolfbait!"

At thirteen years old, Will was used to the old knight's teasing. He'd been raised on it.

"Well, while the wolves are devouring me," answered Will, "I'll be sure to holler loud enough that you'll know where to swing that mighty sword of yours. Wouldn't want your old eyes to mistake a shrub for the enemy. Again."

Osbert sat back in his saddle for a moment before snorting and breaking into a huge grin.

"No, we wouldn't want that," laughed the old man. "Wouldn't want that!"

Osbert laughed himself into a coughing fit that ended in a string of curses. He spit out something wet and nasty-looking onto his sleeve. *Osbert shouldn't be out in this weather,* thought Will. But the stubborn knight wouldn't be left behind. Bold Sir Osbert had never shied away from a battle, even if it was only against a bunch of skinny, half-frozen wolves. But his best days were long past, and he'd traded in battle cries for complaints of stiff joints and damp weather.

Will couldn't imagine the flesh-and-blood enemy who could make an end of the tough old warrior, but this night's biting cold just might.

"I'd hoped it might snow," said Will, looking up at the darkening sky. The clouds had hung gray and threatening all day, but the ground remained dry as dust. "We'd have an easier time following their tracks in fresh snow."

"Ah, Geoff will track them, snow or no. He's part hound, that uncle of yours. And the moon's rising to light our ride home. But a blanket of Christmas white would've been nice, taken my mind off this freezing wind at least. I'm chattering what few teeth I have left down to nubs!"

There hadn't been so much as a snowflake in England this year, despite the terrible cold. But the trees, thick with hoarfrost, still glittered white in the moonlight. The wind blew easily through the bare branches and cut through leather and furs.

This was a sort of cold that settled deep in your bones, and all across England people were suffering for it.

"Weather like this'll have those wolves knocking on the doors of your father's own castle," said Osbert. "That's *after* they've eaten all the peasants, of course. Natural order of things that the peasants go first. Only fitting."

The old man chuckled at his own joke, but his laughter sounded hollow and out of place among those dark trees.

Squinting into the woods, Osbert muttered, "Useless. Not a living thing stirring in these woods. Maybe they've fled back to Sherwood to hunt bandits. Nothing for them here."

Will nodded and tried to picture these trees in the summer, green and lush. These woods belonged to his father, Lord Rodric Shackley. Lord Rodric had sailed off with King Richard to fight in the Crusades, and he'd been gone fighting overseas for over two years. But now the king was coming home, and Will's father with him.

Will and his playmate, Milo, fled here to his father's woods whenever Nan came at them with the kitchen spoon. The last time had been just a few months ago, when they'd stolen into the molasses. Over the course of a few days, the two of them had nearly emptied the larder. It hadn't been hard for Nan to guess the culprits—a pair of sticky boys with stomachaches were easy to spot in a castle full of knights. They'd come here to escape her spanking spoon, but the trees had looked so much friendlier then. On a cold winter's night like this, the branches reached for you like bony fingers, the comforting hum of crickets was replaced with the howling wind, and instead of a sack of stolen sweets, Will now wore a heavy sword.

The wolves had gotten overly bold this season, coming all the way from Sherwood Forest into his father's woods and stealing into farms to threaten man and beast alike. People told stories of winters gone by when the wolves of Sherwood had been so thick the men had to ride out to meet them on the field of battle, like an invading army. Osbert claimed the wolves had even stitched their own war banners from rabbit hides. Osbert liked to tell stories.

The women back at the castle told different stories. Will had heard them this morning as he loitered near the kitchens. These weren't natural wolves, they whispered. These wolves were accursed, sent from the pit to punish England for her many sins. A farmer, they said, had cut off the paw of one of the beasts as it came for his hens. He wrapped the thing up in a sackcloth to bring to Lord Geoffrey, but when he delivered the bloody package, the paw had gone missing and in its place was a human hand.

Who actually saw this? Nan, Will's nurse, had asked in her characteristic suffer-no-fools voice. No one, it turned out. But they'd all heard it was true.

"You ever seen a pack hunt?" asked Will, eyeing the trees as they passed.

"I've seen worse than that," answered Osbert. "I've seen what they leave behind, which is precious little, I can tell you."

"It's the howling that chills you," added Hugo, his family's skinny steward. "More so than this winter's air. A single howl gets your attention; then the chorus starts. That's when you know they've got your scent. When you've gone from hunter to hunted."

The men grew quiet. Will was listening for howls on the wind when Osbert loudly announced to the hunting party that he'd grown cold enough to fart snow.

The frozen men burst into laughter, their icy beards cracking with their smiles. It only grew worse when Hugo told Osbert to stop exaggerating and Osbert invited the steward to lean close and see for himself. He threatened to fart up a blizzard for him.

Will laughed until his face hurt, but it helped to unclench the fear he'd been holding in his gut ever since they'd ridden into these woods. He was wiping away the tears of laughter before they could freeze to his cheeks when his uncle Geoff rode up next to him.

"Old Osbert tells the same jokes he told your father and me when we were boys," he said. "But somehow they never get old."

Will looked at the white-haired knight hunched over in his saddle, his hands so arthritic and curled that they could barely grasp the reins. But those big arms could still swing a sword with more strength than Will could muster.

"Just how old is he?" Will asked, and not for the first time.

"Haven't you heard? Sir Osbert dined with the Romans, just so he could tell Caesar his roads were too bumpy." Geoff shook his head. "Truth is, he was little more than a lad when he first rode to war with your grandfather, God rest his soul. He and Osbert were boys together. Around about your age, I'd imagine."

Will winced at his uncle's reference to his being a boy. He knew that's what the men here thought of him. The only son and heir of Lord Rodric was a boy overly fond of his play games, and of trouble in general. And who'd been shielded from manhood by an overprotective mother while his father fought alongside good king Richard against the infidels. Will knew his father's men were fond of him, even if they teased him mercilessly, but he also knew they feared he lacked the spine to rule.

That was why he was out here tonight. Talk was getting out of hand. Men were wondering, out loud, if Geoff might be the better choice, and Geoff would have none of it. As Rodric's younger brother, he wasn't officially in line, and he certainly wasn't a man of ambition. Geoff reveled in being free to hunt and fight without worrying about the responsibilities of leadership. But while Lord Rodric was away to war, Geoff's rule as regent had been strong and fair. He'd become more popular than ever, and if Will failed to show his mettle . . .

"How's the armor?" Geoff asked. Will wore a shirt of chain links beneath his thick fur-lined cloak. The shirt alone weighed thirty pounds. Add to that the plate-metal greaves on his legs and the gauntlets on his hands, and it was exhausting work just getting on and off his horse.

"Metal's cold," said Will. "Even through my underclothes. Glad I don't have to armor my arse."

His uncle chuckled. "I meant did you have anyone check it after you strapped it on. Won't do much good if it's dangling open."

Will felt his cheeks warm, despite the weather. "I know how to armor myself, Uncle. I do it whenever I train in combat lessons."

"I didn't mean . . . Look, I'm just keeping an eye on you, understand? Your father will be back in England by the thaw, so just try to stay alive that long? As a favor to me?"

Will's father would be home by spring, if not sooner. After two years, it seemed hard to imagine, but they'd gotten word. King Richard's crusade was over. He and his knights, Will's father included, were sailing back to England. Will's heart was full of joy at the thought of his father's return, but also a bit of fear. What if he was a disappointment to his father? At thirteen, he was now of age, and expected to act like the heir to his father's title. That meant he should spend his days at study, he should join his uncle on his hunts, he should learn politics and history and governance. He should stop stealing Nan's molasses.

They rode on for a few minutes without saying much.

Eventually, Geoff motioned to Will to follow him, and the two trotted to the front of the line, out of earshot of the rest. They were getting deep into the woods now. The trails here were narrow and crowded for a troop of men on horseback. Stinging branches whipped against exposed cheeks and necks. At least Osbert would have something else to complain about besides the cold.

"This trail is a game path," said Geoff. "And there's wolf spoor all along here. I'm sure we'll find them soon."

Will peered at the trail, but in the night one patch of fallen leaves looked like another. How his uncle could track that well in these conditions was a mystery, but Geoff had a nose for this that couldn't be denied. A born huntsman.

"I suppose you heard me arguing with Lady Katherine earlier," Geoff said, not taking his eyes from the trail.

Will nodded. His uncle and his mother had had disagreements before, but nothing like their row today. Voices had been raised, and his mother had reverted back to her native French to call Geoff names that would make Osbert blush.

"She thinks you're not ready to be out here with us tonight," said his uncle.

"She thinks I'm still a boy."

Geoff let out a long sigh. "And she's right. On this, your mother has right on her side. No question."

Will looked at his uncle, but the regent of Shackley held up his hand. "She's right as a mother, but she's wrong as the lady of Shackley. You are the son of Rodric Shackley, and heir to his house. You must be seen as such. I'm not your father, but I owe it to him to see that you are ready to rule. When he sailed off with Richard, you were still a boy, but when he returns, you'll be a man. Your days as young Will Scarlet, scourge of the castle servants, are over. You'll be Lord William before you know it."

Young Will Scarlet. Nobody but Geoff called him that. A play on his name and a tease. Whenever he'd been brought before his father for some terrible offense against Nan or the kitchen staff, he'd always blushed a bright crimson. Geoff said it was his tell, and that they always knew when he'd been up to no good by his shade of red. Will's father would grow grave and disappointed, while Geoff smirked over his shoulder.

Young Will Scarlet's rear will match his face after Nan's done with her spanking spoon! Geoff would sing.

"Killing wolves is supposed to teach me to be a great lord of men?" asked Will. "Aren't there any books on the subject?"

"No," said Geoff. "But sharing in your men's hardship, their danger, that's a start. And they are your men, Will. Despite Osbert's taunts, or even mine. We will be yours to command one day."

Geoff put his hand on his nephew's shoulder and gave it a squeeze. "Still, stay near me or Hugo tonight. We'll find the pack if Osbert's bellyaching hasn't scared them all back to Sherwood already. But if we do catch up with them, hold your reins tight and stay clear. Prince John's been offering real silver for wolf pelts, and hunters have been driving them out of their woods to haunt us. Cold and hunger will make any creature desperate, Will. Add the fear of the sword, and that makes them dangerous."

As his uncle steered his charger, Samson, over the frozen ground, Will tried to follow the same path. Samson was a destrier, a warhorse, who'd carried Geoff over many hunts, and he was sure-footed even on this icy track. But Will's horse was a young mare named Bellwether, and although Will loved her, she was still skittish. Not that Will blamed her. This wasn't a fit night for any creature.

"Uncle," he said, checking to make sure the men were

still out of earshot. "In the kitchens this morning, I heard the women talking."

"Yes, they do that. Passes the time, I'm told."

"No, they were talking about the farmer who came to visit you the other day with a . . . hand wrapped in a sackcloth. They said that when he'd cut it off, it had belonged to a wolf."

His uncle could barely suppress his chuckle. "A wolf? Is that what they said? Well, really . . . The man's name is Gamel, a tenant in terrible debt. Gamel, it would seem, listens to the very wrong kind of advice, because someone told him that if he were too maimed to work his land, he'd be relieved of his obligations to his lord."

Will turned this over in his head. "So, this Gamel . . . he cut off his own hand? To escape his debt?"

Geoff shook his head and sighed. "Not as thick as all that. But nearly. No, he tried for just his thumb. Didn't even manage that properly, though. All he brought me was the knuckle upward. Tell the kitchen gossips that it was a half thumb that had once belonged to a half-wit, not a wolf."

Of course the wolf story wasn't true. How could Will have believed the kitchen women's tales? And yet, for a moment, Will couldn't tell if he was relieved or disappointed.

They rode until the woods opened onto a large stretch of lonely fields and moorland. Somewhere on the other side of those vast moors lay Sherwood Forest, and not even the brave knights of Shackley House would venture into that far-off forest. Bandits and worse called Sherwood home. Worse than wolves, to be sure. It was said that the devil himself walked beneath those boughs on moonless nights and turned men into wild beasts.

But Sherwood was far away still, and here, out of the trees, the full moon was easily visible in the clear sky. The ground frost reflected the silvery light so that the earth seemed covered in riches just there for the taking. If they weren't so miserably frozen, the men might have paused to appreciate the beauty, but as it was, they were eager to turn south toward home. Back to warm fires and heavy blankets and bed.

Geoff had just given the signal to turn back when Hugo held up his hand. Sitting up tall in his saddle, he tensed, listening for something.

"What is it?" asked Will's uncle.

"He's realized he's frozen off his necessaries and wants to backtrack to find them, my lord," laughed Osbert.

"Quiet!" said Geoff.

They listened for a moment. At first all Will heard was the wind on the hills; then he heard something more. An animal howl.

"They're on the moor," said Hugo, hefting his boar spear.

"Probably laughing at us while we gathered nettles in our backsides all night long," said Osbert, scowling at the woods.

Geoff steered Samson to the front. The rest of the horses seemed anxious, pawing at the ground. Bellwether was already straining against her reins. Only Samson stood iron-still, steadfast.

"Hugo, you take that closest hill," said Geoff. "See if you can't flush them out to us."

"Won't need to, my lord," said Hugo. And he pointed to the closest rise.

Will squinted. Even with the bright moon, it was hard to make out details in the dark. The hill's crest was a ragged silhouette of rocks, but when several of the rocks moved . . .

"They've got our scent," said Geoff.

No sooner had his uncle spoken than the moor began to echo with howls. Two, three, more and more.

That's when you know you've gone from hunter to hunted.

"God's blood," swore Osbert. "How many are there?"

"Even half dead with hunger, they won't try six men together on horseback," said Geoff. "Stay in formation and use the boar spears. Watch your horses' flanks."

The pack rushed down the hill but stopped within a stone's throw of the mounted men. Their hackles raised, they snarled and snapped at the air but would come no closer. The horses whinnied with worry.

Will counted nine of the beasts, including a large coal-black leader. They were sad, wiry things except for him. He had meat and muscle on his bones, having earned his pick of the kills.

"On my mark!" said his uncle. "Charge!"

Geoff spurred Samson forward, and they all pulled ahead as one. The wolves scattered at the men's charge but did not retreat. Hunger kept them in the fight.

Hugo drew first blood, skewering one on his boar spear. It died with a quick yelp. Osbert missed his as the creature dashed between his horse's legs, leaving the old man's spear stuck in the frozen earth and a curse on his lips.

Out of the corner of his eye, Will saw Geoff run down another, trampling it beneath Samson's hooves. But Will couldn't focus on the hunt for long. He was busy holding Bellwether's reins tight. She wanted to bolt from the battle, and it took all of Will's strength to keep her within the circle of riders.

His ears rang with snarls and cries, with men's shouts and the stomping of hooves on the frozen ground. Will's mouth had gone dry, and his heart beat wildly in his chest.

Geoff's orderly charge dissolved into chaos as men and wolves clashed on the moor. Will found himself cut off from the rest when the big black one bore down upon him. Bellwether reared up to try to avoid the black's snapping jaws, even as Geoff turned Samson to come to Will's rescue. But the black snapped Bellwether on her hind leg. She let out a cry and she kicked out with all her might, sending the wolf rolling into the dirt.

But there was no calming her now. She bolted away from the fear and pain straight into the woods, heedless of the path. Will lost the reins in her charge, and all he could do was hold on to her mane as she barreled through the trees and brush. Branches swatted his head and scraped his cheeks, but still deeper into the wood she galloped.

Will was reaching forward with his left hand, groping blindly for her bridle, when a sturdy branch caught him on the shoulder and spun him around and off the saddle.

The trees, the ground, and the night sky suddenly stopped flying past him as he hit the forest floor. He tried to breathe, but the air had been knocked from his lungs, and panic grabbed hold of him.

Where was he? How far had Bellwether taken him in her mad dash, and had anyone watched him go?

After a few minutes, he found his breath again and pulled himself to sitting. Pain radiated down from his left shoulder, but he could still move his arm, flex his fingers. His face felt wet and sticky from a gash along his right cheek, but otherwise he didn't seem seriously hurt, which was lucky.

He stood to get his bearings. The path was nowhere to be seen, and at this edge of the woods one tree looked like another. He and Milo had never ventured as far as the moor, and regardless, a deep woods looked nothing like itself in leafless winter.

Bellwether had disappeared. Will whistled for her, but she was long past hearing or caring. He felt a sharp stab of alarm at the thought of her alone in these woods. She wouldn't last the night in this cold, with the wolves.

Neither would he if he didn't act soon. The way he saw it, he had two choices. He could set off in search of his uncle or stay put and try to get a fire going and wait for dawn. If he started marching off blindly, he might take himself in entirely the wrong direction and get even more lost, but it didn't feel right not to try. He decided that if no one had answered his calls by the time he'd walked a hundred paces, he'd stop and try to start a fire. There was flint and steel in his belt pouch, and a warm fire would help signal his uncle while hopefully keeping predators at bay.

He'd barely counted twenty paces when he heard something approaching. At first he thought it might be his uncle, but the sounds were too subtle for Samson's hooves. Nothing moved in the trees that he could see. But he *heard.*

It was the padding of soft feet on crackling leaves. Getting closer.

He grasped the hilt of the broadsword at his waist and found it frosted over. It took an extra tug to clear the blade from its frozen scabbard. When he hefted the heavy sword up, he winced in pain as fire shot down his shoulder to his fingertips. But he didn't release his grip. Besides the broadsword, the only weapon he had was a long hunting knife at his side—his own spear was still strapped to Bellwether's saddle, wherever she was.

The wolf emerged from the trees directly in front of him, teeth bared in a snarl. Will brought his sword's point down to prepare for a charge, just as he'd been trained. But his arms were already shaking, and the heavy blade quivered in his hands.

The beast took a step forward and then paused, its head

tilting slightly toward the ground. That's when the real attack came, as the big black one came bounding out of the brush to his right, a barking growl in its throat.

Will had just enough time to pivot and bring his sword to bear, but the giant wolf dodged the point easily and clamped its jaws over his left wrist. Will dropped the blade when the beast's mouth closed over his arm like a trap, but the metal gauntlet held, keeping his wrist from being crushed in the monster's mouth.

The black shook its head and pulled Will off his footing and down onto one knee. His right hand searched his belt as the wolf released him, freeing its teeth to make a lunge for Will's unprotected throat.

It found the tip of Will's hunting knife instead. The force of the creature's own leap managed to drive the knife's point home. Will was shoved backward, landing with a crash into the brush, a dead wolf sprawled across his chest.

While he struggled to roll out from beneath it, the first wolf found his shin, and this time sharp teeth pierced flesh. But the armored greave saved him from the worst of it. He kicked with his free leg and hit the beast squarely in its muzzle, but it didn't let up. Will tried to yank his caught leg from the wolf's mouth, and with a sudden snap he was free.

The wolf fell back a few steps with a metal greave in its jaw, the leather straps dangling loose. Apparently, Will hadn't secured them as well as he thought—lucky for him.

He scrambled across the leaf-strewn floor to his sword, grabbed its hilt with one hand, and swung it in a great sweeping arc behind him. He didn't even have time to look at what he was hacking. He just felt it connect.

Again and again his sword struck the wolf, until Will's strength failed him and he fell panting and sick to the ground.

❄ ❄ ❄

He was half frozen when Geoff found him two hours later. The leg had stopped bleeding, but he could barely unclench his fingers from his sword's hilt. He'd been standing there that whole time, listening for the next attack, which never came. But he'd kept his eyes on the carcasses, waiting for them to transform into men. They'd stayed wolves. Just dead wolves.

When Geoff appeared in the brush, Bellwether in tow, Will finally allowed his sword's point to fall to the dirt, but he still couldn't let it go.

Osbert swore loudly as he looked over the scene. Geoff wrapped a thick woolen blanket around Will's shoulders.

"Well, I'll be bloodied," Osbert said. "Wolfbait, my foot! All hail young lord *Wolfslayer*!"

The men cheered and clapped Will on the back.

"Now," said Osbert, "can we please go home? It's cold out here."

TWO

That lord is named Sir Guy of Gisborne, the Horse Knight.
A name that in certain parts of the kingdom inspires worry.
In the rest, fear.
—THE SHERIFF OF NOTTINGHAM

Will's toes hurt worse than anything. It had stung when Nan sewed the cut on his cheek closed. His shoulder, covered in a deep blue and yellow bruise, throbbed painfully whenever he moved, and the wolf bite on his ankle had swollen to an angry red. But nothing compared to the excruciating torture of having his frozen toes thawed in a pot of hot water.

The pain began as nothing more than a slight tingle. Then what were once stone-numb toes came alive with tiny needle pricks, which grew into stabbing thorns and, ultimately, molten spears of hellfire. He pleaded with Nan.

Please, please, put my poor toes back on ice, he'd begged.

Not if you want to have those toes in the morning, she'd said. *You're lucky they haven't blackened and turned frostbit as is.*

I don't need them all, he'd cried. *I can do without one or two if it'll make it stop!*

In the end, he managed to suffer the torment and keep all ten, and once the ordeal had passed, he slept, not dragging himself from bed until well after first light. The castle was frigid even though the servants kept roaring fires going throughout the night, and Will had to crack a layer of ice from his waterpot just to wash his face and hands. The shock of the freezing water woke him up, at least. A bad-tasting film covered the inside of his mouth and tongue, and he discovered that he'd bitten his cheek last night and not even known it. After rinsing his mouth out with ice water, he scrubbed his teeth clean with a twig of hazel.

His mother surprised him by delivering breakfast to his room. She said little but hugged him in a tight embrace. He ate bacon and a butter roll, and Nan brought him a steaming bowl of porridge. With the first bite, Will realized it was sweetened with molasses. Nan watched him eat, arching her eyebrows but saying nothing.

Will thanked them both while silently preparing a plan to find Nan's hidden molasses stash. She'd practically dared him to.

Lessons for the day were canceled, and so he was left to his own devices, free to roam. Normally, this would be a very dangerous thing, but Will was still too sore to get into any real mischief. Shackley Castle was an old keep, not nearly as grand as the large stone castles of other lords. The main building's wooden walls dated back to Will's great-grandfather and the Norman conquest of England. In the years since, the foundations and outer walls had been reinforced or altogether replaced with solid stone. The ancient wooden hallways he traveled this morning were chilled enough; Will could only imagine what a winter morning like this must feel like in a fortress all of stone. As it was, Will had to wrap himself in a thick woolen shawl just to keep his teeth from chattering.

His wounded ankle had stiffened up during the night,

and as he limped through the castle halls, he was met with greetings of *Lord William* and, by some, *Wolfslayer.* Last night's events had already made the rounds of castle gossip, no doubt helped along by Osbert. Will wondered just how many wolves he'd killed in the old knight's version of the story and if they were wolves at all. More likely it was Celt barbarians mounted on wolfback.

Geoff was busy that morning welcoming a visiting lord, an emissary from Prince John, and so Will wouldn't get to see his uncle until the evening's feast. Nan had told him that they would feast that night to celebrate his father's imminent return and to honor the killing of the wolves. Truth be told, Will was in no mood to celebrate.

He'd killed those wolves, to be sure, but they'd practically fallen on his blade. Hunger had made those beasts overly bold, and they'd charged to their deaths. It was as Geoff had warned—they were desperate, and it was desperation that had gotten them killed, not Will's skill in battle.

And when he closed his eyes, the wolves were still there. His dreams last night had been haunted by snarling faces and lonely howls. He'd been scared to look out his window for fear that the woods would be full of yellow eyes.

Will was so lost in remembering his wolf dreams that he nearly knocked over a pair of servants carrying long pine garlands and a thick white log.

"My apologies, Lord William," said Henry, the stable master. "I didn't see you there."

"My fault," said Will. "I wasn't watching where I was going. What brings you inside?"

Henry smiled. "My lady's brought in the stable staff to work indoors today, on account of the cold. Just enough of us left outside to tend fires, and we're doing that in shifts, my lord."

That was a kindness. Will's mother had a gift for managing the house staff with decency, and they loved her for it.

"Jenny here's helping me string the wreath." Nan's niece Jenny mostly helped out in the serving hall. She was older than Will by at least two years, but she still smiled prettily at him whenever they passed each other. Her cheeks dimpled when she laughed. Though she had been one of his childhood playmates, along with Henry's son Milo, Nan made it her unofficial duty to keep the two of them apart as much as possible these days. It was unseemly, she said, for a young lord his age to be alone with a serving girl.

"What do you have there, Henry?" asked Will.

"It's my lady's Yule log for tonight's feast!" said Jenny, smiling. There were the dimples.

Will glanced down at the white knotted log in Henry's hands. He'd nearly forgotten! The burning of the Yule was a tradition that his mother had brought over from her family in France, one that marked the winter solstice and the beginning of . . .

Christmas.

And with Christmas came presents. Glorious, wonderful presents. Perhaps his father would be home in time to spend Christmas with the family.

Will grinned so big his stitched cheek hurt.

"Henry, my good fellow," he said, clapping the stable master on the back. "I've just remembered something I must do. A lord's duties are never finished, you know!"

Will risked a wink at Jenny—Henry would never tell—and then he set off down the hall with a new lightness in his step, despite the limp, and a new glint in his eye. Wolf dreams forgotten for the time being. Last night's hunt was over, but the hunt for presents had just begun.

❄ ❄ ❄

Feasting began in the early afternoon and would often last late into the night. On days like this, it seemed to the casual watcher that the job of the nobility was to sit and eat all day long, with frequent breaks to scratch one's backside. And while this was true on the surface, what the common man did not see was the real work that went on during these massive meals. Negotiations, decrees, and acts of diplomacy were all accomplished between the pouring of the first cup of wine and the serving of the last sweet cake. Will's father often said that peace treaties were best hammered out between the fish and meat courses (thus giving the diners plenty of time to digest both the meal and the unpleasant terms of the agreement). Feasting was serious business of state, and a lord's duty.

Which was to say Will hated all of it. His rear was asleep before the first course was over, and now that he was a young lord-in-training, he was expected to actually listen to the adults' conversations. After, his mother would sometimes test him on what had been said and who'd said it. He was expected to study the guest lists and memorize the lands and lineages of everyone at his table. In short, it was terribly close to *schooling.*

Tonight's feast turned out to be an exception. Tonight, embarrassment was heaped atop the boredom. Osbert and his drunken companions shouted "Wolfslayer!" repeatedly as they used Will's newfound fame as an excuse to toast to his health—in excess. Although Will had been allowed watered wine since he was young, he avoided it. Wine made men loud and gave Will headaches.

But while Osbert carried on, Geoff was unusually quiet. Not that he was ever the garrulous sort, but tonight he was as quiet as a ghost. Will wondered if it had anything to do with the strangers seated at the end of the table, a fat lord and his man, who'd arrived at the castle earlier that day. The lord had an ugly smile, and he used it to leer at the serving girls. His man was hard-faced and had a strange accent when he spoke, which was rarely. He'd ridden into the castle wearing a gruesome suit of armor fashioned from horsehide rather than chain. The other lords at Geoff's table gave him a wide berth.

The newcomers provided a bit of mystery, but even they couldn't hold Will's attention for long. He was too worried about the presents. Stacked at the far side of the chamber, they were precisely where Will had discovered them, unwrapped them, and carefully wrapped them up again. There were fine silks for Mother sent from her family across the sea. There were history and philosophy books and—his favorite—a fat book of tales. A fine ornamental dagger from the neighboring lords of Tumley and an exquisitely carved hunting horn decorated with grinning goblins.

But beneath all that treasure was another present. A parcel wrapped in blue and silver cloth. Will had been excited to open this particular one, as it had come all the way from Scotland, from his faraway cousins. What he'd discovered was a carefully wrapped package of salted venison, which normally would have been a treat fit for the king himself. But the meat hadn't been properly cured, and it had spoiled during the long journey. The instant the wrappings came off, Will was assaulted by the smell of rotting meat—he'd nearly lost his breakfast. And no matter how he tried, he could not rewrap the stinking thing well enough to contain the smell again. It was as if the English air had wakened the foul Scots odor, and no craft of man could put it to rest again.

But whom could he tell? If he told, he'd reveal that he'd been at the presents, that he'd snuck a peek. He'd been warned before that if he was caught peeking at even one present, he'd risk losing all of them. Nan would find particular pleasure in such a punishment, as she was always going on about the pagan wreaths and the coarse custom of giving presents on such a holy day. If she had it her way, Will would spend the whole of Christmas in prayer or, worse, singing those terrible songs.

But the longer he went without telling, the worse the smell got. Even now, men and women in the hall were wrinkling their noses at an unidentifiable stench. The waves of freshly cooked food masked the source, but not for long. And soon Mother's silks and Will's books would all smell of rot. One hunk of sour deer meat might ruin Christmas for them all.

Resolved to save Christmas without also earning himself a swat from Nan's spoon, Will told his mother that he needed to stretch his legs and took a turn around the hall. By this time, the men were on their feet. Some sang bawdy songs, while others huddled together throwing dice. The point was, no one was paying any attention to Will. His plan was simple—if he could get close enough, he could *accidentally* bump one of the drunker men into the presents. After several profuse apologies, the servants would be brought in to rearrange the mess, and certainly one of them would discover the stink. If someone else reported it, no one could possibly trace it back to—

"Will Scarlet!" said a voice over his shoulder. "Or I should say Lord William now. Wolf's Bane!"

He turned to see the new sheriff, Mark Brewer, smiling at him over his cup of wine. Besides being the king's authority in Nottinghamshire (and, unhappily for him, nearby Sherwood), the sheriff had once been Geoff's hunting partner and a friend of the family. He'd been present at Shackley House enough times to have heard Geoff's teasing, though he often came to Will's defense. *Stay strong and live up to your name, willful Will,*

Mark had said once after his uncle made up a particularly nasty joke about Will's height—Geoff had offered to build the small boy a stepladder to reach his chamber pot.

Will Shackley had grown taller in the years since then, and Mark Brewer had gone on to become the king's sheriff, in service to Prince John. An ironic achievement for a man who so disdained the prince. But though his appointment was royal, he still walked and dressed like a soldier, and he kept his hair cut short in a military style. He looked out of place in this hall, and yet he possessed a kind of strength that Will admired. It was as if he were daring them all, rubbing his own lowborn status in their faces. It was why he and Geoff had been such good friends growing up, both disdainful of the puff and pageantry of royalty. But Geoff had been forced to take on the role of regent, and Mark was John's sheriff now. Life had strained the two men's friendship in unforeseeable ways.

"It's Wolf*slayer*," said Will, sticking his chest out.

The sheriff tilted his cup at Will and nodded. "So it is. My apologies. All these hero's titles . . . A mere king's servant such as myself is likely to forget."

"I'm sure you'll earn yours soon enough."

The sheriff smiled and tapped the gold chain of office hanging about his neck. "Ah, yes. Sheriff Mark Brewer, Tax Collector! Or perhaps Solver of Land Disputes! Very heroic."

Will laughed and allowed himself to relax a bit. Brewer was still good company, despite his new title. Still, he watched the man carefully, in case he might prove drunk enough to shove into the presents.

"How's the face?" asked the sheriff, gesturing to the cut on Will's cheek.

"I'd forgotten all about it. An evening of lordly talk has bored me numb."

The sheriff laughed. "Bored? You're just not paying close enough attention, my young lord. There's nothing boring about tonight's talk, I assure you."

He put his arm around Will's shoulders. "Look there," he said, pointing to the two strangers at the end of the table. "Do you know who those new faces are?"

"Some lord and his man," answered Will. "Arrived today."

"That lord is named Sir Guy of Gisborne, the Horse Knight. A name that in certain parts of the kingdom inspires worry. In the rest, fear."

Will watched the soft-faced lord wink and pinch at the passing girls—poor Jenny was serving that end of the table and was getting the worst of it. Anger suddenly welled up inside Will, surprising him, as he watched the obscene fat man grin at Jenny's retreating backside. He could tell from the stern set of Geoff's jaw that his uncle was barely tolerating the man's presence. Barely.

"Geoff is afraid of *him*?" asked Will.

"Your uncle? Oh no. Geoff's not afraid of any man, even when he ought to be." The sheriff took a long drink of his wine. "More's the pity."

"Well, Geoff's not going to fear a fat lord who brings an armed thug with him to a royal feast."

The sheriff raised an eyebrow. "Armed thug? My, you *haven't* been listening tonight, have you? The brooding one in the horsehide armor isn't a thug, *he's* Sir Guy."

Will stared at the sullen, armored knight in open amazement. He'd assumed that the man with the rich clothes and soft flesh, the man making an ass of himself, was Sir Guy. But his quiet companion, the one who'd dressed for dinner as if he were dressing for battle, was the real lord. Will began to understand why people might fear such a man.

"Then who's the other one?" asked Will.

"His manservant. That's his official title, but he's well known to be Guy's bribes master."

Now it was Will's turn to raise an eyebrow.

"There's all sorts of unsavory talk associated with Sir Guy," said the sheriff. "He's a landless knight, a mercenary captain who sells his swords-for-hire to the highest bidder. And there's no higher bidder than Prince John at the moment."

"Why would Geoff welcome such a man into court? Father wouldn't have stood for it."

"Yes, he would've," answered the sheriff. "He would've done just as Geoff is doing now, because Guy is Prince John's man. And the prince, it seems, has taken an interest in Shackley House."

"The prince? Really?"

Brewer took another drink from his cup. "Good Prince Lackland himself. Happy Christmas."

The sheriff called King Richard's brother Prince Lackland because when Richard returned, the prince would find himself lacking any lands of his own. It wasn't a name anyone used to the prince's face. Will had overheard his uncle and the neighboring barons grumble plenty about the prince's rule ever since King Richard had ridden off on his crusade. They said John wanted to be king himself, but that was all about to change now that the rightful king was returning home. The barons' petty complaints seemed rather boring anyway.

The way the sheriff made fun of the prince, on the other hand, well, that *was* entertaining. Will was about to ask if the sheriff had any nicknames for the King of France when he heard the banging of someone's cup on the table and shouts for quiet.

"Ah," said the sheriff, smiling. "Evening's entertainment is about to begin, I think."

Osbert had walked to the middle of the room. He opened his mouth to say something, but a loud belch came out instead.

"Oh, pardon, my lord," he said. "It's the sausages. Play havoc on an old man's stomach."

Geoff waved away the old man's apology amidst the lords' snickers and said, "You have something you'd like to say to the hall?"

"Indeed," said Osbert. "I'd like to ask the hall to join me in raising a cup— Heavens! Is my cup empty? What does an old man need to do to wet his lips in this castle? I'll die of thirst before age can take me!"

There was more laughter as Osbert chuckled at his own little joke.

"Let's raise a cup to our young lord William Shackley!" he said. "When we rode out together last night, he was still a pimply-faced boy who'd soil his bedclothes at the thought of drawing his sword! A milk-fat mother's boy—no offense, milady—more interested in straw dolls than strapping on a suit of mail! A . . ."

The laughter grew louder throughout the hall. Several lords were twisting their necks around to get a look at Will. He tried to melt away into the wall, but the sheriff put a hand on his shoulder, keeping him put. The evening's entertainment indeed.

Thankfully, Geoff interrupted the old man with a raise of his hand. "Perhaps we could move along to the toast, Sir Osbert?"

"Hmm? Oh, of course," said Osbert. "He rode out a boy, but he found his strength! While the rest of us more *seasoned* warriors were riding down the runts of that terrible wolf pack, Lord William was facing down four of the beasts alone!"

Two, thought Will. *Only two.*

"To William!" he cried. "Wolfslayer!"

The hall raised their cups and shouted "Wolfslayer!" together. The men gave him respectful nods. A few even bowed.

Had Osbert ended there, it would have been a fine toast, despite the teasing. But the old man did not know when to stop.

"I've not seen such born-and-bred bravery since King Richard!" he continued. "It's a God-given strength that does not grow on every branch of the tree, does it?"

Will felt the sheriff stiffen next to him. There were a few murmurs of agreement from the hall, but just as many were suddenly silent.

"Will's father possesses it! His brother, Geoffrey, possesses it! The wisdom to know how to hold a lord's chair for him till his return! Not growing too comfortable in a borrowed throne . . ."

Now no one cheered. An awkward quiet had fallen over the hall, and the only sound was the crackle of the hearth fire.

"Old fool," the sheriff whispered.

Again, Geoff interceded. He stood and held his cup high. "To William!"

Relieved, the men drank.

"Now, good old Osbert," said Geoff. "Enough talk. Won't you join us up here for some dessert?"

"If I could beg your lord's indulgence," called a voice from the end of the table, "I'd like to propose another toast."

At his full height, Sir Guy stood at least a head taller than Osbert. *His* wine cup, Will noticed, had barely been touched.

"To John," said Guy. "Long may he reign."

Up until now, Will had felt a step behind. He'd felt the room hush as Osbert went on with his toast, though he hadn't quite understood why. He'd suspected it had something to do with Prince John.

But Sir Guy's toast was something else, and there was no mistaking it. The prince shared power with a council, and he was only a temporary regent—he ruled in King Richard's stead until he returned from the crusade, much like Geoff was doing for Will's father. And the customary toast would be to wish John good health and for *Richard's speedy return*.

To wish anything else was to challenge Richard's claim to his own throne. Men were frozen. Their cups halfway to their lips, eyes glued to Geoff. They were waiting for their lord's signal.

But Geoff had grown quiet. His own wine untouched. His eyes angry as he glared at the Horse Knight.

Sir Guy didn't relent.

"No? I'm sure the hero of the evening will join me in my toast," he said, pointing to Will in the crowd. "What say you, Wolfslayer? Will you toast Prince John's benevolent rule?"

"Carefully, Will," whispered the sheriff. "Carefully."

All eyes were on Will. Geoff couldn't or wouldn't step in to save him this time. His mother looked ready to leap from her seat, her face full of fear.

"I'll . . . I'll raise my cup," said Will. "To England. To Prince John, King Richard, and the house of Plantagenet! And to my own father, Rodric Shackley, and his safe return from foreign lands."

This last got a round of "Hear, hears" from the gathered lords, and Will felt the tension in the room lessen slightly.

Even Guy took a drink at this, but his eyes never left Will. The sheriff whispered again in his ear.

"Well done, lad," he said. "You may have just spared us some bloodshed tonight."

As men wandered back to their dice games and their songs, Will lost himself among the crowds and the noise. He ended up staring down at the pile of wrapped presents. The smell of decayed meat wafted up as the spoiled present festered and ruined the rest. There were plenty of drunks standing well within pushing distance now. He could still follow through with his plan and save Christmas.

But what was that the sheriff had said?

You may have just spared us some bloodshed tonight . . .

Will left the presents where they were.

THREE

I won't start a war. Much as I'd like to.
—GEOFFREY SHACKLEY

It was easy to find his uncle the next morning: all Will had to do was follow the shouting. He'd woken early from the kind of restless half sleep that only makes you more tired the more you get of it. This was two nights in a row of poor sleep, and it was beginning to punish him. Will's eyes were sticky and red, and he felt sick to his stomach.

It was too early for breakfast—a red sun had just cracked above the trees in the east—so Will found himself outside Geoff's rooms, listening to his uncle arguing with someone. He could've eavesdropped, but something in him this morning made him bolder, or perhaps reckless. He knocked instead.

He was surprised to find the room full of adults. Mother and Geoff were inside, seated with the sheriff at a table. Osbert sat near the fire. Everyone was in the same clothing they'd worn the night before. Not a one of them had slept.

Something was wrong.

"Will," his mother said. "What are you doing up? It's late!"

"Mother," said Will. "It's not late, it's early. It's past dawn."

His mother glanced out the window and rubbed her eyes.

"So it is. Then why don't you go down to the kitchens and have some breakfast. There's cheese and fruit left from last night's feast. We'll join you later."

"He should stay," said the sheriff. "Perhaps he can talk some sense into you all."

"He's a boy," Will's mother said.

"He's Rodric's heir," said Geoff. "He should have been here from the start."

"Well said," added Osbert.

"Close the door behind you, Will," said Geoff.

"Is this about last night?" asked Will as he stepped inside the room. "Is this about that knight, Sir Guy?"

"Sir Guy arrived yesterday with news," said Geoff.

"Rumors!" said Osbert. "Nothing more!"

"Will," said his mother, taking a deep breath. "King Richard's ship hit a storm near Greece, and he was captured."

"By whom?"

"The Duke of Austria. He's holding him for ransom."

"What about Father? Is he with him? Was he captured, too?"

His mother opened her mouth to answer, but she seemed unable to speak. The sheriff answered for her.

"The king's companions have all been imprisoned with him," he said. "That's all we know."

Will looked at the faces of his family. His father wouldn't be home by Christmas, if he made it home at all.

"I'm afraid it's true, Will," said Geoff. "We know the king was taken. I sent riders out yesterday and had it confirmed by reliable men. Soon the whole kingdom will know. But the prince sent Sir Guy to deliver another message meant for the barons and lords only. He's spreading lies that King Richard is already dead."

Will's mind was whirling. King Richard the Lionheart dead? He was a legend, a hero that every boy idolized. He couldn't die.

"If that's true—"

"It's not," said Osbert.

"But if it is, then what does that mean for Father? Why would they keep Father alive if the king is already dead?"

"Listen to me, Will, and listen well," said the sheriff. He put his arms on Will's shoulders and looked him straight in the eye. "This is about money. King Richard is being held for ransom by the Duke of Austria, and he's not worth anything unless he's alive and well. The same goes for his companions, the same goes for your father."

"There's only one person who would benefit from rumors of the king's death, and that's his brother," said Osbert.

"I don't understand," said Will.

"That snake in the grass Prince John has been sniffing around the throne for a long while now, and he's hoping that by spreading rumors of the king's death, he'll gain support for his own claim to the throne. The king's most loyal lords, like your father, sailed with him on his crusade. There's no better time than now for the prince to make his move."

Will swallowed hard. He wouldn't cry in front of these men. He would be strong, for his father.

Geoff picked at a loose splinter in the table. He looked like he'd tear the whole table apart if he could.

"The prince is sending out his dogs to sniff out the loyalties of the lords and barons," said Geoff. "Guy was testing us last night to see who we'd stand with—John or Richard."

"And between Geoff's sulking and Osbert's *show,* he got a very clear answer, I'd say," said the sheriff. "The only one of you who performed with anything near diplomacy was the Wolf-slayer here."

Now Geoff got to his feet. "What place does diplomacy have in this? Richard's the rightful king, and the barons must send a clear message to Lackland! If he tries for the throne, we will rise up against him. United! Prince John doesn't have half the courage Richard does. He'll never go through with it."

"Only you aren't united," said the sheriff. "And John may not be brave, but he has the one advantage Richard does not."

"Which is?" asked Geoff.

"He's here and Richard's there. Prince John doesn't have to take what's already his."

A loud sigh escaped Osbert as he pulled himself to his feet. "Then we'll shove the prince out kicking and screaming. We'll give the whelp the whipping he deserves and send him crying for his nursemaid and his brother's forgiveness!

"Now," the old man continued, "I'm going to excuse myself so that I may vomit in peace. You learned men and ladies can keep talking of *diplomacy.*"

The last word he practically spat at the sheriff as he stalked out.

"For the royal record, it's not last night's wine that has sickened me this day."

There was a strained silence in the room as they watched him leave and listened to him stomp down the hall.

After he was gone, Geoff turned to the sheriff.

"Mark, I can't believe you, of all people, would have us side with Prince John!"

"I'm not saying you should swear allegiance to the prince," the sheriff said. "But until King Richard is freed and Will's father comes back safe and sound, there is no dishonor in looking out for your people and keeping these lands free of bloodshed and civil war."

The sheriff put his hand on Geoff's shoulder. "Lords weather the passing storms, Geoff, and the best way to do that is to stay neutral. Don't come out for Prince John, but don't come out against him, either. Tell Osbert no more foolish toasts, and leave kingly politics to kings."

The sheriff gathered up his cloak and bowed to Will's mother.

"Sir Guy will doubtless be gone by midday, off to report his chilly reception to the prince. Meanwhile, send an official invitation to John to spend Christmas here at Shackley Castle. I'll deliver the message myself, if need be, including assurances of your neutrality. Prince John will likely refuse, now that he knows you won't be the ally he'd hoped for, but he won't make life difficult for you.

"You are right about one thing—the prince is weaker than his brother. If someday he ends up on the throne, he'll be fearful of his claim to it. Easily swayed. John may not be the king we want, but we can make him the king England needs!"

As the sheriff was leaving, he winked at Will. "I hope you were taking notes, Lord Will. This'll all be your problem one day. Heaven help you."

After the sheriff was gone, Geoff turned to Will. "There's one thing I agree with the sheriff on, Will. Your father is alive."

"Do you really think so, Uncle?"

"I do."

Will looked to his mother, standing there so still. Her face was stern, expressionless, but she gripped her arms around her stomach as if she might be sick at any moment. She nodded in agreement with Geoff and somehow managed a smile for Will.

Geoff rubbed his tired eyes. "Will, this is your first taste of how power really works in England. What do you think?"

Will thought for a minute. Should he muster up some false bravado and curse John's name as Osbert would've? Or should he try to put on the sheriff's calm demeanor and argue for something that made logical sense but just felt wrong somehow? In the end, he decided honesty would be the best policy.

"I think . . . I think the wolves were easier," he said. "At least then I knew who the enemy was."

Geoff nodded with a small smile. "Well said, lad. Well said."

"Lady Katherine," said Geoff. "It seems we are losing friends. Osbert will abandon us if we don't openly support Richard. The sheriff will abandon us if we do."

"The sheriff will not put his head on the chopping block for you, Geoffrey, but he won't oppose you, either. Mark Brewer has been our friend for years."

"Yes," said Geoff. "He's also ambitious, and he's the prince's own appointed sheriff now."

"He doesn't love John, and he came here to warn you," she said. "That counts for something."

"My brother left me the care of his people until his return. I won't start a war. Much as I'd like to."

"It's because of that the prince has his eye on us, Geoffrey," said Mother. "You are the loyal brother to Rodric. You are steadfast in your devotion to him, and it reflects poorly on Prince John by comparison. He knows the other lords would rally to your cause if you declared against him. The sheriff thinks you can stay neutral, but I don't know if that will be enough."

Geoff slammed his fist on the table. "I will not throw my lot in with Sir Guy of Gisborne and his kind! Brutes and robber-knights, that's the sort of lord that'll support John."

Suddenly and without warning, Geoff sank into his chair. He looked deflated, like an empty wineskin. Will had never seen his uncle look so tired, or so small.

"How I wish Rodric had stayed put, and not run off to fight in Richard's bloody war."

"I wish that every day. And every night," said Mother softly. "Every lonely wife and mother in England wishes that."

Geoff waved them away. "I need sleep. We'll talk more on this later."

He plucked distractedly at the table, tearing at a fresh splinter. "John won't become king in a day."

Will was wandering the halls looking for a place to take his troubled thoughts when he heard his name. He turned to see Mark Brewer, the sheriff, coming toward him. He was wearing his riding gear and a set of warm furs.

"Leaving already?" Will asked.

The sheriff nodded. "I'd rather be going to bed, believe me, but I have duties to attend to back in Nottingham. The peace doesn't keep itself."

Will walked with the sheriff a ways, past servants going about their morning chores. Despite the early hour, the castle around him was already alive with its regular morning routine. Most would be breaking their fast on leftover bread and cheese, but the kitchens would already be working on the midday meal, and the smells of roasting mutton and honeyed pork would soon start wafting through the halls. Outside, wood was being chopped for the never-ending fires, the horses rubbed down, and stable stalls cleaned. The servants went about their work, ignorant of the problems of their lords, or of England as a whole.

The sheriff stopped in front of one of the shuttered windows that overlooked the courtyard. The latch was stuck closed with frost, but after a moment's fumbling he managed to pry it open. It swung outward and let in a blast of frigid morning air. The sheriff leaned his head out and breathed deep.

Will pulled his cloak tighter around him, but the wind still found its way past his clothes.

"Are you trying to freeze me to death?" he asked.

"It's invigorating," answered the sheriff.

"Says you. You've got your traveling furs on!"

The sheriff smiled but didn't make any move to close the shutter. "When I was young, I spent so much time here. Geoff and I used to play knights and castles down there in that very courtyard. Just as you and that stableboy do—blast, what's his name?"

"Milo," Will said.

"Yes, Milo. I should've known that. He always takes such good care of my horse. . . ."

The sheriff turned and looked at Will.

"I've been away from this place too long, but that's what happens when you grow up. I used to dream of having a manor house like this, of being an important man like your father, like your uncle. So I worked hard, I bowed and smiled at the right people, and when the prince appointed me sheriff, well . . . I learned there's a point when you stop doing the things you want to do and you start doing the things you have to do. I don't think your uncle understands that yet."

"What do you mean?"

The sheriff didn't answer right away. Instead, he reached out a hand and tousled Will's hair, something he hadn't done since Will was a young boy.

"Stop it," said Will. "It gets all tangled as it is. And it'll be your fault if Nan comes chasing after me with a comb!"

The sheriff laughed. "The Wolfslayer is afraid of Nan's comb! God, that's rich. You know, Will, you mustn't tell your uncle this, but you really are my favorite person in this stubborn little house. Fools that you all are."

"Is that supposed to be a compliment?"

"It is what it is," he said.

Then the sheriff bowed and walked down the hall toward the front doors. He didn't bother closing the shutters, so Will watched him enter the courtyard below. Milo was already waiting for him there with the sheriff's horse. Even from up in his window, Will could hear the sheriff thank Milo by name as he slipped him a coin.

Then Will closed the shutters (his teeth were chattering by now) and wandered off in search of something to take his mind off his troubles.

FOUR

We mustn't let lawlessness go unpunished.
—SIR GUY OF GISBORNE

Will would've wandered down to the kitchens, but after all the talk of fighting and intrigue, he wasn't in the mood for company. Avoiding people wasn't difficult, as most were happy avoiding him in turn. The servants knew that trouble followed the young lord like thunder followed lightning, and many had been struck more than once.

But the trouble brewing inside Shackley House today was not of Will's making. It was barely within his understanding. Richard was the rightful king of England, but while he was locked away in a foreign prison with Will's father, the king's younger brother John was scheming to steal the throne of England. And Will's uncle was being asked to choose sides. No, not asked. He was being forced, as they all would be soon enough.

In truth, Will couldn't care less about who wore the crown. All he wanted was his father back. These last two years had been hard on the family. Geoff did his best to look after his brother's estate, but responsibility weighed heavily on him, and where he was once a joyful, laughing soul, now he scowled more than he smiled. Will's mother endured the lonely days by hugging Will even closer to her, smothering him one moment and scolding him the next.

And Will was just lost. He knew that his childhood was over, but he had no earthly idea how to be a man. He had tutors and combat masters, and he had Geoff and Osbert, but they were all poor substitutes for his father. They meant well, but Geoff would lecture him on the importance of responsibility in one breath while railing against it in the next. Osbert advised him to get into fights. The more the better.

In his most secret thoughts, Will almost resented his father. Why did he have to choose King Richard over his family? Why was royal duty more important than duty to his son? Will was angry that he'd been gone so long, and terrified that he wouldn't come back at all.

Will wondered how many days he'd carelessly run through these halls, laughing and playing while his father carried some secret worry in his own heart. If this was a taste of what it was to be a man, Will wanted none of it.

Feeling shut in by the narrow hallways, Will bundled himself up in his thick winter woolens and took a stroll in the crisp morning air down to the stables. Perhaps giving Bellwether a nice brush down would take his mind off lordly troubles.

The mare was always excitable, but she settled some as Will hand-fed her thick-cut oats. Once she was calm, he checked the poultice on her injured back leg—even a small wound needed to be watched carefully when inflicted by a wild animal. They'd both been bitten, so perhaps they'd turn feral together and transform into beasts by moonlight. A wolf-boy riding a wolf-horse through the forests. That would earn a place in Osbert's drinking stories.

"Will! Will!"

Will turned to see Milo poking his head into Bellwether's stall, his face barely recognizable beneath a ridiculous fur cap that had been sized for a grown man and kept sliding over the boy's eyes. Milo had been Will's playmate since he'd been able to walk. In that time, Will had dragged the poor boy into one spot of trouble after another.

"I was wondering when you'd show up here," Milo said. "Haven't seen you since you rode out on that wolf hunt. I heard you slew five of the devils and the rest changed back into men and ran all the way to Scotland!"

Will shook his head. The kitchen gossips had outdone themselves this time—not that Milo wasn't easy prey.

"Don't believe castle whispers, Milo," Will said. "They were *Irish*, not Scots at all. And they didn't run home, they swam."

The young boy wrinkled his nose as he chewed over this new fact.

"Aww, you're just having a go at me now, aren't you?" he asked. "Why would they swim when they could hop a boat?"

Will laughed and Milo joined in, although he didn't look entirely sure what they were laughing about. It felt good.

"She's still spooked, poor Bellwether is," said Milo. "But her wound will heal up nicely. I made that poultice myself. Vinegar and mint do the trick."

Milo treated these horses better than most people treated their own families. "It's fine work, Milo. I'm grateful."

"Have you seen your presents?" asked Milo, his face lighting up. "I heard talk that they're stacked up to the ceiling! Don't think I could resist taking a peek myself. I love Christmas."

"They're not quite to the ceiling," said Will, feeling suddenly self-conscious. "And most of them are for Mother and Geoff anyway."

Milo rubbed his hands together. "Still, I bet there's some

kingly gifts in there, hey? I peeked at my presents last year and found a fine woolen cape with a jeweled clasp—you remember the one? I called it my wizard's cloak!"

Will did remember the cape, a gift from Milo's mother. The clasp was inset with a gaudy glass bead, not a jewel at all. And he remembered that he had teased Milo mercilessly about it all last winter. He'd called it Milo's ball gown, casually and callously insulting the one gift Milo really loved. His only gift, and Will had ruined it.

Will realized that Milo hadn't worn it at all this season, despite the cold.

"It was a nice cape," said Will. "Even if I didn't say so."

Milo shrugged beneath his too-big cap. Another gift from his mother, no doubt. "Doesn't matter now. Still, I wouldn't mind getting a look at those royal presents! If you're up for a little sneaking."

"Actually, I don't know if today's a good day. Maybe tomorrow . . ."

A cry interrupted him. A girl's voice, from somewhere in the stables, shouting. Without waiting for his friend, Milo ran out of Bellwether's stall toward the sound. He was the son of the head stable hand, and these were his horses—the stable was his domain.

Will followed swiftly behind, and as the two of them reached the far end, they found Jenny backed into an empty stall, cornered by a fat man wrapped up so tight in gaudy furs he looked like a stuffed hedgehog.

As Will got closer, he recognized the man as Sir Guy's bribes master, the one with the wandering hands. They hadn't left the castle yet after all. In one fist he held a horsewhip, and he seemed to be brandishing it at Jenny.

"What's . . . what are you doing in here?" asked Milo.

"I found this wench sneaking through my saddlebags," said the bribes master. "Looking to steal from her betters, she is."

"That's not true!" said Jenny. "I was just fetching some wood for the kitchen, and I stopped to pet the horses! I wasn't anywhere near the saddlebags."

"Well, you're both spooking the other horses," said Milo, eyeing the bribes master. Guy's man was twice the stableboy's size, and a head taller than Will.

"Jenny, why don't you come with us," said Will. "We'll sort all this out inside."

As she took a step toward them, the bribes master reached out and grabbed her by the wrist.

"I'll let bygones be bygones," he said. "For a kiss!"

Will started to protest, but Milo was quicker. The small stable hand rushed to Jenny's defense, shoving the fat bribes master and freeing Jenny.

"Get away from her!" Milo said.

The fat man cursed as he stumbled backward, but he found his footing fast enough and swung his horsewhip at Milo, catching the boy across the ear with an ugly-sounding crack.

Jenny cried out as Milo cowered beneath the man's whip. Will caught the strong scent of ale on the man's breath—he was still drunk from the night before.

"You know who I am?" he asked. "I am William Shackley, nephew of Lord Geoffrey!"

The man licked his lips nervously. "Aye, I know you," he said quietly. "And since I don't care to whip lordlings, why don't you run along now."

Will could call out. He could call for help, and someone would come running. And then the bribes master would be hauled away to face Geoff's justice. Eventually, help would come, but in the meantime the future lord of Shackley House would have just stood by and watched as this beast beat on a poor stableboy.

Will imagined what Geoff would do in this situation, or Mark the sheriff. He looked around for some sort of weapon, a shoe iron, something, and found a scabbarded broadsword leaning against the opposite stall. How had that gotten there? No one left such weapons just lying about, but there wasn't time to question his good fortune.

He drew the sword from its scabbard—the handle was well-worn leather—and put the bribes master on guard.

"I command you to stop!" he shouted.

And he did. For a moment, the bribes master was frozen, whip in hand and eyes on Will's sword. He didn't like the look of that blade; his fearful eyes betrayed that much.

But he didn't yield. He let out a nasty laugh and swung the whip at Milo. And picturing wolves, Will swung his sword.

He aimed for the bribes master's arm but missed. The fat man shifted and Will struck the man's thick thigh instead. The blade connected with something hard beneath the man's furs, armor perhaps, but it also cut into something softer.

With a cry, the bribes master dropped the whip and fell to the ground, clutching his wounded leg.

Will stepped past the bribes master without lowering his sword. He hoped the man couldn't see his knees shaking.

"Milo, are you all right?"

The boy nodded. His face was wet with tears and snot, his hands were a pattern of red welts, yet he made far less noise than the whimpering fat man.

Jenny knelt next to Milo and pressed the hem of her dress against his bleeding ear.

"Do you all know who my master is?" said the man, as he held his bleeding leg.

"Do you know whose castle this is?" Will shouted. He suddenly wanted to hit him again.

"This is the castle of Lord Rodric Shackley," answered a strangely accented voice from behind them. "And you are his only son and heir."

Will turned to see Sir Guy standing there, watching them. He was dressed the same as he had been last night, in his hideous horsehide armor, but this time something was missing. His belt was empty.

"And that is my man you just wounded. With *my* sword."

The Horse Knight smiled and shook his head. How long had he been in the stable, watching? Will wondered. And why hadn't he stopped it?

Something had happened here that Will wasn't seeing. None of it made any sense. None of it.

Why was Sir Guy smiling?

"I think we should speak to your uncle about this," said Sir Guy. "A stolen sword, a wounded servant . . . We mustn't let lawlessness go unpunished, eh, Wolfslayer?"

FIVE

England is plots within plots.
—LADY KATHERINE

Will arrived at his mother's chamber just as Milo was leaving it. The stable hand practically ran over the young lord on his way out. Milo's bandaged hands looked painful, and his ear was red and swollen where it'd been tacked back together. But the boy's smiling face was sticky with honey.

At first Will wondered what business his mother would have with Milo, but when he saw his friend's sugary face, he realized—Lady Katherine had been plying him with sweets.

His mother wanted answers; she wanted to hear Milo's side of the story, away from the intimidating lords and the shouted accusations. A smart move. She'd probably interrogated Jenny as well. After a day of Sir Guy's rather public hysterics and cries for justice, Lady Katherine was conducting her own investigation into the matter.

The day had been dizzying, dreamlike, ever since the fight in the stables. Though he'd been so calm and cool in the stables, when Guy went before Geoff to air his grievance, he transformed. His bribes master had been taken to Guy's room, where the physician stitched up his leg, and Guy carried the man there himself. When he returned to Geoff's hall, he hadn't even bothered to wash the blood from his hands. He was the perfect picture of a lord offended, and in front of everyone, he condemned the lawlessness of Geoff's halls and Will's thuggery. His man had been wronged, and therefore he had been wronged. Will hadn't seen a better performance.

Geoff had endured Guy's raving with a clenched jaw and barely concealed fury. On the thievery charge, Will knew he and Milo might be suspected—everyone in the castle knew their history of mischief making. But not a man or woman would believe that he and Milo had physically attacked the bribes master unprovoked or that Jenny was somehow involved. That lie went too far.

Will would've liked a moment alone now with Milo himself, but the door was open and he could glimpse his mother inside waiting for him.

"How are you feeling?" Will asked his friend.

"Hurts," said Milo, holding up his fingers. "But your mother's surgeon stitched me up properly. Says I'll heal well enough."

Will smiled, and as he brushed past his friend, Milo whispered, "Think we've really stepped into it this time, Will."

The fire was roaring inside Lady Katherine's chambers, and the air smelled of honey. Two chairs were set at the front table, and honey rolls and a bowl of sweet cream sat in between them.

Will's mother ignored the desserts and pointedly did not invite Will to help himself, which was a shame because it was the first food he'd spied all day that set his stomach to rumbling. Instead, she sat on her cushioned stool near the fireplace and took up her embroidery.

Will was left to stand.

"Um, am I in trouble?" asked Will.

His mother did not look up from her stitching. "Will, you are the heir of Shackley House, and you are too old to be afraid of a scolding from your mother."

Will let out a breath. "Oh, I thought that—"

"That being said, yes. You are in trouble."

"What? Mother, that's not fair!"

Finally, Lady Katherine looked up from her embroidery. Her face was full of exasperation and something else. Her blue eyes had made her worthy of many portraits in her youth, and she was still considered a great beauty. But tonight those eyes were bloodshot, puffy. Had she been crying?

"Sit down, my son. We need to talk."

Will pulled a chair over to the fire. He lingered near the sweet cream for just a second but left it, sadly, untouched.

Once he'd settled into his seat, his mother watched him for a bit, saying nothing. Will knew better than to interrupt whatever thought she was mulling over, but he did wish he had a nice plateful of cream and perhaps a honey roll to pass the quiet. Maybe this was a part of his punishment, this torture by pastry.

"You look like your father when you sulk," she said, smiling slightly.

"Father?"

"What?" she said. "You think a great lord of men doesn't know how to pout? Not when he's holding court, to be sure. But you remember the year when he wasn't allowed to journey to France to ride in my father's jousting tourney?"

Will nodded. "He twisted his ankle, and Geoff rode in his place."

"And Lord Rodric Shackley sat in that very same chair and grumbled for weeks. You have his frown."

Will squirmed uncomfortably, adjusting the cushion beneath his bottom. He hadn't been frowning, had he?

"But you have something else of your father, too. You have his instinct. His sense of justice and fairness. It's lordly and you wear it well. I'm proud of you for standing up for your friends, Will. You should know that."

He kept his eyes on the fire. He hadn't been expecting praise and wasn't sure what to do with it. Was this part of her interrogation?

"But you haven't been caught stealing from Nan's larder this time," she said. "Sir Guy is a favorite of the prince, and while he was enjoying the hospitality of our castle, his man was wounded. By the Shackley heir himself."

"But I've already told you I was protecting Milo and Jenny. That man would've whipped Milo to shreds!"

"Yes, but Guy refutes your story. He claims that his sword went missing in the night and that he sent his man out to search for it in the morning. And that his man found the three of you *playing* with it in the stables. When the man tried to retrieve his master's sword, you turned on him. He defended himself with his horsewhip, and you cut him down."

"That's not true!" said Will.

"Can you prove it?"

"I have witnesses!"

"Co-conspirators, Guy calls them."

"Mother! I'm innocent!" Will found himself shouting, while all the while his mother sat calmly before him, her voice level and her stare hard. Did she really not believe her own son?

His mother took a deep breath as a sad, small smile cracked her otherwise stony expression.

"Oh, my son," she said. "Of course you are. No one believes Sir Guy or his repulsive bribes master. But innocence and guilt have nothing to do with this now. Sir Guy wants to take you to Westminster. To be tried by the royal court there."

"Westminster? Why, Mother?" asked Will. "Couldn't we summon the sheriff instead? Why must I travel to London?"

"You won't," she said. "Geoff won't allow it. He'll let Guy shout himself blue, but he won't give you over to Prince John."

Prince John? What does the prince have to do with a brawl in Shackley Castle?

His mother must've seen the look of sudden understanding dawn upon her son's face, because she nodded. "England is plots within plots," she said.

This wasn't about a wounded servant at all.

"The prince wants me in London so that Geoff will be forced to support him," said Will. "The prince wants a hostage."

"Yes," said his mother. "He'll lock you up in the Tower while he delays the trial for weeks—months, if need be. Just long enough to pressure your uncle to back his bid for the throne."

Will felt his legs go wobbly. If he hadn't already been sitting, he might have fallen over. There were stories of lordlings who went into the Tower of London and never came out. How had this all happened so fast?

"He'll lock you up in a room befitting your station, of course," said his mother. "A well-furnished prison, but a prison nonetheless."

His mother rested her hand upon Will's arm. "But Sir Guy and the prince miscalculated. The royal court is not a place to try a lord for brawling with a servant, no matter how favored that servant may be. No crime has been committed worthy of Westminster, and the rest of the lords would see through the prince's ploy easily."

Will looked into his mother's eyes. "So I don't have to go?"

"No, my son. Geoff has already sent for the sheriff, and Mark Brewer will ask that we pay Sir Guy a fine for his troubles and offer up an apology. Such an apology will stick in your uncle's throat like a chicken bone, but he'll do it. Then we'll send the Horse Knight on his way and pray he never darkens our door again!"

Will let his head fall into his hands. He was relieved beyond words not to have to make the journey to London, but at the same time he felt his cheeks burning a bright red with the shame that his uncle would have to formally apologize to Sir Guy for a crime that Will was not even guilty of. It made Will so sick that even the sweets laid out before him lost their appeal.

"How are you sleeping?" his mother asked after a moment.

"How did—"

"I'm your mother."

Will sighed. "I have bad dreams. Ever since the wolves."

"Your father never sleeps well, either. And he dreams of worse than wolves, I'm afraid."

Will's mother reached out and took him in her arms, hugging him close. "Oh, Will, how I wish you didn't have to grow up yet. I'm not ready for it."

"Honestly, I don't know if I am, either," said Will, his voice suddenly thick in his throat.

Lady Katherine released him. "But we don't have a say in the matter, my young lord William. The time has come."

Wiping at his eyes, Will stood and headed for the door. He was glad Geoff wasn't here to see this.

"Will?"

He stopped at the door and turned to her. She was staring at the fire again, her back to him, the embroidery forgotten on her stool.

"Yes, Mother?"

"Bad things are happening in England right now, and we both miss your father terribly, but we must not lose faith. We must never, never lose faith."

"Yes, Mother," Will said as he tried to find a smile to comfort her with, but it was difficult. As he shut the door behind him, he thought he could hear his mother crying.

That night exhaustion and worry finally overtook him. He slept fitfully, and it was late the next morning when he was woken by Hugo banging on his chamber door.

Groggily, Will opened up.

"Yes?"

"Geoffrey has asked for you to come at once, my lord."

"Why? Has something happened?"

The thin steward swallowed, his Adam's apple bobbing along his throat like fish in a stream.

"The sheriff arrived this morning with soldiers."

"Well, good," answered Will. "They can escort Sir Guy from the castle."

"My lord, the man you wounded, Sir Guy's bribes master . . . he's dead."

Will felt the floor shift beneath his feet, threatening to drop away. Somewhere on the edge of last night's sleep, the wolves howled.

SIX

Shall I fetch his corpse?
—Sir Guy of Gisborne

Will followed Hugo through the halls of Shackley House as panicked servants bustled back and forth. Everyone seemed to want something to do, but there wasn't anything. The gates had already been opened to permit the sheriff's entrance before the news of the bribes master's death had spread. And now the sheriff was inside the castle with a score of armed men.

As Hugo led him past a window overlooking the courtyard, Will spotted Geoff, Osbert, and the rest of the castle guards assembling before the sheriff and his men. Luckily, no swords were drawn. Yet.

Hugo led Will to a door that he recognized. To most of the house staff, it was an old unused storage room, but Will knew the family secret. At the back of the closet was a hidden passage that led down to a tunnel. That tunnel would take you beyond the castle walls to a secluded copse of trees and safety. An escape tunnel for the lord's family.

"Come," said Hugo. "I'm to escort you and Lady Katherine to safety. She's out there already, waiting for you."

"Leave?" said Will. He couldn't believe what he was hearing. "Mother wants me to run away?"

"My lord, these are your *uncle's* orders."

Geoff. For all his talk of making a man out of him, here he was treating Will like a boy. Hiding him away with his mother until the danger had passed.

But this danger was Will's fault, and he would face it with the men of his house. He hadn't run from the wolves; he wouldn't run from the sheriff.

He would, however, run from Hugo. He knew the family's steward wasn't above dragging Will into that passage by the ear if that's what it took to follow Geoff's order, and though the man was skinny, he was still a good deal stronger than Will.

Will made a show of peering into the dark storage room. "How will I see inside that passage?" he asked.

"There's a lantern on the wall there."

"Where? I don't see it."

"Here," said Hugo, stepping past Will and into the room.

And that's when Will slammed the door shut behind him. Then he turned and sprinted back down the hall, even as he heard Hugo shouting and fumbling for the latch in the dark. It wouldn't keep him long, but it gave Will a head start.

Past the worried servants he bolted, the groups gathered at the windows and near the doors, round to the front doors and straight out into the courtyard.

When Geoff saw him appear, he shot Will a look that promised daggers, but Osbert gave Will an approving nod. Will tried to catch his breath and walk calmly to join his uncle, as a true lord of Shackley would.

The sheriff watched Will approach and smiled. Sir Guy stood off to one side, watching as well. He was unarmed, which Will took for a good sign, at least.

"My lord William," said the sheriff. "I am glad that you've joined us. And I hope that you can talk some sense into your uncle."

"I am regent here," said Geoff. "The boy's protector. And I have said my piece. He isn't going anywhere."

The sheriff's smile faded. "Geoff, be sensible!"

"Yes, *Mark*? Are we dispensing with titles now? You come into my castle with armed men and suddenly I'm your friend again, is that it? And who are these men? They wear your colors, but I don't recognize their faces."

"This is no longer about a fight. A man is dead," said the sheriff. "A trusted servant of Sir Guy's, but I cannot officiate a murder trial against Lord Rodric's only heir. I don't have the authority. Westminster is the only choice."

"I didn't kill him," said Will. "I only wounded him!"

"He bled out in the night," said Guy, frowning. "Seems your sword arm is stronger than it looks, Wolfslayer."

"Our physician examined his wound," said Geoff. "He said it was a flesh wound, nothing more."

"Then you need a better surgeon!" shouted Guy. "My man's dead. Shall I fetch his corpse?"

"No, but perhaps you could fetch the blade you used to kill him?"

"How dare . . ." If Guy had had a sword on him, he would've drawn it then and there. And Geoff was ready to match him.

But the sheriff stepped between the two of them.

"Enough! You can hurl all the accusations you like at Westminster. This is now a matter for the royal court, and it is my duty to escort Sir Guy and William there."

He stepped in close to Geoff, and his words were soft enough that only those closest could make them out.

"I give you my word, Geoff. Will won't come to harm. He'll be treated according to his station and title."

"He'll be a prisoner!" answered Geoff. "John's hostage."

"He'll be alive! Don't you see what's happening here?" The sheriff gestured to the men squaring off, their hands on their weapons. "I tried to warn you."

"You are not the prince!" said Geoff. "Your word means nothing in Westminster. I will not let you take my brother's only son from his own house!"

There was an excruciating moment when neither man said anything. Will didn't know what to do. He didn't want to go to London, but he couldn't let men fight and die on his behalf. He'd have to trust the sheriff.

"I'll go with him," he said.

"Will," said Geoff.

"It's my choice. Either I'm a man or I'm not, Uncle. And I'm allowed to make my own decisions."

The sheriff let out a sigh of relief and, turning to Will, said, "Lord William, indeed."

But then Will looked over at Sir Guy, if for no other reason than to show him that he was unafraid. As he did, he saw Guy give a quick nod to one of the sheriff's soldiers.

Two men stepped forward, and one of them grabbed Will and threw him to the ground while the other pulled a pair of irons from his belt. It was unexpected, and Will hit the earth with a painful thud.

The sheriff shouted at the men to stop, and they paused but didn't back off. One man placed his foot on Will's back as he looked to Guy for what to do next.

It became clear at this moment whose men these soldiers really were.

Geoff was in the sheriff's face, shouting again even as the sheriff barked orders at the soldiers to stand down. The sound of several swords being drawn at once rang out through the courtyard. A battle cry, a bearlike roar that seemed improbable for his age, came out of Osbert's mouth, and he swung a heavy fist at the soldier standing on Will. Osbert caught the man along the jaw, knocking him to the ground.

Then the courtyard erupted into chaos.

Will rolled away to avoid being trampled by a stampede of booted feet as the soldiers descended on the castle guards. He barely dodged a pair of men who'd dropped their weapons and were now pummeling each other with their armored fists while they wrestled on the ground.

Will reached for his side but realized he hadn't bothered to buckle on a weapon. The courtyard was filled with fighting men, and here was Will unarmed and unarmored. He searched for his uncle's face among the crowd, but there were more soldiers than Shackley men. Already the line of castle guards had broken. Fists and booted feet, clubs and the flats of swords—Will was in the middle of a free-for-all castle brawl.

He spotted Osbert's white head among the fighting—he and a small group of guards had formed a tight unit and were fighting back to back against the undisciplined soldiers. The old warrior was grinning madly as he bashed helmeted heads together. Will had just started to pick his way there when he saw one of Guy's men, the one who'd been ready to put Will in chains, break away from the fighting. Holding a brutal-looking cudgel in his fist, the man stalked toward Will.

The soldier's bloodlust was up, and he swung wildly at first as Will ducked beneath his blows. Will was fast—faster than this armored thug at least. But he couldn't dodge forever, and the soldier pressed his advantage now, cutting off Will's escape and pinning him against the courtyard wall. There was nowhere left to run.

The soldier saw this and smiled. Worse, he took his time and aimed his next blow. He'd crack the boy's skull wide open. This time he couldn't miss.

Or at least he *wouldn't* have missed had he not at that moment been hit on the head with a large clay chamber pot. And a stone water jug. And then a basket of laundry and some eggs.

It had suddenly started raining crockery and kitchen slop. Will looked up to see Milo and several other servants leaning out of the topmost windows. They had joined the fight, throwing whatever they could find onto the heads of the enemy below. Milo waved at Will and grinned. He was loving this.

As was Osbert. Will could hear the old man's shouted curses even above the din, and he only cursed that much when he was really having fun. Will, on the other hand, was simply trying not to get his head bashed in.

He was easing along the wall, ducking and weaving out of the way of fighting men, when Geoff appeared at his side. He had a nasty cut over one eye, but he, too, was grinning. Were they all mad? He knocked one of the sheriff's men out of his path with the flat of his blade, then grabbed Will by the shoulder and pulled him away from the courtyard and the fighting. Opening one of the side doors into the main keep, Geoff shoved Will inside.

"Get back in where it's safe, Will," he said. "Leave it to us to send these mercenaries out of here on their heads and the almighty sheriff back to Nottingham with his tail between his legs!"

Then Geoff turned and started back toward the courtyard, but he didn't see the figure stepping up behind him. Only Will saw, from his hiding spot in the doorway, as Sir Guy of Gisborne emerged from the shadows.

Before Will could shout a warning, Guy wrapped an arm around Geoff's neck, grabbing him from behind.

"You wanted to see the knife that killed my man?" he said into Geoff's ear. "Here it is!"

Geoff stiffened, his eyes going suddenly wide. A spot of blood bubbled at the corner of his mouth as he started to say something, and then he slumped forward. He landed face-first in the dirt, a knife handle sticking out of his back. He didn't get up.

Will froze as Sir Guy turned and disappeared into the brawling crowd. A moment passed before Will could even understand what he'd just seen, what he *alone* had witnessed—before he could throw open the door and scream Geoff's name in a cry loud enough that it pierced the clatter of battle. Men stopped their fighting and looked around to see what could have made such an anguished sound.

One of them spied Geoff's body on the ground and cried out in turn. Then another.

A strong arm wrapped itself around Will's waist, and he fought against it, hitting and kicking at his captor until he saw Hugo's face.

"We go now!"

He didn't wait for Will to agree. Hugo half carried, half dragged the boy away as the sounds of the battle began to change. This was no longer just a soldiers' street brawl.

Lord Geoffrey was dead, and more blood was about to be spilled.

PART II

Sherwood

SEVEN

Hey, you alive or dead?
—John Little

Much got her nickname from something her father used to say. When the neighbors asked what use a daughter was to a poor miller who needed strong hands to work his grindstone, he'd frown and shake his head. *What use is a daughter to a poor miller?* he'd ask. *Nothing much.*

But when they were alone together, when he'd tucked her in at night and brushed the hair from her eyes with his cracked, callused hands, she'd ask him her own secret question: *Is there anything that would make you happier than me?*

Nothing much, came his reply.

That wasn't the whole truth. Much saw how lonely he was, how on certain gray days he'd sit in his chair and stare at her mother's dusty lockbox. She'd seen him fingering the fine dress he kept stashed within. She'd noticed the way he blinked and wiped at his eyes when he spoke of his wife, dead these five years.

Much's Christian name was Marianna, same as her mother's. And that, perhaps more than anything, was why her father had refused to use it. It was just too much.

Some griefs are too strong to face head-on. She understood that now. She'd learned it the minute her father coughed his last tired breath and she found herself alone—an orphaned daughter of marrying age with nothing but debt for a dowry. Some memories were too painful to live with, and some reminders best forgotten. So she'd cut her hair and buried it along with her father's body and her mother's dress. She'd traded her sewing needle for a walking stick and a pair of breeches. Marianna the miller's daughter was buried in that small plot of earth with her parents. Much the miller's *son* set out to carve a new life far away.

"Much! What are you doing up there, you daft boy? We're supposed to be setting up the trip line down here *on the ground*!"

Stout called up at her in what he clearly thought was a clever whisper. Truth was, Stout was hard of hearing, and his whispers were loud enough to stir the pope from his bed in Rome.

Behind Stout, Much could see John Little shaking his head. The big man also knew that anyone within a quarter mile of the South Road had just learned that outlaws were setting about to ambush them.

Scowling, Much climbed a few branches higher to get a better view down the road and see if Stout had scared off any potential customers. From her high vantage point, she could see an empty stretch of road, made of well-used dirt and rotted leaves. Deep grooves cut by heavy wagon wheels were etched into the newly thawed earth, but they were old tracks. No one had come this way in quite a while.

"It's clear," she called down, not bothering to whisper.

"Why don't you just announce it to the whole bloody forest?" Stout whisper-shouted again. John sighed at the stupidity of their thick companion.

"He's just said that the road's empty," said John. "There's no one to hear. Lucky for us."

"But that cart entered south Sherwood at daybreak," argued Stout. "Surely they'd have made it this far by now."

"Maybe the lookouts were wrong," answered John.

"Or maybe Crooked's Men got to them first," said Much, peeking through the branches.

"South Road's our territory," said Stout. "They wouldn't dare hunt on Merry Men's ground."

"Crooked would dare just about anything," said Much. "He's mad."

"And what does a pip-sized boy know about it, hey?" asked Stout.

"He knows that Tom Crooked didn't get his name from his bad posture," answered John. "I wouldn't put it past him to go poaching on our territory."

John hefted his quarterstaff over his shoulders and gave his back a twist. Even halfway up the tree, Much could hear the cracking and popping of the big man's joints. In his winter furs, he didn't look quite human. She'd heard tales of the bearbaiting in London and of the size of those terrible beasts brought over from the Continent. John in his furs matched the picture in her mind. Much's own clothes were thinner—wool and a bit of banded leather. The days were getting warmer now that the long, brutal winter had finally given way to spring, but the mornings were still chilly with the wet spring thaw. Much had less protection from the cold, because she couldn't afford to be slowed down by cumbersome furs. John didn't rely on speed, not with his size, while Much needed every advantage her small frame could give her. The Merry Men said that it was easier to snatch up a mouse than lay a hand on Much the Miller's Son.

On the ground below her, John and Stout double-checked their homemade weapons and bits of stolen armor. It was a poor showing. John's staff was well used and half again as long as a man, but Stout's mace was little more than a club hammered through with nails. Stout had stuffed his round belly into a greasy leather jerkin made for a thinner man and thrown a fur cape atop that. Much hadn't seen the suit of armor big enough for John.

Stout scratched at a piece of flabby belly poking out between the leather seams. "Well, if Tom did make a grab for that cart, he'll end up with a gut full of arrows."

John made a low noise in his throat but said nothing.

Much counted her knives. Staffs and clubs were for grown men with the muscle to make them count. For a "boy" like Much, survival meant staying out of sight and out of reach. But if it came to a scrape, she had pretty good aim with the knives.

"We sure it's not one of the sheriff's carts?" asked Stout. "Have to let 'em pass if he's got an escort from the sheriff."

The Sheriff of Nottingham was the law in Nottinghamshire, and that included Sherwood Forest. But the good sheriff had a special "arrangement" with the forest bandits—for a bit of monthly bribe money, he left them alone, just as long as the bandits left his own people alone in turn. This meant that he could escort Prince John's taxes safely through, as well as any fat merchants willing to pay for the sheriff's escort. It was always a sad sight to see a well-furnished carriage come rolling along with a couple of the sheriff's guards attached. But every bandit in Sherwood felt it was worth it to keep his neck free of the hangman's noose.

"The cart may arrive yet," said John. "You and me can set up the trip lines, Stout. Much will stay up his tree and keep watch."

Stout grumbled something about everyone doing his fair share as he set about burying a thick rope across the road. When he looked up, Much smiled down at him and made a show of stretching out on a tree limb. Truth was, it was awfully uncomfortable balanced between two uneven branches, but for Stout's benefit Much did her best to look like she was relaxing on a lord's soft featherbed.

As the two men hid the ropes and tied them off, Much watched the road and listened for the sound of hooves or the creak of a cart. If Tom Crooked hadn't already taken the cart, then it should be coming this way within the hour at the latest. That was assuming they didn't stop, and people didn't stop in Sherwood Forest unless they had no other choice. The devil walked this forest at night, folks said, and brigands and cut-throats hunted it by day.

Brigands like Much. And Stout, John Little, Rob, Wat, and all the rest of the Merry Men, as they laughingly called themselves. A troop of bandits that had laid claim to the southern road through Sherwood Forest. A troop of bandits led by the deadliest bowman in all of England. A man without pity or compromise—Gilbert the White Hand.

He could split an arrow in mid-flight, it was said. Stout idolized and feared him. John tolerated him, and Much knew well enough to stay out of his way. Gilbert had taken the "boy" in because they needed someone sneaky. Someone who could scout the town and the woods without raising an alarm. After all, who feared a poor, starved beggar boy?

Much had a place in their band as long as she was useful and for as long as she kept her secret safe. She was another mouth to feed and another split of the loot (although her share was pathetically small). If she displeased Gilbert or became lax or lazy, he'd give her a head start before cutting her down with an arrow in the back. And he didn't look kindly on bandits who came back empty-handed.

John and Stout set the trap and then set about waiting. If a cart came this way, Much would whistle a signal and the two men would hoist up their ropes, both in front of and behind the cart. The rope nets wouldn't stop a horse at full gallop, but they would box in a slow-moving cart well enough. Once the customers saw that they were trapped, they would reach for their weapons. One look at John, and they would drop them again. Then they'd do business with the Merry Men (the Merry Men's business being the robbing-you-of-all-your-coin-and-most-likely-your-boots kind).

The minutes crept by and there was still no sign of the cart, so they sat and passed the time, each in his own fashion. Stout picked the lint from his hairy belly button; John cut a sapling into useless strips of green wood, tied them into knots, and then started in on another. And up in the tree, away from the prying eyes of her companions, Much carved pictures into the bark. She'd never learned her letters, but she'd gotten good at carving the sun and the moon, for father and daughter. She'd marked countless trees throughout Sherwood Forest this way, a hidden tribute to a dead girl named Marianna and her father.

It was another hour before she saw the horse. It came into sight at a slow trot, its rider slumped over the saddle. The creature was breathing heavily, foaming at the mouth and lathered in sweat. The rider must've ridden the poor beast hard before collapsing himself. The pair seemed alone, rider and horse.

Much gave the warning signal, two quick birdcalls in succession, to her companions below.

"Is it the cart?" answered a harsh whisper from the trees. Much held her breath, but the rider did not stir. He was most likely unconscious or dead.

The horse kept coming. Much slowly eased herself down from the branches until she could see John standing there with his huge hand over Stout's mouth. The fat bandit's eyes were indignant.

Much used hand signals to communicate with John.

A single rider, she signed. *Wounded or dead.*

Faking? mouthed John.

Much shrugged. How was she to know?

John let Stout free and hefted his long staff. Stout spit and mumbled something about John's hands tasting like vinegar as he readied his club and took his position. The two men pulled up the rope lines, trapping the horse and rider between them.

If the horse was at all spooked by the sudden appearance of tall John in its path, it was too tired to do anything about it. It just kept on coming. The rider didn't stir.

Stout stepped out onto the road behind it, mace in hand.

"Ho there," John called to the rider. "Are you in need of aid, my friend?"

"We'll happily aid you in lessening your purse!" said Stout, grinning.

"Shut up," answered John. He called back to the rider, "Are you hurt?"

Still there was no answer.

John motioned to Much, and she stepped out of the trees and cautiously took the horse's reins in one hand, her knife in the other. The beast didn't resist. The rider's face was hidden by a cloak, but there was an ugly wet spot visible on the hood where blood had soaked through.

John came around the other side and gave the rider a poke with his staff. He slid a bit in the saddle but didn't react.

"Hey, you alive or dead?" John asked as he poked again. This time John put his arm into it, and the rider rolled off the saddle and onto Much.

Much could've dodged out of the way, but she'd hesitated a second too long, afraid to release the horse's reins, and the rider tumbled on top of her, knocking her to the ground beneath him.

She panicked at first and tried to wiggle her hand free to fetch her fallen knife. But she soon realized that this was no ploy, no clever trap. The rider was deadweight.

Her alarm quickly turned to embarrassment. He wasn't a big man; in fact, he was slightly built and not very tall, but he was still far too heavy for Much to budge. She was pinned, helpless beneath a dead body in the middle of the road.

Stout was already snickering. "Wait, Much. Leave a little fight for us! You don't need to hog all the glory for yourself!"

"Go stuff . . . your head . . . up your backside, Stout," gasped Much as she struggled to free herself from the corpse.

"Stout, look in the saddlebags," said John. "Much, while you're down there, why don't you see if our fallen friend has any coin in his pockets? The horse is nice, but I'd like some silver to brighten my day."

"Where's the blasted cart?" asked Stout as he began rummaging through the horse's pack.

John shook his head. "That's too fine a horse to be riding alongside a merchant's cart. Even as protection."

After some struggle, Much managed to roll the rider's body off her and onto his back. John was watching her with a bemused smile, his hands resting on his staff.

"You know you could've asked for help, lad," he said.

"Didn't need it," she answered, wiping a smear of something wet off her cheek. The dead man had bled on her.

The cloak had fallen back, and his face was visible now—a young man about her age, his sandy-brown hair plastered to his forehead with dried blood. He had soft features, maybe even handsome if not for the look of death on his pale face and his cold blue lips.

Someone groaned.

"Enough, Stout!" she snapped.

"What?" the fat man said. "I didn't say anything!"

Much looked back at John, but he was shaking his head.

They both looked down at the dead man. His lips were moving.

"Lord," said John. "He's alive!"

John was right. The boy was the very shade of the grave. Eyes closed, but his lips were moving.

Much found her knife in the dirt and then leaned closer, putting her ear next to the boy's lips.

John knelt next to her. "What's he saying?"

"Wolves," she answered. "He said . . . *wolves.*"

EIGHT

What bandit worth his salt won't take a risk now and again?
—MUCH THE MILLER'S SON

On the way back to camp, they talked about one thing only—whether they should try to save the boy's life or let him die and take his horse. Arguing *for* the boy was John, who pointed out that though the lad's clothes were plain enough, he carried a fine sword of rich craftsmanship and his horse was superior, not a bug-bitten nag like the ones they had stabled back at the camp. Perhaps the boy had some connection to a rich house. Perhaps he was a servant, or even a person of importance riding under the disguise of poverty. Such a person would be worth a great deal in ransom, but only if he was alive. You just couldn't get a good price for a corpse.

Arguing *against* saving the boy was Stout, who acknowledged that while he rode a fine horse, he probably did so because he'd robbed and killed the rightful owner. The boy had a sneaky, cutthroat look about him, Stout said, a look that reminded him of himself in his younger days. It would be a waste to nurse the little thief back to health only to have to kill him again once they discovered the truth of his awful character.

No one asked Much her opinion, and she didn't offer it. She didn't know what to make of this strange young rider who'd appeared. He was mysterious, and mysteries, on the whole, annoyed her. For instance, the boy kept mumbling feverish things about wolves, and yet it was obvious enough that his wounds were man-made. She wanted to shake him awake, if only to tell him to stop going on about wolves that weren't there. If he quieted down like a sensible person, then he could live if he liked.

Nevertheless, as irritating as she found him, she didn't like the idea of just letting him die. Not when there was a chance he could recover. She believed in that, in a fighting chance. She'd had to these past few years.

Perhaps that was why, as they led the boy toward camp, his limp frame slumped sideways over his horse, she found herself cooling his feverish forehead and neck with a rag soaked in her own drinking water. She wanted him to have that fighting chance.

The Merry Men's camp was hidden safely away among the tangles of Sherwood Forest, at the junction of a pair of long-forgotten hunting trails. As the little team of bandits traveled the secret paths, they heard the telltale whistles and animal calls of hidden lookouts placed along the way. *Friends approaching,* the calls said. *With a prisoner in tow.*

After they'd passed the lookouts, it was several minutes before they could smell the camp's cookfires. At first the Merry Men's defenses had seemed overly complex to Much—the forest was protection enough. But that was before she'd learned about Crooked's Men, the rival bandit gang that hunted the northern woods. There was a truce of sorts these days between the Merry Men and Crooked's Men, but there'd been violence in the past, and any peace was fragile. Each eyed the other's territory greedily.

The South Road wasn't well traveled, and the most Much and her companions could hope for was passing farmers and tradesmen. The sheriff's tax men used the road as they pleased, but no one would dare rob them. The Merry Men were a sad sight, even by outlaw standards, and there was barely enough to go around, and nothing to spare for an ailing stranger.

Wat Crabstaff greeted them at the camp's gate, which was little more than a few sturdy logs strung together with twine. Wat was missing his two front teeth, and his distinctive smile could be seen through the gaps in the gate.

"Well, the mighty have returned! How was business today, sirs?"

"No cart," grumbled Stout.

"We've a wounded man," said John. "Single rider on horseback, but I think he may be worth something to someone."

Stout snorted at this, but John ignored him.

"At the very least we've a well-bred horse and some gear," added Much, trying to sound more pleased with the day's work than she really was. "Horse good enough for a king, I'll wager."

"Oh, well, won't his lordship be pleased?" said Wat as he swung the log gate open wide. "And if your poor wounded prisoner's ransom doesn't get paid, perhaps Gilbert can use him for target practice?"

The Merry Men's camp wasn't impressive to look at, but it served its purpose. There was space enough for every man in the band to have a bit of privacy. Being the newest member, Much was given a leaky construction that was half moth-eaten tent and half drafty lean-to. But she endured the cold as best she could, and John had lent her a set of thick, if smelly, animal hides to bury herself under during the worst hours of the night. She slept like a burrowing animal under all those covers, and in the morning she'd have to crack the frost off the furs.

It was a typical camp belonging to a typical band of half-starved outlaws, but one thing separated the Merry Men's camp from any other in all of England—the statue of the Horned and Hooded God. One of the many tales told about Sherwood was that of Herne the Hunter, a pagan god of the Celts who was said to roam the woods on the night of the full moon. It had been Wat's idea to build their own Herne, as a kind of scarecrow to frighten away unwanted spirits and, more important, to scare travelers into giving up their coin without a fight.

But Wat turned out to be a poor engineer as well as a blasphemous and superstitious idiot. And in the end, they were left with a mammoth statue of wood and fur so heavy that not even John Little could move it more than a few inches, never mind carry it with them on ambush.

Despite its practical uselessness, Wat wouldn't allow them to take it down, lest they offend the real Herne. The Horned and Hooded God (so named because of his giant potato-sack head and broken buck's rack of antlers) now stood watch over them all, day and night, and made an excellent home for mice.

In time, the Merry Men had come to think of the statue as a kind of grotesque good-luck charm, their good luck being that they'd survived the worst winter in memory and hadn't been forced to eat Wat for his stupidity. But spring was upon them, and there was a new sense of cheer in the air, or at least there had been up until the moment Much and John had dragged a half-dead prisoner into their midst.

"We sent you after a cart loaded with goods, and you bring

us back another mouth to feed?" said Gilbert. He stood next to the fire, arms crossed over his broad chest, scowling. His bow was leaning, thankfully unstrung, against his tent. On his left hand began a patchwork of burn scars that ran all the way up his forearm, the pale shade of which earned him his name. But those scars didn't hinder his ability with sword or bow.

"We waited for the cart, but it never showed," said John. "So when he wandered along, we made the best of it."

Stout stared at his shoes, but John met Gilbert's stare head-on. John never looked away, and maybe that was an inevitable by-product of literally looking down on everyone you met, but Much didn't think so. John Little was simply a proud man, thief or no.

The big man gestured to their prisoner, still slung on his horse's back. The boy had stopped calling out in his delirium, and his color had taken on an even paler shade of white, if such a thing were possible. He needed attention, and soon, if he was going to have a chance of living.

"The horse is fine," offered Much. "And John and I thought he might be worth some coin. A ransom's better than a cart of cheap rugs, surely!"

Gilbert turned his hard stare on Much. He had a craggy, pockmarked face, and Much had never been able to stare him down the way John could.

"A ransom could bring us wealth, to be sure," said Gilbert. "Could also bring us a whole legion of king's men. Could lead their spears right up our backsides, too, depending on just who this fellow really is. Might be the wayward son of a nice plump merchant, or he might be the bloody secret son of the archbishop himself, *but we don't know, do we?*"

"Eh, that's what I told them," said Stout.

"Shut up, Stout," said Gilbert.

John had a look about him that said he'd rather be hitting something than talking. And by calling him out in front of all the other men, Gilbert seemed to be daring him to say or do something foolish.

"But, Gilbert," said Much. She needed to talk fast. "We won't know anything if he's dead. What bandit worth his salt won't take a risk now and again?"

Gilbert smiled at Much. That smile unnerved her more than any amount of shouting or cursing. He drew a small knife from his belt and approached her. Much's hand went reflexively to her own blades, and she felt John stiffen by her side.

"Well said, little thief," said Gilbert. "So he's your problem now."

Much started to protest, but Gilbert cut her off.

"And," he said, "when all's said and done, if he lives and turns out to be worth a nice ransom without bother, then you'll get your fair share. But if he turns out to be something more, if there are people out there looking for him that could cause us trouble . . . well, in that case, you'll be the one to slit his throat."

John put a hand on her arm. "There's no need for that, Gilbert. We all agreed to bring him in, and he's our responsibility."

Much shook off John's hand. He didn't see what was happening here, but she did. The rest of the men had gathered around and were watching the show. Gilbert was putting Much to the test to see if their youngest member really had the mettle to be an outlaw. If she let John fight this fight for her, she'd lose respect in the eyes of the group, respect she'd been fighting for months to earn.

She spat at the knife in Gilbert's hand.

"I don't need it," she said. "I'll use my own if it comes to that."

Gilbert let out a barking laugh. "We'll see, little thief. We'll see."

"But I won't have him in my tent," she said. "He talks in his sleep."

Gilbert started to yell, but she pointed at a dingy little tent set off from the others. Downwind.

"He can sleep there," she said.

Someone snickered. John shook his head. Much knew that she'd just condemned the poor boy to a fate possibly worse than death, but she couldn't—wouldn't—have him in her tent. Not even to nurse him back to health.

"Well," said Gilbert, eyeing the secluded tent. "Maybe the vapors in there will purify the bad blood."

There were sprinkles of more laughter as the captain walked over and kicked the tent.

"Hey! Get your lazy arse up! We've got a surprise for you!"

From within came a long, low moan, like the sound a wounded animal might make as it dragged itself to a lonely spot to die.

Gilbert pulled back the tent flap to allow in the sun, but in doing so, he let the noxious air inside escape. Much and the rest of the Merry Men covered their noses. A few turned away.

And with a roar halfway between rage and pain, the occupant stumbled out into the camp. He was tall, though not nearly as tall as John, and his black beard was filthy and crusted. His clothes were soiled and threadbare, and he clutched at his head with one hand while clawing at the offending sunlight with the other.

"Wine," he croaked. "I need some wine."

"Christ, Rob," said John. "It's still morning!"

"Rob the Drunk," said Gilbert with that same oily grin. "I

wanted to introduce you to your new tent mate. You're both half dead anyway, so what's the difference?"

Much glanced over at the boy's face, so pale and so helpless, and nearly changed her mind. How could she consign him to such a fate?

As if in answer, Rob vomited all over his own boots.

NINE

I don't care. John, Richard, or King Fart the Great,
they're all the same to us out here in the wild.
—GILBERT THE WHITE HAND

"What's your name?" the boy asked. Judging by his size, he was younger than Will by a few years. Small and slight of bone. Delicate features hidden beneath a constant scowl and a thick layer of grime.

"I've told you," Will answered. "Will Scarlet."

The boy snorted. "You'll have to do better than that. No Scarlets hereabouts. No Scarlets anywhere, I'm thinking."

The boy crouched with half his body outside the tent so that he could get the occasional sniff of fresh air. No such luck for Will. He was stuck inside with the stench and the stench's source snoring away beside him. The stale, sour smell of wine and vomit reminded Will of his father's hall after a wild feasting night, only there was no escaping this foul mix. And there was no getting used to it, either.

"You've got to eat if you want to get your strength back," said the boy. He offered Will a bowl of lumpy porridge, but Will made no move to take it.

"Let me out of here and I'll eat," said Will. "I'm strong enough to walk."

"That's why I can't let you out. Can't have you walking off."

Will's fever had broken a day ago, and he'd emerged clear-headed, if still physically weak. Whoever his captors were, they weren't any regular military force. These undisciplined men, with their shoddy weapons and patchwork armor, weren't the sheriff's soldiers or even Guy's mercenaries. Bounty hunters perhaps. Or bandits. Either way, they'd saved Will's life, but they'd also made him into a prisoner—just how valuable a prisoner, they were obviously trying to suss out.

"Since you don't believe my name, how about telling me yours?" asked Will.

The boy hesitated for just a moment before answering. "Much," he said. "My name's Much."

Will smiled. "Not many Muches around these parts, either, I'd suppose."

The boy, Much, grew suddenly angry. "But I'm not the one supposed to be answering questions. You are. And your name matters, mine don't. Yours could mean the difference between living or dying!"

"And why does it matter to you?"

Much looked away. When he next spoke, his voice was low, and he glanced worriedly over his shoulder. "I'm not one for useless killing, that's all. Your clothes are poor, but you rode into Sherwood on a fine horse, carrying a sword worth more than every weapon in this camp. You claim a made-up name, but your accent is flowery. Schooled, like a priest's."

Much looked Will in the eye. "You're not who you're pretending to be, that's obvious to everyone here. So be thinking about who you really are. Too important, and you're too much risk. Easier for you to just disappear. Not important enough, and you're just another mouth to feed food we don't have. Also easier for you to disappear. Make yourself just important enough to live, Will Scarlet. Just enough."

Much set the porridge down next to Will and handed him a wineskin before backing out of the tent, holding his nose as he went.

"And sorry about Rob," he said, looking at the snoring, stinking man on the other side of the tent. "Eat something, if you can."

Much let the tent flap close, and Will was left with the drunk's snores and his own troubled thoughts for company. The last couple of months had been a blur. After they'd escaped from Shackley Castle, Hugo had led Will to his mother, and together they went into hiding with Hugo's kinfolk in the village of Derby. There they waited out the worst of the winter months until it was safe enough to make for the coast. They'd planned to escape to France, to Lady Katherine's family.

It had been Hugo's plan to split Will and his mother up—to take separate ships and regroup when they reached the mainland. That way, they doubled their chances that one member of the Shackley family would escape. After some arguing, Will's mother finally relented, but she insisted that Hugo accompany Will.

When the spring thaw came, Will's mother set out for the coast by traveling south out of Derby, while Hugo and Will took the forest road. The bandits had set upon the two of them soon thereafter. Not these people, at least not from the faces Will had gotten a look at, but other men. Crueler men who were not interested in taking prisoners. And now Hugo was dead. Will had seen his father's loyal steward catch an arrow in the throat. Bellwether bolted after that, outpacing the men on foot, and this time Will didn't fight her. He simply held on until his own wounds overtook him. It seemed that the mare's skittishness had saved his life.

Will wondered if his mother was waiting for him even now, across the Channel, waiting for a ship that would never come. The truth was, Will would never join her there, not even if he managed to escape from his captivity. His destiny lay back at Shackley Castle, and this time he wouldn't run from it.

He was going to kill Sir Guy.

When he closed his eyes, he saw the faces of all his lost friends and family—Nan, Osbert, Jenny, Milo. He prayed that they'd gotten far away from that villain and his mercenaries, but he feared the worst. Life serving a man like Sir Guy would be nightmarish. But they hadn't had a secret tunnel to escape through. They hadn't even been given the choice of cowardice.

Geoff died protecting him. Hugo died protecting him. Even now, his shame burned hot in his chest. His mother hadn't understood. She'd said that as the heir of Shackley House, he had a royal duty to live to fight again. She'd said that when his father returned with King Richard, all would be set right and they'd come back from their exile in France. Will had never recognized it before now, but his mother clung to false hope like it was a ship's mast in a storm. But in that courtyard battle, Will had gotten a glimpse at the way the world truly worked. Bad men did what they liked if they were strong enough to get away with it, brothers stole their brothers' crowns, and fathers did not come back from war.

Now Will was all that remained of the Shackley name.

That night he dreamed of dead wolves that turned to men. He awoke many times to strange sounds outside. Animal cries, some familiar and some strangely alien, some distant and some frighteningly close. He remembered the stories about Sherwood Forest—how it was said that deep in the woods was a cave leading all the way to hell and that the devil walked the woods at night looking for souls to drag back down with him.

In the morning, Will's throat was sore and raw. He was thirsty enough to try to stomach the watered wine, but the skin was empty. The porridge, too, had been eaten, and Will's tent mate slept contentedly on his cot. Will was sure that if he examined the man, he'd find bits of porridge in his beard, but he dared not get that close.

As rusty dawn light crept into the tent, Will examined his wounds with his fingers, gently probing their outlines. The swelling over his eye had gone down as the nasty wound became an ugly scab. He'd end up with a scar there to match the one on his cheek. His face had changed so much in just a few short months.

Will waited for Much to come to him with breakfast, but though he heard commotion outside his tent, no one bothered to look in on him. It was several long hours before Much reappeared, and when he did, he was empty-handed.

"You can walk?" the boy asked as he poked his head inside the tent.

"Yes," said Will. "But I'm thirsty if you have—"

"Then get moving. Gilbert wants to see you. Out here."

Much tossed Will a waterskin and left without another word.

As Will gulped down the leathery-tasting water, he wondered at the boy who'd been so concerned about him yesterday and who seemed too busy to spare him more than a few words today.

Too busy, or too scared. *Gilbert wants to see you.*

Will sat up and waited for the dizziness to pass. His feet

were bare, but he didn't see his boots anywhere. Will didn't want to meet this Gilbert barefooted, but there was nothing to be done about it.

He'd just gotten his feet beneath him when he noticed the drunk, Rob, was awake and watching him. The man had startlingly blue eyes despite the red bloodshot.

"Careful out there, boy," said Rob. "How you say a thing's as important as what you say."

The idea of this thieving drunk offering him advice irritated Will.

"It'd be easier if I had something in my belly," answered Will. "It'd be easier if someone hadn't eaten my food and drunk my wine while I slept."

Rob chuckled. "You're complaining about being stolen from to a camp full of thieves? Hope you can do better than that."

Now he knew why Rob's advice irritated him so—the man was smug about offering it. Even hungover and stinking from his own vomit, the man had an air about him like *he knew better.*

"I'll be on my best behavior," said Will, turning his back on Rob and making for the tent door, albeit somewhat unsteadily.

"I'm serious. Gilbert will kill you if you answer wrong—or more like he'll make Much do it."

Will stopped. "What are you talking about?"

"Gilbert wanted to cut your throat the first time he saw you, but Much stood for you. Gilbert gave in then, but he's a perverse sort, and he's ordered that if you're to die, it'll be by Much's knife."

"I didn't think Much was the sort."

"He's not," said Rob. "But if he doesn't do it, Gilbert will kill him, too. Just for show."

"I see."

"So answer smart and don't put him in that position. You've got two lives in your hands now."

"This Gilbert of yours sounds like quite the leader."

"He's a bloody devil that should be buried to his neck in horse dung. The men hate him."

"Then why follow him?"

"Scared. And they're right to be. He's the best fighter out there. Not a man among them who could take him in a fair fight. Not even John."

Will had caught glimpses of a giant who'd often been at Much's side while Will was still on the mend. That must have been John.

"And that's the pecking order among thieves, is it? Gilbert's the best fighter in the band, so he gets made leader."

"Didn't say he was the best fighter in the band," said Rob. "I said he was the best fighter *out there.*"

It took a moment before Will realized that Rob was referring to himself, but when he did, he nearly laughed in Rob's face. The man could barely stand up straight. Still, if he wanted to boast a bit, Will would let him. He had no time to argue.

"Tell me something before I go," said Will. "Why all this now? You haven't mumbled a word the whole time I've been sharing your tent. Why talk to me now? Is it Much? You worried about him?"

"Gilbert cut my wine rations, but the boy gives me his," he answered. "If you stay alive, I get to keep drinking yours, too. That's twice the wine."

Rob laid his head back down on his cot and closed his eyes. "Good luck to you."

❄ ❄ ❄

Will had seen outlaws before. Plenty of times. Because he was a lord of men, his father was charged with keeping the peace, and Will had had ample opportunity to see criminals assembled in the courtyard, awaiting their lord's justice.

What had struck Will then, and what struck him now, was not how dangerous the men were (some were doubtless fierce enough) but how pathetic they looked. These were hard-scrapping peasants with knives instead of plows. Desperate men who'd given up on hope.

These bandits were no different. They might call themselves the Merry Men, but their eyes were every bit as hopeless as the blank stares of his father's condemned prisoners. And if they'd taken to a life of crime to escape poverty, then they must be terribly disappointed with what they'd found.

They were pitiful to look at, all except Gilbert.

Gilbert stood facing him, a fine chain shirt across his chest and Will's sword at his hip. He fondled it like it was a king's jeweled scepter. He reminded Will of the black wolf he'd killed, the leader of the pack. Like the wolf, this one had earned an extra share of the spoils.

"We're glad you're feeling better," Gilbert was saying. "Who knew that little Much had such skill as a surgeon?"

A few of the men laughed at this—the fat one known as Stout, in particular—but most stayed quiet.

"So it'll grieve me greatly if we have to kill you," Gilbert said.

"That's two of us," said Will.

That earned a grin at least from the bandit leader. Will had guessed that these men would expect a lordling to weep and beg for his life, but Will wouldn't give them that. His insides were all twisted up in fear, and he was wishing he'd had time to use the chamber pot first, but he did his best to appear calm. If they were going to believe his story, then he needed to remain collected.

"Much here tells me you're named Will Scarlet," said Gilbert. "Can't see how the name Scarlet profits us in any way."

"It's not my real name," said Will.

"Really," answered Gilbert dryly. "What a shocking confession."

Will took a deep breath. He could feel Much standing next to him, the tension in the boy's body. He'd been practicing what to say all morning long.

"My father's name is Hugo Blunt, steward in service to Lord Rodric Shackley. But that is not my name because my father never married my mother. He raised me on the grounds of Shackley Castle, but I have no claim to his property, or his name. They called me Scarlet, after my mother."

Gilbert seemed to be considering this as he scratched his pockmarked cheek. Will had heard once that the best lie was the one closest to the truth. The man who'd told him that was Sheriff Mark Brewer, and he should know, since he turned out to be a traitor and a lying coward in the end.

"We heard what happened at Shackley Castle," said Gilbert. "How the lord regent there was exposed in a traitorous plot to kill Prince John."

"That's not true!" The words were out of his mouth before he could stop them. It was dangerous defending his family too fiercely, but he couldn't let Guy's slander stand unanswered, not even before a band of thieves. "The Sheriff of Nottingham allowed Sir Guy's thugs into the castle, and Lord Geoffrey was murdered by Guy himself because he wouldn't support Prince John against King Richard. I saw it happen!"

Gilbert shrugged. "The way I hear it told, he was killed in

a brawl in his own courtyard. Insulted the prince's good name and started a fight he couldn't win. Prince John's since given the stewardship of Shackley Castle over to Sir Guy. But the truth of the matter is, I don't care. John, Richard, or King Fart the Great, they're all the same to us out here in the wild.

"Now," he continued, "where's your father? He alive or dead?"

"Dead," answered Will, and that was partly true at least. Hugo was dead, and Will didn't have to fake tears to mourn the man who'd served him so bravely, but Will's real father might still be alive, somewhere.

"Dead," said Gilbert. "Shame. Dead men don't pay for bastard boys."

Will could see the ice in Gilbert's eyes. He heard the rustle of movement nearby, perhaps a knife being drawn from its sheath.

"You're right that no one'll pay my ransom," Will said quickly. "But I can help you. I know how you can be rich men!"

"I know," said Gilbert. "I've heard the sermons. Work hard, love and fear our good king what's-his-name, and we can all be rich in heaven! No thank you."

"Shackley Castle still stands, and there are real riches inside!" said Will.

"Lovely," said Gilbert. "I'll ask Sir Guy to show them to me the next time I pop in for supper!"

"But I know a secret passage into the castle!" Will said. "It was known only to the royal family and my father. Guy can't have discovered it."

Gilbert held up his hand. No one moved while the bandit leader stared at Will, judging him. Weighing his life against the trouble it was likely to cause.

"I still suspect that half of what you are telling me is pure manure," said Gilbert at last. "And if this half turns out to be the lie, I'll run you through myself. But if you can tell us the location of this passage, you might just live to see the morning, Will Scarlet."

Will let out a long breath. It could have been his imagination, but he thought Much did the same.

"I'll do better than that," said Will. "I'll take you there myself."

TEN

Better a live prisoner than dead target practice.
—MUCH THE MILLER'S SON

A fallen lord. A plot to steal the throne of England. A hidden treasure at the end of a secret passage. It sounded like one of her father's bedtime tales. When Much had told Will to think carefully about what he could say to stay alive, she hadn't expected this load of dung. What a soft-skulled idiot.

Much had listened quietly as Will told them all his fairy story of hidden treasure, and like children they believed it. Truth was, the camp was filled with enough desperation and frustration that they'd have believed anything. Times had never been good, but they'd been getting steadily worse, and once Gilbert discovered that there was no such passage and no hidden treasure, he'd have Will killed in the worst way he could imagine—and Gilbert the White Hand was a frighteningly imaginative man. And if, during the slow process of the boy's dying, it was revealed that Much had encouraged him to lie to begin with, then she'd likely be next.

But for today at least, the camp was abuzz with talk of treasure. The Merry Men couldn't care less about Will's story of the murder of Lord Geoffrey Shackley. What mattered most now was the prospect of silver, and something else—the attack on Will and his father. The two of them had been ambushed by bandits, which was nothing remarkable in these parts. What was remarkable was where the ambush had taken place—the South Road, the Merry Men's road.

Someone else was poaching on their territory.

There was little debate as to who it was. Crooked's Men had threatened incursions before, and the sheer brutality of the attack was Tom Crooked's style. The Merry Men were scum, thieves of the lowest sort and proud of it, but Crooked had assembled a band of vicious cutthroats. Crooked's Men had a saying: "Silver glitters more sweetly when it's painted red."

The ambush was Crooked's work, of that they were certain. What they should do about it was still unsettled. Few were happy about ceding territory to a rival band, but even fewer were eager to start a war with Crooked's Men. Of those that wanted to pay Crooked back in kind, John's voice was the loudest (in part simply because the giant's voice boomed as a general rule). Even more than the slight against the Merry Men, John was offended at the act itself. If Sherwood became known for wanton murder, merchants would find another way around it. As it was, folks took their chances on the South Road because all they were risking was their property, and maybe a bruised pate. Often, hired guards didn't even put up a fight, because they knew that if they simply surrendered, they would live to see their wives and mistresses again. Men were easier to deal with when they were fighting for coin instead of their lives.

For her part, Much preferred to let the matter be. The reason Crooked had started poaching on their territory in the first place was that he had more men. Meaner men. She'd come to Sherwood to thieve, not to march to war. She'd come to Sherwood because she was running away. She'd stayed because there was nowhere else to go, and in time she'd discovered things here worth staying for.

Bloody Will Scarlet. The boy was trouble.

The men in the camp wanted it both ways—they wanted Will's promised fortune, and they wanted to send a message to Crooked. Gilbert devised a plan that would accomplish the two goals at the same time, or so he boasted. But Much had learned long ago that when men resorted to boasting, it was time to start worrying.

As Much packed up her gear, the hunting party assembled outside. In the privacy of her own tent, she changed her shirt and redressed the long bandage she wore wrapped tightly around her chest. As the months passed, it was getting increasingly uncomfortable to wear the wrapping, but she needed more than just a baggy shirt and short hair to pass for a boy these days. It hadn't always been that way, but her body was changing and the truth was getting harder to conceal. The men knew better than to come into her tent unannounced (more than one had earned himself a shoe to the face that way), but she still changed quickly and with her back to the door.

Once properly dressed and disguised, she added two long knives to her belt, plus a smaller blade tucked into her boot. She slung a pack over her shoulder loaded with several days' rations (hard bread and acorns boiled enough times so as to be edible, if not particularly tasty). Lastly, she brushed her bangs down over her eyes. She kept the rest of her pretty face well hidden with filth, but she'd inherited her mother's almond-shaped bright green eyes, so fetching on any other girl her age and so dangerous for her. It was annoying to always have her hair dangling in her vision, but it couldn't be helped—there was no way to dirty up her eyes.

When she stepped outside, she found John waiting with Will. Rob stood off a ways, getting sick in a bush.

Spotting Much, Will gestured angrily at Rob.

"I can't believe that drunk is coming with us!" he whispered.

"He's quite the fighter when he sobers up," said Much.

"But *can* he sober up? For longer than a few hours, I mean?"

John obviously caught the gist of their whispered conversation, because he answered with a laugh, loud enough for Rob to hear. "Rob's a useless pain in the arse when he's like this, but there'll be no wine out there on the road."

"Go bite yourself, *Little John,*" moaned Rob from his doubled-over position.

Much started to laugh, but John caught her eye.

"Don't," he warned, pointing a thick finger at Much's face. "Don't encourage him."

John walked over to Rob and, ignoring the man's curses, helped him onto his horse.

Much leaned over to Will.

"You see, John's family name is Little," she explained. "So Rob calls him—"

"Little John. I get it," said Will, cutting her off. "Why haven't we left yet?"

"We'll be on our way soon enough."

"Not soon enough for my taste," Will said, folding his arms and glaring at nothing in particular.

Much recognized the look, because she'd used it often, back when she'd had the luxury of doing so. Back when she'd still been a miller's daughter instead of a miller's son. Will was in a pout, and he expected it to actually accomplish something here in Sherwood Forest. The boy was a spoiled fool, as well as a troublesome one.

"You do realize you're lucky to be alive, don't you?"

Will answered without looking at her. "I'm a prisoner."

"Better a live prisoner than dead target practice. Which, by the way, is what you'll become if this secret passage of yours doesn't exist. I hope you've thought that far ahead."

"Have *you*?" asked Will, finally looking at her.

"What? What do you mean?"

"I mean, if it turns out I am lying. If I'm more trouble than I'm worth, have you thought about how you'll kill me?"

Much opened her mouth to protest, but no words came out. She'd never intended to do it, no matter what she'd said to Gilbert. But how had Will learned of it?

"Will you knife me in the back then and there, or will you wait until I'm sleeping and just cut my throat?" he asked.

"Neither," said Much. "I don't know who you've been talking to, but I wouldn't do that."

"Never mind," said Will, turning back away. "The passage is real enough. I'll get you all into the castle, and you can ransack the place as long as you stay out of my way. Once my work there is done, I don't care what you do to me."

Much swallowed her shame, and it went down like a bitter pit that stuck in her throat. Will thought her capable of knifing him in the back, and there was no way to make him believe otherwise. And why should he? Since coming to Sherwood, he'd been attacked by bandits, then nursed back to health by even more bandits, only to learn that he was nothing more than ransom. She'd been the closest thing he had to an ally in this camp until he learned she'd been assigned to be his assassin.

It would be pointless to keep arguing, which was why Much was almost relieved to see the two men she despised most—Stout and Gilbert—approaching. Stout was wearing a smug grin (God knew why—it just made him look more like a dimwit) and carried a bright red coat in his hands.

"A change in the plan," said Gilbert. "Stout's going with you."

Stout hooked his thumbs into his belt like he was a man of importance. "Better odds with Stout along, eh?"

"Stout's more muscle, should things turn ugly," said Gilbert.

Much started to protest. "But another man will just make it all the harder to—"

"It's done," said Gilbert. "Done is done. And since young master Scarlet here is wearing clothes that smell like a dead cat, we scrounged up something a bit fresher."

Stout tossed the coat at Will. It was a gaudy thing, the garish coat of a foppish gentleman, dyed dark red. Tassels hung about the buttons, and lace cuffed the sleeves.

"Fitting, don't you think, *Scarlet*?"

"I'm fine in my own clothes, thank you," said Will.

"Wear it," said Gilbert. "It's not a request."

With a sigh, Will removed his shirt and pulled on the coat. He didn't look nearly as terrible as Gilbert had hoped. It actually fit him quite well, although the lace and tassels needed to go. And Much would be relieved not to have to smell his old shirt any longer.

Then Will surprised her by stepping forward and standing face to face with Gilbert, despite his dandy new attire. "I want my sword back."

Gilbert frowned, his hand going to the pommel of that very same blade.

"Well, as I see it," he said, "the Merry Men here saved you out of a sense of Christian charity and neighborly affection! Could've let you die out there on that road, but instead we took you in. Fed you. Sheltered you."

Gilbert smiled as he patted the sword's pommel. "Let's just call this recompense, shall we?"

"Asking payment for charity is not really charity, now is it?" said Will.

"Fine!" barked Gilbert. "Then I'm just plain stealing it! And your horse, too!"

Will, to his credit, didn't back down. He didn't look away. He was a brave boy, Much had to give him that. Brave and bloody foolish.

"Can I have another sword, then?" asked Will finally. "If I'm to be of any help, I'll need a blade."

"Much is the lookout," said Gilbert. "Rob, John, and Stout will do the fighting. *Your* job is to show them the secret passage and where the treasure is. Nothing more. Don't need a sword to point."

Gilbert laughed. "You can have your boots back, though. No one can fit in them."

Then he turned and marched over to the gate, where he had words with John. Rob was leaning over his saddle, his head resting on his horse's neck. He might even have been passed out.

The beginning of another grand adventure, thought Much.

Prince John was well known to be an avid hunter, and in his time as regent he had acquired, or stolen, a number of residences closest to his favorite forests. Some were true castles in their own right, while others, like this one, were little more than watchtowers. When not in use by the prince, these converted hunting lodges were usually manned by caretakers. Gilbert had recently learned of a particular tower, an ancient structure overlooking the road out of Nottingham, that was being cared for by Sir Guy of Gisborne. This was commonly known. What wasn't common knowledge was that Guy kept a number of his men there with swift horses so that they might keep an eye on the comings and goings between Nottingham and London, and there had been many as of late. In short, Sir Guy used the prince's hunting lodge to spy on the Sheriff of Nottingham, whom he trusted not a whit.

A useful bit of intelligence, to be sure, and one that Gilbert had stored away with no particular plan for exploiting it—until now.

It was shortly after dusk when Sir Guy's watchtower spies heard a commotion coming from the stables. A fresh stable and a new set of kennels had been built by the prince to house his horses and hounds for the hunt, but the rest of the tower was ancient. Thick stone walls sunk deep into the soil, strong enough to defend against anything less than a real siege; it was obvious why the prince felt safe there. But while wolves weren't a bother to men within those stone walls, their horses out in the new stables were more vulnerable.

Three of the four men stationed there had just gotten a game of dice going, and the fire was roaring nicely and hot enough to drive away the damp. So they sent the youngest of them down to check on the horses. The young guard took his crossbow and his short sword. He would've strapped on his helmet, but he knew the other men would laugh at him.

In the dark it was hard to see anything truly amiss. They'd been lazy and allowed the courtyard and surrounding field to become overgrown. There were too many places for a wolf—or a man, for that matter—to hide out here. Too many long shadows in the moonlight.

He heard something moving near the stable. Something that was spooking the horses.

The guard stood in the gloomy courtyard, alone. A light burned in the window above, and the sounds of laughter and cursing echoed from within. After a few minutes, he sighed and stepped cautiously toward the stable, crossbow at the ready.

The horses had settled a bit after their initial outburst, but there was still a lot of nervous shuffling and stomping from within their stalls. Whatever had spooked them in the first place could still be nearby. If it was a wolf, he'd run it off. If it was a horse thief, he'd take care of that, too.

The young guard found the rear door of the stable swinging wide open, the latch unhooked. No wolf, then. He had turned to call up to the lighted window and his fellow guards when one of the dark clumps of shadow near him moved. It swung something at his head, and then stars exploded before his eyes.

He awoke with a hard knot of pain on his forehead. Someone was talking.

"You think we should skin 'em, Crooked?"

"You daft idiot! I told you not to go using my name!"

"What's it matter if we're going to skin 'em anyway?"

The young guard's stomach turned at that name. He knew the bandit called Tom Crooked by reputation, and skinning was one of the more merciful ends he could hope for. As his vision cleared, he saw that he'd been stripped down to his underclothes and tied to a table leg inside the watchtower. His companions were tied up and in their underclothes as well.

Standing over them was a powerfully built man with a gray beard. It was twisted up in strange braids that were burnt off at the ends. He wore a black studded-leather jerkin and a dirty white scarf. Tom Crooked.

One of his henchmen stood nearby. Another came into the

room, a man so tall he had to stoop to fit through the doorway. Both had covered their faces with white scarves—the mark of Crooked's gang.

"We aren't skinning them yet," said Crooked. "Unless they try to escape."

Crooked looked them over. "Thanks to your alert guardsman here, we have let ourselves in." He held up the young guard's key ring.

"You got us all captured!" one of the young guard's companions said to him.

The man was answered with a boot to his gut as the fat one kicked him. Hard. He looked ready to do it again, but the tall one stepped in the way.

"At least he was taken while tryin' to do his duty," said Crooked. "You lot lost your pants in the middle of a game of dice!"

The men looked sheepishly around the room, anywhere but at each other.

"Now, here's what we're going to do," said Crooked. "I'm makin' use of those pants a' yours for a day or so. While I'm gone, you'll stay tied up. I'm not killin' you yet, but I'll most likely do so when I return, so's if you have any prayin' or such you need doin', you'd best get to it!"

Hours later and a few leagues away from the watchtower keep, John and Stout measured the cut of newly stolen trousers against each other as Rob brushed wood ash out of his singed beard, returning it to its original black. Then Much used her knife to help him trim away the burnt braids. Stout, Will, and Rob would fit in the stolen uniforms well enough. John could wear the tabard and helm, but no pants fit his long legs, so he had to hope no one examined him too closely. Much gave up on trying to disguise herself in the soldiers' gear. She looked like a boy playing soldier in his father's clothes.

They'd made camp safely out of view of the watchtower and the road, beneath an outcropping of craggy rocks surrounded by tall poplar trees. From there, they could keep an eye on anyone coming and going.

"It was a good plan," Stout was saying. "When those men tell Sir Guy it was Crooked's Men that robbed them, old Crooked's going to be up to his neck in trouble!"

"You didn't need to go kicking them," said Much. "They were already tied up and helpless, if you didn't notice."

"We're supposed to be Crooked's Men, right? Crooked's Men don't care whether you're tied up or sleeping! I still say we should've killed three and left one to tell the tale. Crooked wouldn't leave all four tied up and still breathing."

"Knock it off," said Rob. "If Gilbert's information is right and they keep to schedule, then a rider with provisions will arrive at the watchtower tomorrow. They'll stay tied up till then, which means we've got until dawn to make it to Shackley Castle and Master Will's secret passage. So get those uniforms on and let's get moving!"

Stout and Will did as they were told, and soon four of them were dressed in the armor of Sir Guy's mercenaries, the black and silver stallion insignia across their tunics. Much would pass herself off as a servant if need be.

As they packed up for the ride to Shackley, Will leaned close to Much's ear.

"What's with Rob?" he asked. "He's giving orders and . . ."

"What?" she said.

"He just sounds . . . different."

"He's sober," Much answered, and she steered her horse out onto the road. They had a long night ahead of them, and the most dangerous part was still to come. Bloody Will Scarlet was to lead them all to fortune and glory. God help them.

ELEVEN

All right, where's the treasure?
—Stout

Will thought he'd prepared himself to see Shackley Castle again, but even in the dark, the familiar silhouette brought back too many memories, too fast. There was his home, and inside those wooden walls were the yards where he had played and practiced swordsmanship and the herb garden where he'd stolen mint leaves. Beyond that was the main tower window, where Nan had kept an eye on him. It was a clear night, and even at a distance he could see the glow of a fire within. But it wasn't Nan keeping watch up there anymore.

In the months they'd spent in hiding, Will and his mother had heard rumors that many of the old family servants had been let go or fled from Guy's service. The Horse Knight was suspicious of any who'd been loyal to the Shackley family, and with good reason. The latest tale was that when Guy asked the family surgeon for a headache remedy, he'd been given a constipation cure instead. The surgeon delivered the medicine, then snuck away during the night before the cure had a chance to work. It was said that Guy's shouts of rage could be heard coming from the privy for days afterward.

If Nan was lucky, she'd have been dismissed from Guy's service without having to flee in the night. After all, what use did the Horse Knight have for a nurse? This castle, Will's family home for so many generations, was now by royal decree the property of Sir Guy of Gisborne, and he wasn't one to have children running about the halls.

Sir Guy, who would be dead by morning.

Much had been quiet during the ride from the watchtower to Shackley House, but more than once Will caught the boy staring at him. Perhaps he meant it when he said that he'd no plans to kill him. The boy didn't seem a cold-blooded killer, but there was a hardness in him—something that he was protecting and something he would fight for. Maybe kill for, if pressed.

Will resolved not to let himself get too comfortable with these men. Rob was a drunk, Stout was stupid and cruel, and John might seem a man of honor but in the end was just a bandit like the rest of them. They were using Will because he promised to make them rich, but what they didn't know was that Will was using them, too. He could get them into the castle, but no treasure was waiting there. What was there was Sir Guy of Gisborne, and Will would need these men and their swords if he was going to get close enough to the Horse Knight to kill him.

Much was his only concern. Try as he might, Will was unable to justify leading the boy into danger under false pretenses. True, he was only a few years younger than Will, but Will's childhood was over and it'd died a quick death. Starting with the wolves, and ending with Geoff's murder. Will Scarlet was left with a need for vengeance as red as his name.

If he could, he'd spare the boy. If he couldn't . . . well, revenge was a bloody business, old Osbert used to say.

The towering presence of Shackley House brought up

thoughts of his parents. What would his father think of his only son turned assassin? But he hadn't been there when Geoff died. He hadn't seen the look in his brother's eyes as the life left them. And if Will's father was truly alive out there somewhere with King Richard, and if they were coming back to England, then Will would be counted among the loyal patriots who'd stood up to Prince Lackland and his cronies.

Guy would die, and by Will's hand. Others could judge him as they might.

He found the entrance to the secret passage easily. The copse of trees that disguised it was far enough away from the castle that they could tie their horses there and not be noticed from the walls. Much watched with a strange look on his face as Will rolled away the brush that revealed the hidden grate and dark hole beneath. Was Much surprised that he'd told the truth about the passage? Suspicious? The boy's face was hard to read.

Stout's, on the other hand, wasn't. The fat man was already drooling.

"That there the tunnel to the treasure?"

Will ignored him and turned to John.

"I don't have a key."

Wordlessly, John reached down and put both hands on the grate. It was rusted, and the metal cried out in protest as the big man strained, the veins in his neck bulging with the effort. Then it came loose with a sudden wrenching sound, and the way was open. A short ladder descended into a passage beneath, disappearing into darkness.

"One at a time," said Will. "And, John, I'm sorry, but you might have to squeeze a bit."

John grunted in annoyance. "I'm used to it. The whole world's too blasted small."

"Since we're wearing the uniforms, we three'll go first," said Rob. "It'll be easier to explain ourselves if we're disguised as Guy's hired swords. Will in front, me next—"

"I'll go," said Stout suddenly. "I'll follow the boy."

Everyone looked at Stout. Even with the little Will knew of him, he hadn't guessed Stout the sort to volunteer to march out front—or even second—into danger. Judging by the looks on their faces, Will didn't think the others had guessed it, either.

"Fine," said Rob. "Stout goes second. I'll be third. John, you and Much bring up the rear."

"Much should stay here," said Will.

"What?" said Much. "Why?"

"The boy's sneaky as a shadow, Will," said John. "He'll be useful."

"And if questioned, I can pass as a servant or kitchen boy easily enough," said Much.

Will shook his head. He couldn't let the boy risk his life, not even to get his chance at revenge. "There are patrols," Will lied. "We need you here in case they come this way."

"You never mentioned any patrols," said Rob. "Why wait until now?"

Will took a deep breath. When Rob wasn't drowning in his cups, he had an unnerving stare. Will was starting to prefer the drunk version.

"I . . . I was afraid you wouldn't come with me," lied Will. "I was afraid you'd say no."

"Well, you were bloody right, weren't you?" said Stout. "What if they find our horses?"

"That's why Much stays here," said Will. "The trees will keep the horses hidden, and Much will keep them quiet. And he can have them ready if we need a quick escape."

"I'm not a stable hand!" said Much. "I'm a thief!"

"You're a lookout," said Rob. "And a good one. We should do it Will's way. You stay here and keep your eyes open for those patrols."

"He's right," said John. "We need the horses to make a quick getaway if things go sour."

Rob brushed his hands on his pants. The matter was settled. "Much stays here. The rest of you—time's wasting."

Will lowered himself into the passage, careful to avoid Much's gaze as he disappeared into the hole. He knew what the boy was thinking. He was thinking that Will didn't trust him, that he'd found a way to keep the boy behind to protect himself from a knife in the back. While that might be true in part, it was also true that Will wanted to keep the boy safe if possible.

The irony of protecting the one who might be trying to kill him was not lost on Will. His life had turned upside down and just kept tumbling about him.

The passage was big enough for a normal-sized man to duck through, and true enough, John had to crawl. Though not nearly as tall, Stout found his wide gut to be a problem in spots, and Rob threatened to grease him up like a pig if he got stuck. As it was, he slowed the lot of them down, and on more than one occasion Will had to stop and wait for the rest of them to catch up. Waiting in the dark, surrounded by dirt walls that seemed to be closing in on you every second, was not a pleasant way to pass the time.

The passage turned from dirt to stone as they made their way into the interior of the castle. A ladder led to a flight of stairs that ended in a secret door in a rarely used storage room. Will could hear Stout behind him, out of breath from the climb.

"Don't you . . . don't you get too far ahead," panted the fat bandit. "We're staying together on this one, you and me."

Stout grinned at Will, showing all his yellow teeth. Was that some kind of threat? It didn't matter. Whether Stout trusted him or not was irrelevant to what he needed to do.

"Fine," whispered Will. "But keep your voice down!"

They emerged from the tunnel without making too much more noise, although there was barely enough room for the four of them to stand upright in the storage room. Will doused the little hooded lantern they'd been using for light, and after a few moments of listening at the door for footsteps, they stepped out into the hallway.

The castle was dark, but torches still burned out in the yard, and numerous guards could be seen through the windows warming their hands over braziers of hot coals. Will's father kept just a skeleton crew of guards on the night watch, but Sir Guy was a more paranoid ruler. And he was right to be. Will couldn't be the only one in England who wanted the Horse Knight dead. But it was well past midnight, and the feasts were all done for the day, and the kitchens had yet to start work on breakfast. If there was any time to move around the castle unnoticed, this was it.

"All right," said Stout. "Where's the treasure?"

They all winced as Stout's voice echoed down the hall, but no one came to investigate.

Will pointed over his shoulder. "This way," he whispered. "We have to go higher."

It was nearly impossible to move silently in their stolen soldiers' armor, so they'd have to hope their disguises worked if they met anyone along the way. If they did meet any servants from Will's household, he was hoping that the half helm would disguise his face enough so as not to be recognized. And he'd been given one of the guard's swords at last—it was necessary to play the part of mercenary. He'd need the blade before the night was through.

As they climbed the steps to the main tower, they passed a single servant girl carrying a dirty chamber pot. Will didn't recognize her, but he kept his face turned down just in case. Luckily, she didn't give the four of them a second glance, so she must've been used to seeing armed men in this part of the building, even at this late hour. That was both reassuring and troubling. The servants might not care about unfamiliar faces, but other soldiers would. If they stumbled across the wrong guards, they'd have little choice but to draw steel.

They reached the entrance to a long, curving stairwell, with doors on either side. It was a stairwell that Will had traveled countless times in another life. Rob stepped up beside Will and whispered in his ear.

"These look like they lead up to the lord and lady's living quarters," he said. "I thought we were looking for a vault."

Will hadn't expected any of them to be familiar with castle layouts, but obviously Rob was.

"Lord Shackley never wanted to sleep far from his silver," Will said. "He kept the vault in his room."

Will suddenly felt Rob's hand on his arm, stopping him in his tracks.

Rob leaned in close, angry. "So you are taking us into the lord's bedroom. *Sir Guy's* bloody room? Are you mad?"

Stout and John had stopped as well, curious what the two were whispering about. Will tried to think of an excuse, fast. He was too close to his revenge to have to stop now.

As it turned out, he didn't have time to think at all. One of the side doors opened suddenly and out stepped three men. The first two were guards of the castle, Guy's men. The third stepped out behind them and was holding a large lockbox in his hands. He looked out of place in his woodsman garb, with his dirty white scarf and strange braided beard. The ends of which were blackened and burnt. . . .

The two groups stopped in their tracks, and there was a surprised, tense moment as they looked each other over.

"What are you men . . . ," began Tom Crooked. Will had hoped that their helms and uniforms would be enough to disguise them, but there was one man who was impossible to hide.

"Bloody hell, it's John Little!" Crooked shouted, pointing at the giant. "Kill him!"

TWELVE

This had better be a really big treasure.
—Rob

Tom Crooked had his sword out of its sheath in the blink of an eye, but before the man could swing it, Rob threw a sudden punch at his face, knocking him backward and sending his lockbox clattering to the ground. It landed with the distinct clank of coins being jostled within.

Shouting an alarm, the two guardsmen stepped up to take his place and were met with John's and Stout's steel. Swords clashed around them as Rob and Will drew their own swords and turned to face the sound of booted feet running toward them. Someone else had heard Crooked's call.

"This had better be a really big treasure," said Rob.

From down the hall came three more guards, swords drawn and at the ready. They fought back to back now—John and Stout on one side, Rob and Will on the other. Each pair of men had three enemies to deal with. Bad odds.

Rob's fighting style was wild but not undisciplined. He was always on the offensive, pushing back against two of the guards and forcing them to cede ground, while Will was doing his best to keep his single opponent's blade at bay.

He'd studied swordplay and trained to be a warrior since a very young age. But that's all it was—*training. Play.* This guard was actually trying to kill him, and that changed the dynamics of a fight. The guard swung his sword in long, powerful arcs, but he was hacking away with it like he was chopping wood, trying to use his greater size against a smaller opponent. The impact against Will's own parries was already making his arm numb. But such a tactic left the guard unbalanced. Osbert had shown Will that you never put all your strength into a blow. Just enough to do the job.

Will waited for the man to swing again, then leaped backward. He trusted that John and Stout had his back covered, because he couldn't see where he was landing. The guard's swing went wide with nothing to stop it, and the man stumbled forward as his sword cracked harmlessly off the floor.

The guard looked up just in time to see Will's boot kicking him in the face. The man's head snapped backward and he fell.

There wasn't time to celebrate, though, as Rob was still fending off two men. But when Will turned to help, he backed into someone who shouted his name.

Stout was there, glaring at Will, his own sword raised.

No sooner had Will spotted him than the bandit was forced to fend off a fresh attack from Crooked himself. John was wrestling on the floor with two guards at once (a fight that wasn't going to go well for the guards). Rob had one of the guards on point against the wall. The mercenary had lost his sword and seemed to be surrendering, but the second had flanked Rob and was readying a blow at the man's back. There was no way Rob would pivot in time to avoid it.

The guard swung, but Will was there to parry the blow. Their swords clashed, and the guard backed up, buying Rob enough time to bring his sword around to protect himself.

"You're welcome!" shouted Will. After all, he'd just saved Rob's life.

John had the guards on the ground. Stout was busy with Crooked, and Rob and the last guardsman were now engaged in a furious duel. That left . . .

The guard Will had kicked in the face came back at him with a snarl, charging him even though he was weaponless. Unfortunately, the guard was so nearly blind from his bleeding broken nose that he tackled the two of them into the stairwell, and together they tumbled down the steps and out of sight.

Will came to a rough, skidding stop about halfway down the first flight of steps, landing painfully on his rear. But he was lucky, as the guard had continued rolling all the way down until he lay unconscious in a heap at the foot of the steps.

Will took a deep breath and climbed back up the stairs, wincing and limping as he went. It wasn't possible to actually break one's bottom, was it?

Atop the steps, the fight was over. One guard had surrendered, three were unconscious, and the last was lying dead on the ground at Rob's feet, a bloody wound next to his heart. There was no sign of Crooked.

"There you are," said Stout.

"We have to go," said Rob. "Crooked got away, and he'll alert the whole castle before long."

"He fled like a cowardly dog," said Stout.

"Just what was Tom Crooked doing here?" asked John.

"I don't know," said Rob. "But of course he recognized your massive face. Can't really disguise that, can we?"

"You think he's in league with Sir Guy?" asked Stout. "Would a knight actually partner with an outlaw?"

"Sir Guy pays mercenaries to do his bidding—perhaps he

found Crooked's price," said Rob. "Time to ponder later. The castle alarm's been sounded, so we're leaving. Now!"

"No!" said Will. They were close. So close. The lord's bedroom was just up one more flight of stairs, and that was where they'd find Guy. Will was sure of it.

"We still have time to get the treasure," said Will. "This way!"

Will sprinted off toward the stairs as fast as his wounded bottom would take him. He ignored Rob's calls for him to stop. Each step was painful, and he really was beginning to wonder if he'd broken his backside, but he wouldn't allow himself to slow down. There wouldn't be a second chance at Sir Guy.

Up the stairs past his old room without stopping. The guards that should've been stationed in the family quarters must've been the ones they'd already fought. They'd heard the sounds of battle below and come running.

Down the hall and to the great oaken door at the end. The lord's bedroom, his father's room, which had been empty for years now, ever since Lord Rodric had ridden off to war. An empty bed now defiled by that murderer Sir Guy of Gisborne. Will forced himself to pause before going in, to focus. Sir Guy was no simple castle guard. He was a killer.

Will listened for the sounds of pursuit but heard nothing. Very well. If Rob and the others had fled, then he'd do it himself. Or die in the attempt.

The door opened easily. For a moment, Will remembered opening this door in times past, coming to tell his father about a compliment he'd earned from his tutors or awkwardly confessing some minor crime Nan had caught him in.

He half expected to see his father hunched over his table, his nose in a book.

Instead, he found a dark, unused room. Of course his father wasn't there, but neither was the Horse Knight. The bed was made and hadn't been slept in. The hearth was cold. No one had used this room in quite a while.

So where was Sir Guy?

THIRTEEN

You are calling me a stupid boy? Have you caught a glimpse of yourself in a mirror recently, Will Scarlet?
—MUCH THE MILLER'S SON

Will had lied about the patrols. Much had seen it in the boy's eyes. And if he'd lied about the patrols, then what else had he lied about? Admittedly, it was a shock to find out that the secret passage was real, but every good sneak thief and ne'er-do-well knew that a seed of truth didn't add up to a whole.

If the secret passage was the seed, the rest of the plant was probably rotten. That meant no patrols and, most likely, no treasure.

So what was Will Scarlet up to? Much had watched the boy closely, not just because he was pleasing to look at (and saying that he was a sight prettier than your average bandit wasn't exactly high praise). No, she'd watched him because he'd had plenty of opportunities to escape, and one by one he'd passed them by. Back at the watchtower, during the chaos of the fight, or whenever Stout took a turn at night watch because everyone knew he slept through his shifts. But Will hadn't slipped away. He'd wanted to bring them here, to this castle, and he'd wanted all of them to follow him inside. Everyone except Much.

Which was precisely why she felt justified going in anyway.

Her plan had been simple, and it had seemed like such a good one until she'd gone and gotten herself lost. Following the tunnel had been easy—she'd had room to spare—but once she emerged from the storage room, things got a bit trickier. She had no idea where the men had gone. If Will was indeed leading them to treasure (which she doubted), then they would most likely have headed downstairs. Though she'd never seen one herself, she'd heard that most treasure rooms were kept in the lower levels, beneath stone. But since Will was lying about all this, he could have led them anywhere. He might've deposited them directly into the prisons or marched them in front of the captain of the guard.

With so many unfortunate possibilities, Much had chosen to make for the supposed treasure and see if she couldn't spot some sign of their passage along the way. But after all these months spent sleeping under the stars and using the sky and trees to find her way, her sense of direction indoors had become hopelessly skewed. Before long she was lost. She'd managed to dodge a few passing guards, but her luck would eventually run out if she couldn't find her companions soon. She doubted she could find her way back to the secret passage even if she tried. She pictured the lot of them emerging from the tunnel outside, their pockets filled to overflowing with treasure, while she was stuck in here wandering in circles until she was caught and hanged.

When she heard the cries of alarm, she realized that they were all in serious trouble. The odds that the guards were shouting about some *other* intruders were very slim indeed, which meant that something had gone wrong with Will's master plan. Or, depending on his motives, perhaps it had gone right. What were the chances that he'd led them here to their doom? But if that were the case, why try to leave Much behind?

Too many questions swirled around that boy, and there was no time for answers. Against common sense, Much followed the sounds of trouble. By now, there were enough servants running about the halls in their nightclothes that no one paid much attention to another skinny boy in the mix. Those that did barely had time to spare her a queer look before being carried away by the stampede.

The castle was now awake, and there was nowhere left to hide.

As she rounded the corner, Much slammed face-first into a guard. She fell backward and mumbled an apology as she hid her face behind her hand. The smack to the nose had made her eyes water, and she could barely see beyond the tears. But she knew she needed to play the part of the humble servant if she was going to get past him.

"A thousand apologies, milord," she said. "I should've been careful where I was— Hey!"

A gloved hand grabbed her by the collar and hauled her to her feet. A harsh voice whispered in her ear, "Come with me!" and she was dragged off down the hall, away from the rest of the scattering servants.

Much wouldn't be taken prisoner. With a flick of her wrist, she produced a knife, and though she still couldn't see well, the guard was holding her close enough that she didn't need to. She flashed the knife in front of his face, just inches from his eyes.

"Hey! Hey! Much, it's me!"

The hand let go of her collar.

With her free hand, Much wiped at her eyes, her vision clearing enough to get a good look at the face she was about to stab. It was Will Scarlet beneath that helm.

She lowered the knife. Just a bit.

"Where are the others?" she asked.

Will glanced worriedly at the blade.

"I don't know! We got separated." His eyes drifted from the knife to her angry, accusing eyes. "What are you doing here?"

Much hid the knife away in her belt.

"You lot are not my masters! Just because you tell me to stay behind doesn't mean I have to do it. The Merry Men are free men!"

Will sighed heavily.

"You're a stupid boy who's going to get himself killed."

Much seriously considered drawing the knife again.

"You are calling me a stupid boy? Have you caught a glimpse of yourself in a mirror recently, Will Scarlet?"

The argument ended there, though, as the sounds of commotion drew nearer. This time the voices were accompanied by the clanging of armor and booted feet running. Guards were approaching.

"Come on," said Will. "This way."

He started down the hall, and Much decided to follow. He knew the castle, and if he intended to hand her over to the guards, he could've simply stayed put.

"We can't reach the secret passage," he said as they went. "These floors are thick with guards by now, but there's another way. A slop gate that Milo and I used when Nan was . . ."

He started to say something more but seemed to think better of it. For a moment, just a moment, the stern-faced young man who constantly ground his teeth at the world around him had disappeared. In his place had been a boy. A lonely boy.

But he was gone as quickly as he'd appeared, and Much found herself blushing. She knew what it was like to hold on to a disguise and how it must feel to drop it like that, accidentally. It must feel like a violation. She was embarrassed for him, and for herself, too. It was a shame to find you were the kind of person who needed secrets.

The two of them continued on, pausing now and again to listen for footsteps. They were near the castle's foundation now, where the wooden walls gave way to stone. The air here had a damp coolness about it, and the musty smell of earth and rock. Was he taking her down to the treasure room after all?

"We weren't supposed to come down here," Will was saying, almost to himself, "because it was too close to the cells. But there's a slop gate down here that no one uses much anymore. Not big enough for a grown man in armor to fit through, but it'll suit you and me."

Much nodded. She wondered who Will was talking about when he said *we*. This Milo person he'd let slip? Was he a brother? Friend? And what had become of him now that Sir Guy of Gisborne was lord and master here? The Horse Knight had a wicked reputation even among criminals.

Will put his finger to his lips as they neared what looked like a row of cells. As quietly as possible, they snuck past the hall. An empty stool and pee bucket stood in a corner. The jailer was missing.

"Must've gone to see what the alarm is about," said Will. "We're lucky we can—"

Will was cut off by a low moan echoing from the farthest cell. It was haunting, pained. The sound of suffering.

"What was . . ." Will let his words trail off as he began approaching the cell.

"Will!" Much whispered. "What are you doing? We don't have time!"

But he ignored her as he looked into the cell door's grated window.

"I need light!" he said, pointing at a torch on the wall behind her.

"Will!" Much said.

"Light!" he suddenly shouted. If she didn't do as he asked, he was likely to lead the entire castle-guard down here to them.

Much took the torch from its sconce and held it out to him. She just hoped he saw whatever it was he needed to see quickly.

"Oh Lord," Will breathed as he peered into the cell.

Will grabbed the cell door's handle, but it was locked. He cursed and pulled on it with all his strength, but it wouldn't budge.

"The jailer must have the key," he said, and started back up the way they'd come.

"Are you mad?" asked Much. "Where are you going?"

"To find the jailer," answered Will.

"You'll get caught! You can't go back up there. . . ."

Will spun around, and his face was so full of fury that Much reflexively took a step backward.

"I have to get into that cell!" he said. "Go if you want to. The slop gate is that way."

Then he turned and started back up again.

"Wait!" said Much. "Will, just wait a moment!"

Much turned and knelt next to the door. She searched her belt pouch for an oilcloth. Inside the cloth was a very special set of tools.

"Now *I* need the light," she said.

Will looked at her for a second in confusion, then brought the torch near.

"Wat Crabstaff may be an ignorant lout and a snitch," she

said, fitting a curved loop of wire into the lock. "But he's the best lockpick in Nottinghamshire. And he's been teaching me a thing or two. . . ."

Much had only ever practiced on lockboxes and merchants' chests. That's really all they had call for in Sherwood. But the basic mechanics of picking a lock, any lock, were the same. Trick the tumblers with a wire. Listen for just the right sort of click and . . .

"There," she said, smiling. That was impressive, even she had to admit. "It's open."

Will looked dubious, but when he tried, the latch turned and the door swung open on squeaking, protesting hinges. Much glanced over her shoulder worriedly.

"I hope nobody heard that," she said.

"Here," said Will, handing her the torch. "I need you to hold this for me."

Much followed him into the cell and was at once assaulted by the smell. It smelled of human waste and something else. Death.

In one corner lay a man on a straw mat. He was old, his once-white beard stained yellow and filthy. His skin shone a sickly green in the torchlight and hung loosely on his bones. His brow was beaded in feverish sweat.

Will gasped aloud when he saw him, but he didn't rush over to him right away. Instead, he walked slowly, as if in a daze. As if he didn't quite believe what he was seeing.

Much knew what they were seeing. They were seeing a dying man.

When Will reached the mat, he took the man's hand in his.

"Osbert," he said. "Osbert, it's me. It's Will."

This Osbert opened his eyes and squinted up at Will. For a moment, he didn't seem to recognize him, but then a small smile appeared on his lips.

"Well . . . you are a sneaky one, aren't you?" he asked, his voice little more than a croak.

"Yes," answered Will with something between a chuckle and a sob. "And I'm getting you out of here. I'm rescuing you."

Osbert shook his head.

"I'm not . . . up for traveling, young lord."

The old man lifted a shaking finger and pointed to his feet. A dirty cloth covered his legs, but even in the dim torchlight Much could tell that the angles were all wrong. She lifted the sheet and saw that his legs were broken in several places, and the wounds smelled of rot. He didn't have long to live.

"After Sir Guy took your father's castle," the old man said, struggling for breath, "he assembled all the men before him to swear fealty at swordpoint. Coward that he was . . . he left our hands in manacles."

Osbert took a moment to rest.

"But he left our legs free, so you know what old Osbert did?" he asked.

Will shook his head. "What?"

"I kicked him in the balls!"

Osbert let out a wet laugh.

"Then he did this," said Osbert, pointing again at his ruined legs. "But it was worth it."

"If you can't walk," said Will, "we'll carry you."

"I can't . . ."

"Much," said Will. "Help me."

"Will," said Much. "He won't make it."

"Please," he said. He didn't shout this time, or threaten. He just begged her, his voice breaking, his eyes brimming with tears.

"Okay," she said. "Get your arms under his shoulder. I'll get the other one."

Will tried moving him, but the old man cried out in pain.

"William Shackley," he said, pulling away with as much strength as he could muster. "I don't know how you got here, but the one thing that allows me to die in peace is knowing you are free. . . ."

He pulled Will closer to him, his hands on the boy's face.

"I swore an oath to serve your father. I swore an oath to serve you. I won't have you caught on account of a dying old man!"

"I can't leave you here!"

"You will, my lord. For your father. For your family, for your uncle's memory, you will."

Will looked around the room, as if help would magically appear. Much kept her eye on the door. They were running out of time.

"I'll find Guy," said Will. "I'll not leave until I have his head!"

"Guy's gone," said Osbert. "He rode off on some errand of Prince John's. Can always tell when he's left because the jailer dips into the wine . . . and he never shares."

Will's whole body seemed to crumple. Whatever tent pole of strength had kept him going thus far had broken with this news.

"Leave me, lad," said Osbert. "I'll not last the day anyhow, but you can keep fighting. . . . Please, Will."

Will didn't move. Didn't make a sound. So Much stepped forward and placed a hand on his shoulder.

"Will, he's right," she said. "We need to go. Now."

Will didn't answer, but he stood.

"Leave me a knife," said Osbert. "The jailer is a spiteful piece of work, as well as a selfish drinker. I'd like to get one last bit of payback before I die."

"I'll leave you two," said Much, and she placed a pair of knives into his hands. "You're a tough old man."

"Thank you, girl," he said.

Much's breath caught in her throat. What did he just call her? She glanced quickly at Will, but if he heard, he didn't show it. He seemed lost in his own black thoughts.

As they turned to go, Will looked back at him.

"May heaven open its gates to you, Sir Osbert the Bold," he said. "Finest knight I've ever known."

Osbert nodded. "Long live Lord William Shackley. Wolfslayer."

With that, the old man's head fell back against the mat, his breath coming in labored gasps. He was right—he wouldn't last through the night. But they'd not live that long if they didn't leave soon.

Will led the way out without saying another word. The slop gate was indeed big enough for them to shimmy through, though Will had a harder time of it. It deposited them rather roughly outside the castle onto a slope filthy with rotten garbage and emptied chamber pots. But they were outside, in the night air, where Much could see the stars again.

As they made their way back toward the hidden grove and the horses, Much thought about all she'd heard. *Lord William Shackley. Wolfslayer.*

The boy walking next to her wasn't some steward's son, nor was he a thief. He was the rightful heir to Shackley Castle, and Sir Guy had stolen it from him.

She now understood perfectly why he'd brought them there. Vengeance. A blood quest he'd been denied.

With this revelation, she felt for him, even sympathized with him. Sir Guy had stolen everything from him. But with this new knowledge, Much also feared Will. He'd put them all in harm's way to try to get his revenge, and John and Rob might still be in peril. She knew from experience that someone who'd lost everything was capable of anything.

At least one of her instincts about him had been right—Will Scarlet was trouble.

FOURTEEN

William Shackley is dead.
—*Will Scarlet*

Guy was still alive. Osbert was dying, if not dead already. And for the second time, Will was fleeing from his own castle. Only this time he'd escaped through a garbage hatch.

Wolfslayer. Failure. Coward.

As he and Much trudged through the muddy field back to their hidden horses, Will tried to remember Osbert as he once was—laughing, quick to anger, full of life. He didn't want his last memory of Osbert to be of him broken and dying. The look of hope in his eyes when he'd recognized Will was a cruel joke. The old knight expected him to go on to do great things, and perhaps it was for the best that Osbert would die before he could realize his disappointment.

Will had missed his opportunity to kill Sir Guy because of bad luck. It didn't matter that there was no way he could've known that the Horse Knight was away; he'd still failed.

"So that old man was a knight of your . . . father's? Lord Shackley?"

Much's voice startled Will out of his morose thoughts.

"Hmm? Oh."

Of course. Everything Osbert had said in that cell exposed the truth about Will's family and his own identity. And Much had heard every word.

"He was . . . not himself," said Will. "You saw him. He thought you were a girl. Delusional."

Much wouldn't look at him. Funny that the boy should be so easily bothered by this. He was so small and delicately featured that this couldn't have been the first time he'd been mistaken for a girl.

"But the way you answered him," said Much. "Are you delusional, too?"

Will started to protest but stopped. He'd been in trouble enough times in his life to know when he was caught.

"Are you going to tell the others?" he asked.

"Remember what I told you before? About not being so important that you'd be trouble? Well, you are most certainly trouble."

"I know."

"Where are your parents now? They say the lord of Shackley was killed. . . ."

"That was my uncle Geoff," said Will. "My parents are alive, at least I think they are, but they are both . . . overseas."

His mother, he dared to hope, was safely with her family in France. She would be heartsick with worry, but at least she was safe. His father was a different story. Since they'd fled the castle, there'd been no word of King Richard's captivity. The best Will could assume was that his father was still imprisoned with the missing king. It was a bitter thing when the best a boy could wish was for his parent to be in chains, but better in chains than suffer Geoff's fate.

It was almost more pain than he could bear, and so he

kept it buried deep down in an ugly, dark place within himself, bound up tightly with wire and shackled to his need for vengeance. He had to find Sir Guy. He had to find another way.

"William Shackley is dead," said Will. "I'm Will Scarlet now. I don't know if you can understand this, but . . . I had to become someone else. I had to."

Much stared at him for a long time. At last the boy said, "I understand. I do. But then why are you obsessed with William Shackley's unfinished business? You could've gotten us killed trying to get revenge on Sir Guy. John and Rob might actually be dead, for all we know. . . ."

"They're alive," said Will. "Rob said they were leaving."

"Maybe, but they *could've* been killed looking for your treasure. A treasure that doesn't exist! You lied to us, Will!"

Will took a sudden step toward Much, his anger lit like dry tinder in his breast, and his hands balled up into fists before he could stop himself.

"I lied to my *captors*!" he said. "Or did you forget that I'm your prisoner?"

"I saved your life," said Much.

"Only to make me more valuable to ransom."

"How dare—"

"You weren't nursing me back to health; you were just tending to the money."

Will didn't even see the blow coming, but one minute he was standing over Much with a finger in the boy's face and the next he'd been punched in the jaw. A solid right hook. So Will returned the favor. He landed a blow across the lad's cheek. He might've even given him a black eye.

Much staggered backward as Will shook the sting out of his knuckles. That was settled, then. Lesson taught. The boy might be smaller and younger than he, but Will wasn't going to stand here and let him pummel—

All at once Much was on him like a wildcat. Hissing and hitting and biting—*biting,* for God's sake!—as he tackled Will to the ground. Even though Will was larger and stronger, he couldn't get a grip on the boy long enough to peel him off.

"Gah! Stop it! Leave off!" Will cried.

"Well, well, well," said a voice in return, but not Much's. A man's voice.

Will stopped struggling, and Much leaped off him, the boy's hands going for his knife.

Will looked up and saw Stout standing there, grinning.

"Didn't mean to interrupt your play-fighting," he said.

The outlaw had changed out of his uniform disguise and back into his own gear. Mace in one hand, a sack slung over his shoulder.

"Got to give our young bastard here credit," said Stout. "Tonight was a bounty to remember!"

Will stood up and tentatively examined his swelling lip with his fingers. His ear was bleeding, too, from a number of teeth marks.

"What are you talking about, Stout?" he asked.

"There was no treasure, you dolt," added Much.

"Oh ho!" said Stout. "Really, now? Then what's this?"

He tugged at the sack and out fell a sturdy-looking lockbox. It was the one Crooked had been holding at the start of the fight.

"See for yourself," he said.

Much pocketed his knife and cautiously examined the box. Someone had already broken the lock, so all the boy had to do was throw back the lid. It was filled with silver coin.

Much stared at it, wide-eyed, for a few seconds before

looking accusingly at Stout. Will doubted these bandits had ever seen so much money in one place before.

"Where's Rob and John?" asked Much.

"Now, now," said Stout. "They're fine. By the time we came up out of the tunnel, this area was swarming with guards. Rob and John took a few horses to lead them on a wild-goose chase. I was supposed to wait a bit to see if you all showed up, then meet up with them again."

"They trusted you with the silver?" asked Will.

"More like they knew he'd be too chicken to cross Gilbert," said Much.

Stout glared at them. "And what do you know about what I will and won't do? You think Gilbert trusts you more than me?"

"What's that supposed to mean?" said Much.

But Will had had enough. He was tired of all of it and just wanted to get as far away from this place as possible.

"It doesn't matter," he said. "Just pack up your silver so we can go."

"But that's just the problem," said Stout. "*We* aren't going anywhere."

The fat outlaw moved just a fraction of an instant too slow. If he hadn't gloated, if he hadn't taken the time to taunt him, Will would never have seen him bring up his mace. He wouldn't have seen it swinging for his head, and he wouldn't have ducked away at the very last second.

"Stout!" shouted Much.

Stout growled as Will danced away, drawing his sword as he did so.

"Gilbert's orders," said Stout, slowly closing in on Will. "He said you would be too yellow to do what needed to be done, Much, so he left it to me. His *trusted* Stout!"

"But there's the treasure!" cried Much. "Gilbert's getting what he wanted!"

"And now the rest of the problem will disappear," said Will, understanding. "He never meant to let me live."

Will prepared to meet the man's attack head-on, but just then Stout shouted in pain and dropped his mace to the ground. He stood there staring at his arm, as if not fully understanding what he was looking at. A small knife was sticking out of the meat of his forearm. Stout blinked at the sight. He couldn't quite believe what he was seeing.

"Much!" he cried. "You little turd!"

"Wait," said Will.

He brought his sword up to the man's chin. Stout glanced down at the blade nervously. His tongue flicked in and out between his lips like a snake's.

"Yield, Stout," said Will. "Or we'll have your head."

"You talk big now," said Stout. "I'd have had yours if that runt hadn't tossed a bleeding knife at me!"

He held up his ruined arm for them to see.

"You put a knife in my arm!" he said.

"I'll aim somewhere else next time," said Much. "Unless you do as Will says."

Stout looked fearfully at Much. "I'll yield! I'll yield! I'm no good without my fighting hand anyhow!

"But mark my words," he continued. "This isn't over, bloody Will Scarlet. I'll have your hide. And yours, too, Much! You've both got it coming!"

Stout complained and threatened most of the way back. He carried on so much that Will had to bind up the man's wrists, and by the end he was forced to gag him as well. The sun was coming up, and Sir Guy's men were everywhere. In the distance, Will could hear the baying of search hounds as they sniffed for the outlaws' trail. If they avoided the dogs, Stout's wailing would still be heard for leagues.

So Stout got the gag. Even so, he had to be pushed, prodded, and repeatedly threatened to get him to march. Will and Much took turns riding their only horse, and they made Stout walk the whole way. It was an hour's ride to the rendezvous spot—which meant half a day's walk at Stout's pace. Still, they managed to reach it without seeing any pursuers. It was afternoon when they found the shaded outcropping where they'd first donned their disguises. Rob and John were supposed to meet them there if they could.

Stout fell to his knees the moment they stopped, and for a while Will worried the man's heart would burst in his chest he was breathing so hard. But they removed his gag (which meant they had to put up with his curses) and changed the bloody bandage around his arm. They gave him some water (which he gulped down in between the curses) and dumped him next to a tree. Will left his hands bound but didn't bother tying him to the tree itself. After the long march, the fat bandit was in no physical condition to run away.

They buried their stolen soldiers' uniforms and found their own clothes safely where they'd stashed them. Will eyed the scarlet jacket warily and considered tossing it away, but when he saw Stout watching him, he decided to wear it again to spite the man. He and Gilbert had meant to shame him with the garish coat, but Will thought it fitting. Much nodded approvingly (but when Stout wasn't looking, he helped Will tear off the lace and tassels, which made a vast improvement). They dared not risk a fire, for fear that the smoke would be spotted from the road, so they broke their fast on stale bread and washed it down with water from a nearby brook.

After they'd eaten, Much climbed the tallest tree he could find to keep a lookout while Will sat and brooded. He could leave now if he wanted. There was no chance this band would follow him into Shackley Castle a second time, and what business did he have hanging around a bunch of outlaws anyway? Especially when Sir Guy was still alive. But the question now was, where would he go? Though he worried about his mother, he wasn't about to give up his revenge and make for France.

He couldn't forget the look in Osbert's eyes. The old man hadn't wanted Will to throw his life away, but he wouldn't want him to tuck his tail between his legs and run to his mother, either. He would want Will to stay in England and fight. No matter the odds. Will had to find another way to get to Sir Guy.

And after that—if he survived that—the sheriff was still out there. Guy was a murderer, but Mark Brewer had betrayed them in his own way, too. He'd brought Sir Guy's mercenaries into the castle. He'd been so afraid of angering Prince John that he'd betrayed his friends, and now Geoff was dead.

After Sir Guy. Once Guy was dead, then Will would confront the sheriff.

Will was still wrestling with his thoughts when John and Rob finally arrived. Much spotted them well in advance, so they had time to prepare. Or, more precisely, to plan their explanation as to why they had Stout tied up under a tree. Will was nervous about how they would react, but Much promised him that John and Rob had no love for Stout in the first place, and even less for Gilbert the White Hand. They could be trusted.

He hoped.

Much and Will greeted them as they rode into their little camp. Both men were haggard and dirty from a night of hard riding. They obviously hadn't slept.

They spotted Stout's bindings right away and shared a look.

"Well," said John. "Why didn't we think of that?"

Upon seeing them, Stout hollered and cursed up such a racket that Will was forced to gag the man again. Neither John nor Rob made any move to stop him.

Much explained to them all that had transpired, about Stout's attack, all except the part about Will's real identity. An omission that Will was both surprised at and thankful for.

"So, Master Will," said Rob. "Sudden betrayals notwithstanding, I'm curious—after we were separated, did you ever find your hidden treasure?"

Will didn't like the way Rob asked the question. As if he'd long ago guessed the answer.

"There's your treasure," said Will. He pointed to the lockbox of coin sitting at his feet. "More than you'd get robbing merchants' carts, I'd wager."

"Ah, yes, we're rich men now!" said Rob. "Minus Gilbert's share, of course."

"Gilbert?" said John. "Rob, haven't you been listening? We have a problem here!"

"Eh?" said Rob. "So Stout got greedy and tried to cut out one man's part of the loot. Hardly surprising for an outlaw."

"I'm not just talking about Stout," said John. "It's Gilbert. You knew it'd come to this someday."

"Come to what?" asked Rob. "He hasn't hurt me. Nor you."

"He's ordering the murder of boys now! You can stand for that?"

"Bah," said Rob. "No one's dead."

But John wouldn't let up. "Stout would've killed the boy—you know it's true. And Much, too, if needed."

"Oh, just stop it, John!"

"Why? You need to hear more?"

"What I *need* is a bloody drink!"

With that, Rob stomped off to the edge of the camp. There he sat, staring off into space. Will could see the man's hands shaking despite the warm sun.

John began unpacking their horses, all the while muttering under his breath. Will stood staring for a time at Rob. He'd misjudged the man. He'd thought him a drunk and a scoundrel at first, but he'd come to realize he was something more. Still a scoundrel, yes, and certainly a drunk, but there was something else in him, a kind of strength that made others listen when he spoke. It was a quality Will's father had possessed, one that Will had dreamed of having.

Much pulled Will away, and the two of them began unpacking their rations for a late lunch. Eventually, John joined them, but Rob stayed where he was. He looked to be getting worse, and his face was pale and sweaty. Will began to worry about the man's health.

"He hasn't been sober for this long in . . . a long time," John explained, finishing off a piece of crusty black bread. "It's hard on him."

"Why's he like this?" asked Will. "Why does he do that to himself? The drinking?"

John leaned back against the rocks and began tearing long strips from one of the nearby saplings.

"Want to hear how Rob and I met?"

"What's that got to do with—" began Will, but John kept on talking, and Much motioned to Will to stay quiet. It was best to let the man talk.

"Rob and I became friends because one day we both wanted to cross the same bridge at the same time," John continued. "I wanted to go one way, Rob wanted to go another. Both of us too stubborn and too full of our young selves to give the other man the right-of-way."

"So you argued?" asked Will.

"Argued? We fought! Stupid reason to, but there it is."

John tied a few strips of green wood into a knot and then held it up to the sun.

"A pointless, dumb fight over who got to cross the bridge first. As pointless as this here knot of wood. But like this knot, it was something to do."

"Men are fools," said Much. "*Grown* men, I mean!"

John laughed. "I'd say men of a certain age are foolish, yes. Just old enough to be dangerous but not yet old enough to be careful. Like young master Scarlet there."

Will felt his cheeks redden to match his coat. He'd very nearly gotten the lot of them killed, but so far no one was taking him to task for it. But it was unspoken among all of them.

"So who won the fight?" Much asked.

"I did," said John. "Because I cheated. I called a truce, and when Rob's back was turned, I kicked him into the water face-first."

"And he fell for that?" asked Much.

"Of course he did," said John. "He's a man of honor among thieves."

Will looked over at Rob. He'd curled up in the shadow of a poplar and pulled his cloak over his face.

"That still doesn't answer why he drinks like he does," said Will. "What's honorable about killing yourself with wine?"

"Nothing," answered John. "But I will tell you lads two more truths about that man that might help explain. One, Rob there is the best longbowman in all of England. Better than Gilbert even. And our fearless leader knows it."

"What?" said Much. "I've never seen him touch a bow."

"That's 'cause of the drink. Can't aim an arrow when your hands are shaking. But trust me, he's the stuff legends are made of. And being that good at something—I mean the best—well, that does something to you. Sets up expectations, you see. Unreasonable expectations."

It was true that Will had seen Rob swing a sword well enough, but that was mostly bravado. But he had a hard time picturing Rob steady enough to aim a bow.

"Fine," said Will. "Rob's a legend. What's the second thing?"

"Second is, be careful of women," said John.

"That's it?" said Will. "Are you trying to say a woman did that to Rob?"

"Not just any woman," said John. "Believe me, Mari— Look, I shouldn't even use her name, but just know that she was the kind of woman that men do stupid things for. Wars have been fought over women like her. Rob loved her and, to everyone's shock, she loved him back."

"So what was the problem?" asked Much.

"She was a royal, the daughter of a well-respected house. And Rob is . . . Rob."

"How did it end?" asked Will.

"Badly. It ended badly." John shook his head. "Now, I've said too much about another man's business already. Time to get some sleep, my young lads. Dream about the women who'll break your hearts someday!"

Then John stretched his long arms out and clasped them behind his head, finally closing his eyes.

"Too dangerous to travel by daylight, but we'll be safe here until nightfall," he said. "And it never pays to make plans when you're this tired. Besides, Rob and I were extra careful to disguise our trail. We could hole up here for days and no one would be the wiser. Believe me, there's no two better woodsmen in all of England!"

FIFTEEN

The many do the bidding of the few in merry old England, Will. Remember that.
—Rob

It seemed to Will that he'd been asleep only a few minutes. He'd been dreaming that he and Much were sharing a bowl of porridge sweetened with stolen molasses when he heard the howl of wolves outside his window. They were near.

"Will, wake up!"

Will blinked awake to find Much shaking him. The boy's face looked worried, and the sweet molasses was gone. But the wolves were still there. He could hear them getting closer.

"We have to go!" Much was saying. "They have our scent!"

Hounds. Not wolves at all. Sir Guy's hounds had picked up their trail. Will could hear baying in the distance. But getting louder.

Will leaped to his feet, shaking the life back into his still-heavy arms and legs. The sun was a pale orb low in the west. Dark rain clouds had gathered overhead, and the wind was picking up.

"How long have I been asleep?" he asked.

Much put his hand up to the sun. He seemed to be measuring the number of hand widths from the sun to the horizon.

"We've about an hour of daylight left," he said. "Come on, we have to hurry. Again!"

Will glanced around the camp and saw that Rob and John had climbed the outcropping and were peering over the top.

"There they are," Rob was saying. "Ten riders at least. Must've found your trail."

"Not mine," said John. "You're the one can't cover your tracks. I told you to ride on the rocky ground."

"It's those giant feet of yours," said Rob. "Can't hide giant feet."

"I was on a horse!"

Much grabbed Will by the arm, pulling him away from the two men's bickering.

"Come on," he said. "They'll catch up."

There were only three horses left, and two of those were still exhausted from last night's ride. Three horses and five people.

"Will and Much, you two will have to double up," said Rob, jumping down from the rocks.

"What about Stout?" asked Will.

"He'll have to ride with me. . . . Oh, blast it all!"

Will followed the other man's gaze over to Stout's tree, only there was no Stout.

"Must've run off when the dogs started."

"We shouldn't have turned our backs on him," said John.

"Do we follow him?" asked Will.

"No time," said Rob. "He'll take his chances with the hounds like the rest of us. Only he'll do it on foot!"

Will climbed atop his horse and helped Much take the saddle in front of him. As they rode out of the camp, Will felt the boy stiffen when he put his arms around his waist.

"You don't have to hold me," said Much. "I won't fall."

"Don't be foolish," said Will. But the boy still shoved his arms away.

"Fine," said Will. "But if you tumble, I'm not stopping to pick you back up."

The baying of hounds grew steadily louder as they left the shelter of the trees, and now Will could see the riders' dust cloud in the distance. They were coming for them at full gallop, the hounds mad with the scent. Will remembered Geoff's dogs and how they'd get when they caught a fox's trail. Nothing could stop them.

"They're on fresh horses," said John. "We'll never outride them!"

"We can make for the river," suggested Much.

"Those are trained hunting hounds," said Will. "They can track us downstream."

"Then what do we do?" Much asked.

Rob looked up at the darkening sky. He kicked his heels into his horse and rode.

"We ride hard," he shouted. "And pray for rain!"

Will didn't know if any of the others had actually followed Rob's advice, but the prayers worked. Or maybe they were just lucky. Either way, the combination of night falling and a sudden, soaking downpour threw the dogs off their scent. The rain started with a light drizzle but soon became a violent, blowing gale. For a time, they could still catch glimpses of their pursuers outlined in the brief flashes of lightning, but eventually they outpaced them altogether, losing them in the crags and hollows of the moors and behind the sheets of rain.

But their escape was not without casualties. Will's horse lost its footing among the slippery rocks and stumbled, throwing both its riders. Will and Much were lucky enough to end up with just a few scrapes, but the horse broke its leg. Much hid his eyes as John put the poor creature out of its misery.

That left the four of them with only two horses, both of which had been ridden nearly to death already. And they were soaked down to the bone and exhausted, and there was no way they would make it to Sherwood that night.

They needed a place to hide and wait out the storm. They needed somewhere dry. It was Rob's idea to make for a nearby farmhouse. He knew the family who lived there, the Walthams.

Through the pelting rain and clinging mud Will traveled alongside his captors. No, they were no longer his captors since he could have left at any time. His companions, then? Certainly not friends, these outlaws. But what was he now if not an outlaw, too? What else would you call a lord without a land? He was cold, wet, and hungry—that was for certain—and these men were his only chance to get to some place warm and dry.

It took several straight hours of marching through the night to find the farm, and when they did, Will was sure Rob had made a mistake. When Will thought of the tenant farms on his family's land, he pictured snug thatch-roofed houses and tall steepled barns. Smoke wafting up out of the chimney and the air smelling of baking bread as men tended to rolling fields.

Farmhouse was a generous word for where Rob had led them. It was, Will supposed, technically a pig farm in that it had people and pigs sharing the same tiny patch of earth, but the Waltham farm consisted of a single flat-roofed one-room shack for the people, a rickety lean-to sty for the pigs, and a weather-beaten old hay barn that had collapsed on one side. The rainwater had collected in pools on top of the shack, and the overflow ran down in steady streams along the outside. The yard was nothing but mud and pig droppings up to your ankles. And the whole place smelled, just not of baking bread.

Rob spent long minutes at the front door talking with Farmer Waltham, though their words were lost in the roar of the storm. From the stern look on Waltham's face and Rob's wild gesticulating, Will guessed that the old farmer wanted to know why he should open up his house to four waterlogged bandits on the run. Will couldn't think of an earthly reason why he should, but apparently Rob had made his case, because he came back and told them they'd be allowed to hitch their horses up in the barn.

Inside, they found room enough to dry and brush down their remaining two horses, even though one whole half of the barn was little more than fallen debris. Will still felt sorry about the horse they'd had to put down. It made him worry about Bellwether back at the Merry Men's camp, but she was Gilbert's possession now. So he let the men have a bit of a breather and offered to brush down the horses himself. Perhaps if he took extra-special care of these animals, it would go a little way toward making up for the loss of the other. Milo would have liked that he tried, at least.

Will wondered where the stableboy was now. Hopefully he escaped Sir Guy's cruelty. Milo, Nan, Henry, and pretty Jenny. Maybe they were together at one of those farms that smelled of bread. It was a nice fantasy, if nothing else.

"Could do with a little work," said Rob, looking around at the ruined structure. "Roof sags a bit on the left."

"It's good the horses will stay dry while we're in the house," said Will.

"Inside what house?" said John. "You're sleeping with the rest of us here."

Will noticed then that his companions weren't merely catching a rest. They were unpacking and hanging up their wet clothes to dry. They were settling in for the night here in this ruin of a barn.

"Oh," said Will. "So we're . . ."

"Sleeping with the horses?" said John. "Yes. Welcome to the luxurious life of an outlaw on the run!"

"Waltham couldn't possibly fit us inside his house, Will," said Rob. "He's got four children and a wife in that one room already."

Will nodded, embarrassed that he'd assumed they'd be given the royal welcome by these peasants. That was the kind of assumption William Shackley might make, not Will Scarlet.

Sleeping out in the barn would be no great comfort, but it was mostly dry. The wind blew the rain in through the cracks near the corners, but there were enough piles of dry hay about to be used as makeshift beds.

By the time he'd finished brushing down the horses, John and Rob had already stripped to near nothing. Their dripping clothes hung steaming from each and every hook they could find. But Much still sat in a corner, shivering. The boy had taken off his boots and cloak but kept on the rest of his soggy clothes. He hugged his knees to his chest for warmth.

As Will hung up his own wet clothes, he glanced over at John and Rob. John saw the concerned look on Will's face.

"It's no use," John whispered. "He won't change out of those wet clothes."

"He'll catch his death," said Will.

"Everyone has a reason for being the way they are," said John. "And pushing them doesn't help any."

The boy stared at his feet, his teeth chattering so hard Will feared they'd break off. He wanted to follow John's advice and leave him be, but he couldn't just watch Much shiver like that.

"I think we need a fire," said Will, loud enough for all to hear. "I could use something hot."

Much looked up at the mention of a fire, but he didn't say anything.

Rob glanced around the barn, at the piles of hay. "That a good idea?" he asked.

"We'll be careful," said Will. "Besides, we're not going to burn the Walthams' barn down in this rain. Come on, Much. Help me see if we can find some dry wood around this place."

In the end, they got a small fire going with some old rotten boards and a pile of hay for the tinder. It smoked terribly, but it put out welcome heat. Much sat as close to the fire as he dared without setting himself aflame, and after a time his shivering stopped and his cheeks eventually returned to their healthy rosy color. The little fire lifted all of their spirits and it brought some real warmth to the end of a long, cold night.

The fire also allowed them to have a hot meal for the first time in days. They heated Much's store of boiled acorns and spread them across hunks of black bread like butter. When they turned in for the night, they had warm, full bellies. As he lay down to sleep, Will tried not to think about what sorts of creatures he was sharing his bed with, but exhaustion soon overtook his squeamishness and he fell into a sound sleep.

By the time he awoke, the rain had changed to a thick morning mist. The fire had died out during the night, leaving the air chilled once more. Rob was the only other one awake, and he sat at the barn door, wrapped in his cloak, watching the sun struggling to break through a flint-gray sky. Much slept in a ball near the cold fire pit, and John lay across from him, snoring away like a tree saw.

"I had to douse the fire," said Rob when he saw Will was awake. "Can't risk the smoke in the daylight. Even in this half-light. Guy's soldiers will have resumed the search now that the sun's up."

Will drew his red coat tight about his neck and joined Rob at the door. It was hard to believe that this man was the smelly drunk he'd met just days ago.

Rob gestured to the pigsty across the yard, where Farmer Waltham and his sons—a few of them around Will's age—were trying to corral two pigs into a makeshift pen.

"One of Waltham's hogs died from a fever yesterday," said Rob. "This morning there are two more sick, so they're trying to separate them from the rest."

There was a sudden squeal, and one of Waltham's boys went headfirst into the mud as a pig scurried out of reach.

"Can't be easy to grab hold of a wet pig," Rob said.

"What happens if they can't get them separated?" Will asked.

Rob looked at him. "I look like a pig farmer?"

Will shrugged.

"The others will get sick, too, I suppose," said Rob. "Maybe die."

Will examined the sorry state of the Waltham farm. In the daylight, it looked even worse, more like a ruin than an actual home. Gaps in the house were filled in with mud and straw, and Will doubted that the occupants of the house had been much drier last night than he. But worst of all, Will saw how thin the boys were. Their sunken cheeks were visible even at a distance.

Rob nodded, as if reading Will's mind. "Only reason Waltham let us sleep in his barn was he needed the coin."

"You're paying him?"

"Four of us for a halfpenny. He wouldn't risk the trouble with Guy otherwise. And I don't blame him."

"The boys are so . . . skinny," said Will. "Don't they have enough to eat? I mean, they're pig farmers, so couldn't they just . . . eat bacon?"

Rob laughed, but it had a bitter ring to it. A bark more than a chuckle.

"You think those are *his* pigs? Waltham is a serf, Will. None of this belongs to him. He works it for his lord and master and gets a pittance in return."

The front door of the house opened and out stepped a tall woman with stringy hair and an infant at her breast. She called Waltham and the boys in to breakfast, eyeing the barn nervously.

The old farmer waved at her but didn't stop his work. They had one pig corralled in its pen, but the other was proving difficult.

"Maybe we should help them," said Will.

Rob shook his head. "They don't want our help. She doesn't want us here at all. Too afraid of what Guy would do if he caught us here. Having us out in the open working would just add to the risk."

"Sir Guy." Will spat the name. "It's unforgivable that he lets his people live like this."

Rob looked at Will for a moment. The man's blue eyes were inscrutable.

"These are Guy's serfs now, it's true," he said. "But they

weren't a few months ago. They belonged to Lord Rodric Shackley. We're still on Shackley land."

Will blanched. He looked back at the run-down shack, the skinny family, their sunken cheeks.

"B-but," he stuttered, "surely this didn't happen in just a few months. . . ."

"Things are worse under Guy, to be sure. He's a brutal man, and his enforcers are thugs. But this family has been poor all their lives. They've never known what it's like to eat your fill. They've never known what it means to be free."

Rob patted him on the shoulder. "The many do the bidding of the few in merry old England, Will. Remember that."

Rob stood and stretched. "By the way, I like the coat," he said, gesturing to Will's red jacket. "I know Gilbert meant it as an insult, but you wear it well, Will Scarlet."

Then Rob went to scrounge up some breakfast, and Will was left alone. So he straightened his coat and stepped out into the misty yard. He waved to the woman as he approached. For her part, she nodded politely but didn't drop the scowl.

"Thank you for offering us the use of your barn," Will said. "It's most kind."

"Nothing any Christian wouldn't do to help a group of travelers in that storm," she said. "But you'll be leaving now that it's passed."

"Of course."

She looked back to where her husband and sons had cornered a pig. Will noticed that she'd called them travelers, not outlaws or brigands. He thought it best not to correct her.

"This farm is on . . . was on Lord Shackley's lands?" Will asked.

The woman answered without looking. "He was lord of the manor. Family's been indebted to Shackleys for generations."

"And now Sir Guy of Gisborne?"

Again she nodded.

"Tell me, if you would," said Will. "How is the new lord compared to Lord Rodric?"

The woman snorted. "It ain't like I ever met either one of them. Who am I to say?"

"Of course," said Will.

"Look, I've a table to set, and you've all got to pack your things. You're leaving, yes?"

"Of course we are," said Will. "But just one more question, if you don't mind?"

The baby in her arms began fussing. It was rooting into her shoulder, looking for a meal. The woman was so thin, Will wondered how she was able to feed the infant at all.

"Quick," she said. "Baby's hungry."

"You're serfs, are you not?" Will asked.

"Yes."

"So how much . . . I mean, how much debt do you have to pay off? What do you owe your lord?"

She looked at Will as if seeing him for the first time, her eyes wide. For a moment, Will feared that he'd somehow offended her.

"We'll never pay off our debt," she said. "We were born serfs. We will die serfs, and so will our children. Now, if you please, I need to feed my baby."

Will bowed as she let herself back into the house. She'd die a serf, she'd said. Her children would die serfs. They would die in slavery. And there hadn't even been a hint of bitterness in her voice. Just resignation, which seemed somehow even worse.

Will couldn't believe what he was hearing, what he was

seeing. Had his life back at Shackley Castle really been that sheltered? Had his mother seen these people? His father? Will went back to the barn and stood outside the door and watched a man and his half-starved sons chase a sick pig through the mud. A man who up until recently had been his.

SIXTEEN

They've found us! Why do they always find us?
—ROB

Much wanted to clear out of Sherwood and Nottingham altogether. Take the silver they'd robbed and make for the north. Or west to Wales. Anywhere they could escape the reach of men like Sir Guy and Gilbert the White Hand.

Trouble was, once men like that had your scent, they never stopped hunting you. The original plan had been to blame the robbery on Crooked's Men, to make a tidy sum and exact a little revenge on the side. But that was before they'd come face to face with Tom Crooked himself—in Guy's own castle, no less. What he was doing there with a chest full of silver was anyone's guess, but it didn't take much figuring to guess that Tom was now in the Horse Knight's employ.

Crooked had recognized John, and he would make sure that everyone knew who'd really been behind the robbery. Soon Sir Guy would know that it was the Merry Men who'd stolen into his castle and made off with his silver. When the watchtower guards whose uniforms they'd stolen told their story, Crooked would figure out that the Merry Men had been trying to frame him for the crime. In the span of a single night, they'd made several powerful enemies, and those enemies would travel far and wide for their revenge.

So the debate now was whether to return to the Merry Men or flee as far as possible, with Much arguing that they take their winnings and run.

John, who'd never been farther than nearby Barnesdale and had no interest in "exotic locales," wanted to stay and fight. Return to Sherwood and take their chances with Gilbert was his plan.

Will was silent on the subject of what to do next. He'd been in a quiet, glum mood all morning long, which irritated Much. Even more than usual. Last night's fire had been an act of rare kindness on Will's part, and it was touching that he'd been concerned for her. The two of them had even shared a bit of talk over dinner. But by this morning, he was back to his black mood and spent most of his time at the door or outside watching the Walthams go about their miserable lives. He'd even turned away breakfast.

Which was fine with Much. Will Scarlet was trouble and best avoided. Much had so adjusted to her life as a boy that she often forgot she was anything but. She could roughhouse and carry on with the Merry Men as if she were one of them. She could spit and curse and fight like a boy—better than. Except when Will was around. For some reason, he made her feel the difference, keenly.

While she sat with Rob and John and argued over what their next move should be, Will sat outside the door and stared at the fog.

Fine. Bloody Will Scarlet.

"We could divvy up the silver and go our separate ways," John was saying. "But I for one think we'll last longer if we stick together."

"Don't worry, Little John, I'll keep you safe," said Much.

"It's appreciated," he answered with a grin. "When all this trouble blows over, I think I'll use my share to build myself an inn. I've always wanted to have my own place. Roaring fire and fine food in the front room, dice games in the back. And music constantly. There'll be music and dancing from dawn to dawn!"

"And what'll you name it?" asked Rob.

"Ah, but there's the best part! The Little Inn by the Road, but it'll be huge! You see, the joke's that it's not little at all. . . ."

Rob and Much blinked at John.

"Hilarious," said Rob dryly.

"Ah, what do you know?" grumbled John.

"And what about you, Rob?" asked Much. "What do you plan on spending your silver on?"

The bearded man sighed and stared down at his water cup. "I've drinking to do. Real drinking."

Much scowled at him. The man seemed determined to drink himself into the grave, and Much couldn't think of anything sadder than that.

"But we haven't solved our current problem of how to stay alive long enough to spend the coin on anything," said John, bringing them back to the subject. "If we're staying together, then I say again, we head back to Sherwood."

"What about Gilbert?" said Much.

"The man's had it coming for a long time," said John.

With that, he looked pointedly at Rob, who had dug into the last of the morning's cold breakfast of leftover acorn mush and the last of their pack rations.

"Oh, sod off!" said Rob. "I'm not in the mood to think about Gilbert."

"And what to do about Will?" said John, his voice low. "He

knows that Gilbert ordered him dead. You think the lad should just forget about it?"

Will Scarlet. Lord William Shackley in disguise. What Rob and John *didn't* know about Will just might be enough to get them killed. Always their troubles revolved around him. Much had been wrestling with whether to tell Rob and John Will's secret. After all, she was one of the Merry Men, and she had a loyalty there, especially to John, who'd looked after her like a brother. Will's secret could spell real trouble for them all in the end.

But Much had her own secret, too. And if nothing else, she understood that about Will—the need for secrets. And she'd keep his for as long as she dared. That was a bond the two of them shared, whether Will knew it or not.

"Will . . . is free to go his own way," said Much after a moment. "If he wants. I don't think his path is the same as ours anyway."

Rob started to say something, but he was interrupted by the sudden sound of someone shouting outside the barn.

"What the . . . Where's Will?" John asked.

Much looked over to the doorway, but Will was nowhere to be seen. The shouting outside grew still louder.

"They've found us!" said Rob, leaping to his feet. "Why do they always find us?"

"Grab the silver," said John.

Much reached for the lockbox they'd hidden under her bed of hay and discovered it wasn't there.

"It's gone!" said Much. "The box is gone!"

Outside, the shouting was joined by a scream. A woman screaming.

Rob drew his sword as John hefted up his long staff. The

two men exchanged a grim look that Much recognized. If they'd been found, then the yard would be crawling with soldiers, but they weren't going to stand by while the Walthams were slaughtered.

"Much, stay here and hide," said John.

"Sod off," she answered, drawing her knives.

With a nod, Rob threw open the door, and the three of them charged out into the yard. John took the lead, bellowing an improvised battle cry in his deep bass voice.

"Ah! Prepare to have your heads split open, you motherless sons of— Huh?"

John stopped so suddenly that Much almost tripped over the big man's legs. She barely found her footing again, and only then did she see what had stopped the giant in his tracks. What had stunned him into silence, mouth agape, his staff nearly dropping from his limp hands.

The Waltham boys were still shouting. The wife was still crying. But these weren't shouts of fear or tears of sadness. The tears accompanied all the laughing and hugging and dancing that was going on, careless of the mud and pig filth they were stomping around in. They clutched handfuls of silver to their chests.

And at the center of it all stood Will, the open lockbox in his hands. He was looking at the three of them, a small smile on his lips.

"I've decided what we do," he called. "We robbed this silver from the rich . . . so now we'll give it to the poor!"

PART III

CHARITABLE OUTLAWS

SEVENTEEN

Huzzah!
—LITTLE JOHN

The first rule of banditry that Will learned was you could lie in wait all day and not catch a single thing, which was why the really good bandits did the necessary legwork. That's why Rob had sent Much into Nottingham to find a promising fellow—wealthy but not too well guarded. Sufficiently corrupt and deserving of a bit of a scare.

The boy had come back with the tale of the pardoner. He was due to come along the South Road around midday, riding comfortably in a cushioned cart bought and paid for by the selling of indulgences to those who could barely afford bread. He was a wicked one, rolling into town crying about sin and hellfire, scaring every last soul till they couldn't sleep at night for fear of demons and devils. Then he'd be waiting for all those sinners in the morning, offering confession, penance, and, most important, absolution. Everything for a price, and a hefty one at that.

The churchman had done so well for himself that he could even afford the security of armed guards, reported Much. Two of the sheriff's men, paid by the day. They must've made him feel safe and secure as he took the South Road through notorious Sherwood Forest.

But he was about to learn that his feeling of security was as false as the relics he peddled, as fake as the absolution he sold.

It was hard for Will to believe, but after weeks of filling the pockets of the poor, they'd finally run out of stolen silver. All except for a small sum that John insisted they keep to feed themselves. A smaller sum, he grumbled, than he would have liked.

When that silver had run out, they'd started replenishing their stock with the coin of the occasional lazy toll collector or corrupt priest. Like today's pardoner. No one important enough to draw attention to themselves. Just a purse here or there, which they then divided up—a quarter for themselves, three-quarters for those who needed it more.

Charitable outlaws, Rob called them. And the very idea of it tickled him so much that he was in brighter spirits than any of them could remember. He took to singing so often (and so wildly out of tune) that Will found himself sniffing the man's breath for traces of wine.

Will secretly wished they'd do more, strike at Sir Guy and the sheriff where it would hurt the most by cutting off their tax route to Prince John entirely. But to ask Rob and the others to do such a brazen thing, Will would have to confess to Much that he hadn't given up on his quest for vengeance. He'd already put their lives at risk once, when he'd convinced them to rob the castle, and he couldn't do it again.

Yet Will believed in their new mission as well, so much so that he surprised even himself. In just a few short weeks, they'd changed the lives of many families, and as word of their generosity spread, they'd given hope to even more. His days were filled with excitement and danger, but his nights were still haunted by his unfinished business, by the voice whispering in his ear, like a ghost calling on the wind, that Sir Guy was still alive.

Much watched him like a hawk. The boy knew Will's secret, and he'd kept it this long. But Will had no doubt that Much would tell all if he felt that Will was putting them in danger just to sate his desire for revenge.

So they hunted the outskirts of Sherwood and the outlying roads, far from Gilbert's Merry Men and Crooked's Men alike. At night they slept out beneath the stars or took shelter with some grateful family. But they were careful not to stay in one place for long. All was well that ended well, sang Rob. Gilbert and Sir Guy both could go hang themselves among the trees for all he cared.

Today they set up to ambush the pardoner near a bend in the South Road that wound around a tall hillock, just outside the forest. It was a favorite spot of theirs, bordered on one side by a lone fir tree, which provided excellent cover for a lookout. The two guards traveling with him were the only concern. These men must've cost the priest a pretty penny. They were a signal, a sign to the local outlaws who had an arrangement with the sheriff, that this man was not to be touched. As long as they accompanied him, he had nothing to fear from the Merry Men or Crooked's Men or any of the thugs who paid the sheriff's bribes. That was how the arrangement worked—for a fee, the outlaws could rob with impunity so long as they left the sheriff's men alone.

But Will and his companions no longer played by the sheriff's rules.

For today's work, Will was put on point with a bow. He warned them about his poor aim with the weapon, but Rob explained that it didn't matter whether he could hit anything with it, just that the guards saw it. A strong English longbow could pierce armor, and those guards wouldn't know if he could use it or not, but they wouldn't risk finding out.

Will was about to suggest that Rob take the bow instead when he caught a warning look from John. Rob might be sober, but he wasn't yet ready to be the longbowman he once was.

And so the plan was for Rob and John to emerge from their hiding places on either side of the road, weapons drawn, and calmly explain the lethality of the situation. Then they'd encourage the guards to drop their swords and the pardoner to hand over his coin purse. Much would stay up in his tree, eyes and ears open as he watched their backs.

The plan was all a cleverly orchestrated show meant to threaten terrible violence while aiming to avoid it entirely. But even the best plans go awry.

"Hello there, my good men," called Rob as the pardoner's cart rattled up the road. He stepped out of the bushes, his sword twirling in his hand and a smile on his lips. Will had noticed something about Rob since he sobered up—the man liked to show off.

John then appeared on the opposite side of the road, his long quarterstaff in hand. The guards reached for their swords at once as the pardoner threw himself onto the floor of his cart.

"Eh, eh," said Rob.

That was Will's cue. He appeared atop the hill, his red coat standing out against the verdant hillside. He had the arrow cocked and the bow drawn, and he hoped he looked fearsome enough.

"My friend there's an expert marksman," said Rob. "And—"

But he didn't finish, because that was when their plan fell to pieces. The pardoner, besides being a cheating fiend, was also apparently a wily fighter. One moment he was cowering beneath his seat, the next he had a crossbow aimed straight at Rob.

All Will saw was a feathered flash fly through the air and suddenly Rob was on the ground. The following moments were a blur. Will returned fire with the bow, but the arrow went wide, snapping uselessly against a rock. He'd had lessons as a boy, but his eyes were just not that sharp this far away. He really was useless with a bow.

With Rob down, the guards found their courage and attacked John. Two mounted men were more than a match for any fighter on foot, but John stood his ground and swung his long staff in a powerful arc, catching one of the soldiers square in the head. Unfortunately, that left John open to the second rider, and Will heard his shouted curses as the second rider tried to run him down beneath the horse's hooves.

Meanwhile, the pardoner, who'd shot at Rob, was getting away. He whipped his horse and drove the cart forward, careless of whom he ran over in the process. That unlucky person turned out to be the soldier John had struck on the head. He'd fallen from his horse and into the path of the carriage. But the pardoner didn't stop. He kept on without slowing down for the sickening, crunching bump beneath his wheels.

They hadn't rigged a catch line, since the threat of Will's bow was supposed to keep the cart from trying to escape, and if the pardoner made it past the bend onto the straight open road, they'd lose him for sure.

That's when Much jumped. Just as the cart passed under the boy's tree, he dropped from his perch and landed in the back of the cart. The horse had been whipped into a panic by now and was galloping onward regardless, so the pardoner, seeing the new threat, threw down the reins and drew his dagger.

He came for the boy just as they were clearing the bend in

the road and passing out of the shadow of the hill. Will's bow was useless, but he wasn't about to let Much fight the pardoner alone. Tossing the bow aside, Will took a running leap off the hill and landed on the edge of the cart. He just managed to grab the railing and avoid being trampled beneath the spinning wheels.

The cart barreled on. Much was crouched near the back, squaring off against the pardoner. Will dangled off the side, barely managing to hold on. In the next instant, just as the pardoner looked ready to attack, the cart struck a dip in the road and lurched to the side. The pardoner's dagger went flying, and he was left swinging his arms wildly just to keep his balance on the edge of the cart. He looked like a man desperately imitating a bird, hands flapping uselessly in the air.

Will saw his chance, and holding on to the cart's railing with one hand for dear life, he used his other to grab the hem of the pardoner's robe. Then he yanked it as hard as he could. The pardoner screamed as he somersaulted over the side to land face-first on the dirt road.

It took Will and Much quite a while to get the runaway cart back under control, to calm the poor horse and then convince it to turn around and go back the way they'd come (Much turned out to be very bad with horses. Will suggested that the boy might be part mule and therefore victim to a natural rivalry.) But together they did manage to bring the cart around eventually and make it back to the ambush site, where their friends were waiting. Rob, thankfully, was standing. He had a nasty cut along his temple where the pardoner's crossbow bolt had grazed him, and half his beard was still slick with blood, but he was grinning.

John was limping and sported a fat lip, but his two opponents had fared worse. The poor guard who'd been run over by the fleeing pardoner had a broken leg, and his companion had taken a beating with John's staff and lay moaning on the ground, calling out for his mother. Apparently, two mounted soldiers were no match for one Little John.

The pardoner was alive, but tied to a tree. His nose was a swollen mess from his dive to the ground, and both eyes had deep purple bruises underneath. But that didn't stop him from cursing when he saw Will and Much approaching with his purse of ill-gotten gains.

In all, Will's companions looked only slightly better off than the men they'd just defeated. They waved when they saw him, and when Much held up the heavy purse, they all cheered.

John let out a bellowing "*Huzzah!*" before spitting out a bloody tooth.

They loaded the guard with the broken leg into the cart along with the pardoner and let the other guard drive the three of them back to Nottingham. Besides the coin purse, they kept the soldiers' horses and weapons, and they urged them to find better employment.

That night, after supper and a bit of bandaging, they visited the Tilley family. Jean Tilley had been a somewhat successful furrier until a fever robbed him of his sight. A widower with no one but his two young sons to take care of him, Jean was now in dire need. His older boy, Gerard, tried to keep up his father's work and put food on the table for his baby brother, but the harsh winter had made game scarce. And if he was caught hunting deer in the king's forest, he'd be hanged.

Will smiled in spite of himself as he pressed the silver into Jean's hand. It was a look of shock at first as the old man traced the outlines of the coins and realized what they were. Then tears welled up in his sightless eyes as he realized what they *meant.* The pardoner's stolen silver would keep the family fed, Gerard's neck clear of the hangman's noose, and old Jean from dying of grief.

It was a good day to be an outlaw.

EIGHTEEN

Peasants are full of stories. It keeps their minds off their empty bellies.
—THE SHERIFF OF NOTTINGHAM

Much hated towns, all those bodies squeezed together in a pushing, pulling mess. Towns made it hard to breathe, and Much counted every step she had to take before she was free to make for the open road. Nottingham was unbearable on a good day, but Much had never seen it like this. Every foot of open space was taken up by people shouting their wares or by heavy-booted soldiers marching by. Beyond the town walls, tents fluttered in the breeze and a massive crowd sat on benches along a makeshift causeway, cheering on the stampeding of horses and the clang of metal against metal.

The Sheriff of Nottingham was hosting a tournament for nearby lords. Games, sword and shield combat, and the always-popular joust. All of which meant that the population of Nottingham had swelled to half again its size in the span of a few days as knights arrived with their courtiers, entourages, and hangers-on. Peasants from local villages swarmed the area, hoping to catch a glimpse of Lord So-and-So beating the snot out of Sir What's-His-Name. Then, their bloodlust sated, they'd return to the village to drink themselves numb.

And it was in this stew of humanity that Much was to do her scouting.

Fishing, Rob called it. He'd told Much to simply think of herself as casting about for the fattest fish in a pool of fat fishes. All she had to do was point to it, and they'd snatch him up. Just as they'd done with the pardoner.

Problem was, the fat fishes stank. And they stepped on your feet without so much as a "Beg your pardon."

God, but did Much hate towns.

Still, it did her no good to mope. The sooner she found a new target, the sooner she could get out of there. Thus far today, she'd eyed a spice merchant who whipped his servant something awful just for daring to loiter near the bread stand and a petty clerk collecting fees for the sheriff. She'd watched the clerk collect fees from the tourney lords all day long—a fee to pitch a tent, a fee to tie up a horse, a fee to empty a chamber pot. Most of the coin went straight into a heavy lockbox guarded by a trio of stern-faced soldiers, but a little (she noticed) went slyly into his own substantial coin purse. Should he leave Nottingham, that purse would be a tempting target indeed.

As Much waited for the clerk to make his rounds, she decided to pass the time by watching a knight lay his armored head across a blacksmith's anvil—the man must've fared poorly in the competition, because the blacksmith was forced to beat the dents out of his helmet just so the knight could take it off. Men really entertained themselves in the most foolish of ways. She'd just settled back with a handful of roasted pine nuts to see the knight struggle to free himself from his own armor when a fast-moving shape in the crowd caught her attention. A cleric walking deliberately, cursing those who didn't get out of his way fast enough and kicking at stray dogs in the street. This by itself wasn't remarkable, since as far as Much could tell, this sort of behavior was what the residents of Nottingham called "being civil." But what caught Much's attention was the man's two black eyes and nose swollen to the size of a round ripe plum.

The pardoner was back in Nottingham and making his way toward a gathering of tents near the tournament grounds. Much decided to shadow the pardoner, following him from a safe distance so as not to be recognized. And if he did catch a glimpse, she wasn't overly worried. Today she was disguised as a sickly beggar boy, complete with bandaged hands and feet. He'd need a really good look at her face to recognize her. Still, better to keep him in view so they didn't accidentally cross paths up close.

She'd figured that he'd pass the tourney grounds and hole up in a local tavern to nurse his wounds. But he surprised her when he arrived at a large, plain tent on the outskirts of the competitors' pavilion. This one was larger than most but also plainer, without any of the gaudy trappings or silky banners that decorated the rest. A pair of town guardsmen stopped the pardoner at the door, and after a moment of chatter, he was let inside.

If Much had one professional weakness, it was curiosity. There was absolutely no good reason for her to linger there any longer. The pardoner was about whatever business he was about, and it was high time for Much to return to her clerk. She still needed to find out when the man was leaving Nottingham and by which road.

She repeated this very logical reasoning to herself as she slipped around the back of the tent and, looking over her shoulder to make sure she wasn't in plain view, used a knife to cut a small peephole in the rear tent wall. Then she bent down and pretended to be rewrapping her foot bandages. Funny what a wide berth people gave you when you looked to be unwrapping a festering sore.

From her peephole, she had a good view of the pardoner. He was talking to another man, who was strapping himself into a suit of well-worn armor. Much recognized the man by the gold chain of office that hung about his neck—the Sheriff of Nottingham! Much only knew the man by sight, as Gilbert had had dealings with him in the past. Bribes that were paid in the form of tribute. There must have been a lull between tournament contests, because the cheering and boos had died down, and in the relative quiet the men's voices carried well.

The pardoner was red-faced and furious.

". . . all of it!" he was saying. "Every last farthing! And what good did your *protection* buy me? Not a bit."

"I told you," the sheriff answered. "These must've been new. Brigands stopping off along the road for a quick robbery. They'll have moved on by morning."

"Moved on with my silver!" The pardoner was practically spitting he was so mad. "I demand recompense! I demand—"

The man cut off the pardoner with a wave of his hand.

"You'll demand nothing of me. You'll go about your business of saving souls for profit, and you'll remember to put in your daily prayers a special thank-you that the Sheriff of Nottingham hasn't put you in the stockade just for being a horse's ass."

The pardoner paled. "You wouldn't dare. . . ."

The sheriff laughed. "Try me. You're a thief—no better than those highwaymen who took your coin. As far as I'm concerned, it's a case of dogs biting dogs.

"Now," the sheriff continued, "if these bandits don't move on, then I will deal with them, but that's to keep my roads safe for honest folk, not because I was threatened by a fake holy man like yourself."

With that, the sheriff turned his back on the pardoner and resumed armoring himself.

"We're done," he said. "In case you hadn't noticed."

The pardoner backed his way out of the tent, his face a good deal paler than when he'd first come in.

As soon as the pardoner was out the door, the sheriff's demeanor changed. He let out a long sigh and angrily swatted aside a sheaf of papers on a nearby table.

"You see?" said a new voice, strangely accented. "What did I tell you?"

Someone was in the tent with the sheriff. Someone sitting in the shadows beyond Much's field of vision.

"He's a panicked fool who had a bit of bad luck," said the sheriff. "Nothing more."

"You can tell yourself that if you want," said the voice. "But my people tell me that these outlaws are hunting the edges of Sherwood. They aren't going anywhere."

"Yes? And who would your people be? Tom Crooked and his gang of murderers? How do you know that Crooked himself isn't behind all this?"

"Don't be so self-righteous!" said the hidden man. "I understand you've had dealings with him in the past. Your hands are not as clean as you like to pretend."

The sheriff spun around and faced the man in the shadows.

"My arrangement with the bandits of Sherwood kept the greater peace. Let them hunt there so that they stay out of Nottingham. But you are giving them commissions. Making them your mercenaries and enforcers! It's a dangerous game."

"You don't like my methods, look the other way," said the man. "But I've gotten the peasants talking. They say these new outlaws are led by a bandit king. Gives silver to the poor. I think they're trying to spark a rebellion."

The sheriff laughed. "And I think it's a story. I also have one about the Witch of the Forest, who sours milk with a gaze and gives you the pox whenever she sneezes. Peasants are full of stories. It keeps their minds off their empty bellies."

There was the creak of leather as the man from the shadows stepped into view. He wore a terrifying suit of armor that seemed crafted from animal hide, and in his arms he held a helm shaped like a horse's skull. He looked nothing like the shining knights of the tourney. This man looked like a barbarian.

"They stole from me," said the man. "They came into my castle and stole from me."

"Your castle?" said the sheriff. "It still belonged to Rodric Shackley last I checked."

"Prince John in his wisdom has asked me to act as regent until Lord Rodric returns. It's a shame what happened to poor Lord Geoff, killed in a traitorous brawl of his own making. But people get hurt in brawls. Even die."

The sheriff was quiet for a moment. "Geoff was no traitor."

"No matter," said Sir Guy. "It's ancient history. He's dead. Rodric's wife and son are fled to France, and it's my right as the new regent to hunt down these criminals who stole from me!"

"I will catch them," said the sheriff.

"I'm not here to ask your help. I'm here to tell you that I'll find them my own way. I've already begun. You see, I have names. . . ."

At that moment, a loud cheer went up from the tournament grounds, and the two men's voices were drowned out by the noise. Whatever was being said, the sheriff looked none too happy about it. Sir Guy shoved a piece of parchment into the Sheriff's hands, and whatever was written there just made the man angrier. When the cries finally died down, he was practically shouting.

". . . don't do anything so stupid! The peasant folk are already on the verge of open revolt, and the bandits *pay* to be left alone. If you go about kicking hornets' nests, I'll be the one to deal with it!"

"I'm not asking permission, *Sheriff*," answered the man. "I'm just giving you fair warning. I'll catch the robbers my way. You stick to tax collecting—you're good at it."

With that, the man turned to go. "But call me stupid one more time and I'll knock your pate down your neck," he added.

The sheriff called out after him. "Sir Guy, not even Prince John will be able to save you if you go too far."

But the man didn't stop and he didn't look back.

Much snuck away from the tent until she was far enough away that she could run. She kept her head down as she scurried quickly through the crowds. Perhaps too quickly for a supposed sick beggar boy, but she didn't care to dawdle here any longer. It was time to leave Nottingham behind.

Sir Guy of Gisborne. She'd finally gotten a good look at the man Will had sworn to kill, and she knew he couldn't do it. Since joining the world of outlaws, Much had developed a sense about them. She could tell, more or less, the men who skirted or even broke the law because they had to. Because they genuinely believed they had no other choice. But she could also tell, more or less, the men who did it because they enjoyed it. Thrill seekers, some, but the real bad ones had a taste for the chaos.

The violence of it all. Sir Guy was one of those men. He might have a knightly title, but he was an outlaw of the worst kind, and there was no way the skinny boy in the red coat could face that iron-cold killer and live. None.

Much hadn't feared many things in her life, but she feared him. And more, she feared for Will.

NINETEEN

One king's as bad as another.
—MUCH THE MILLER'S SON

After hearing Much's report from Nottingham, Will and his companions never made camp in the same place twice. Most nights they slept out on the windswept moors; others they sheltered beneath the leaves. But occasionally they found warm beds and hot meals with the families they'd helped.

The Horse Knight was hunting them, en force. Much was worried. John was angry and Rob was concerned. For Will's part, the news created in him a mix of fear and pure joy. While he worried about his companions, that he'd hurt the Horse Knight, that their robbery had angered him so, made up in a small way for his own failure at revenge. If he couldn't kill Sir Guy outright, he'd have to settle for driving him to distraction. For now.

But Much had also heard Sir Guy claim to have names, and if Tom Crooked was really in Sir Guy's employ, then he'd have given up the name John Little for sure. He might even have told him about Rob and the Merry Men. While Gilbert and the rest would be safe in their hidden camp, they would have no idea that Sir Guy was out there somewhere waiting for them.

No one cared a bit for Gilbert's safety, but Wat Crabstaff and the rest of the Merry Men would also be at risk, and it didn't feel right letting them go about heedless of the danger.

Unfortunately, the weather turned sour again before they could decide what to do about it, and they were forced to hole up with the old furrier Tilley and his sons until the storms passed. They took shelter in the rear room, while the Tilleys slept in the front. After a day and a night of solid storms, the sun finally reappeared, if only briefly, and Rob and John took advantage of the break in the bad weather to do some scouting and see if they couldn't get some information on Guy's movements. It was agreed that if the roads were clear, they'd all leave in the morning. They'd already been in one place longer than any of them liked.

As the day turned to evening, and without anything else to do, Will decided to teach Much how to play a game. There was a decent fire going in the back room of the house to keep away the lingering damp, but nothing could drive away the boredom, so Will had taken to carving as a way to pass the hours. He'd managed to create a rather rough set of game pieces and turned a sheet of vellum (a "gift" he'd lifted from one of the tax collectors) into a game board by decorating it in rows and columns of squares, some white, some blackened with charcoal. The physical game was complete; now all he needed was someone to play it with. He just needed someone patient enough to learn the rules.

"This is a stupid game and I'm not playing it anymore," said Much.

Will sighed. At least Much hadn't knocked the pieces over this time. That was an improvement, surely.

"Why can't I move this one forward and kill your man?" she asked.

"Pawns only attack on a diagonal. And they don't kill, they capture."

"Well, that's stupid," said Much. "Here's an enemy sitting right in front of him and he won't be bothered to do anything about it? Stupid."

"It requires strategy," said Will. "Let's look at your other possible moves."

Much sat back with his arms folded across his chest and scrunched his face up into a pout as Will reviewed, for the tenth time, each piece's name and its capabilities.

Will could tell the boy was barely listening. "Where'd you learn this?"

"My father," said Will. "He learned it from a traveling Moor."

"A Moor?" said Much.

"From northern Africa and the Arab lands."

"A heathen?"

"Yes," said Will. "But my father said the Moors were honorable people. Men of great learning."

"Wasn't King Richard fighting the Moors on that crusade of his?"

"Yes, but it's possible to honor your enemies," said Will. "If they have honor themselves. Besides, the war is over now. And he learned this game from them years ago. They came to our castle once to trade."

"If they were trading this game of yours, then I hope you didn't give them much in return. It's terrible."

Will began putting the pieces back to their original positions. Maybe if he started over, things would seem clearer.

"Don't get too focused on each piece," he said. "Start with the objective—to defend your king—"

"I don't want to defend my king," said Much. "What's he done for me? The king can go rot for all I care."

"I'm not talking about the real king!" said Will, losing his patience. "Fine, imagine it's King Richard you're defending."

"Don't want to," said Much. "One king's as bad as another."

Will stopped setting up the pieces. "Richard is not John. John's stealing the lands of loyal noblemen while his cronies bleed the people dry. King Richard is a good man."

"Tell that to all those Moors he killed in that war of his," said Much. "Those honorable men of great learning you were telling me about. I wonder if they think he's such a great king."

Before he'd even realized what he was doing, Will had slammed his fist down on the board, sending the pieces flying.

"My father fought with him!" Will shouted. "He's locked up in a prison with the king somewhere, if he's not dead already, and while my father was gone, his brother was murdered and his castle stolen! It has to mean something."

Will stood up and stalked over to the window. He opened the shutter and let the air in to cool his blood. "What do you know about it, anyway? You've probably never even been out of Nottinghamshire."

It was quiet for a while as Will breathed in the night air. When he heard the clatter of wood behind him, he turned around and saw Much picking up the pieces he'd sent flying and dropping them into the little lockbox Will stored them in. Empty now of silver, it made the perfect carrying case for his set.

"Here," said Will, kneeling next to him. "Let me do that. I threw the tantrum, I can clean up the mess."

"I forget sometimes," said Much. "I forget you are . . . who you are. I didn't mean it."

"Yes, you did. And you were right." Will scooped up the last of the fallen pieces—one of the pawns had chipped, but he wouldn't mind making another. He set the box on the table and sat down heavily in his chair.

"The thing is, Much, living in my father's house was like living in two worlds. His world was one of knights and laws and countless other dull daily tasks of ruling. My world was seeing how much mischief I could get away with. Whether anyone would notice if I snuck off to see the mummers play instead of doing my Latin lesson, or if Nan would figure out I was the one who peppered Osbert's wine."

"Latin?" asked Much, eyes wide. "You know Latin?"

"Would've known more if not for the mummers. But my point is, there were only two worlds—my childhood and the royal court. But I realize now that both were false. Illusions."

Will gestured to the little room around them, with its drafty thatch roof and soot-stained walls. "This is the real world. Where people starve because they weren't born with the name Shackley. We were wrong—wolves don't kill peasants, hunger does."

Much shook his head sadly. "That's how it is all over England, Will. You said I've never been out of Nottingham, but I have. I traveled lots of places before I ended up here, and I can tell you your father was no worse than any other lord. Probably better than most. I just can't stand the whole lot of them, is all."

Will rubbed his eyes. His father had always seemed such a hero, and in Will's heart he still was. He missed him dearly and prayed every night for his safe return. As a man, as a father, he was still Will's idol. But as Lord Shackley, he'd come to represent something else, a branch of a much larger rotten tree. A tree that would someday collapse under its own weight.

"And what about you, Much?" Will said. "You know all

my secrets, and yet I know next to nothing about you. Except you're a terrible chess player."

"My story's not as interesting as yours," the boy said, scooting closer to the fire. "No palace intrigue. No daring escapes."

"Where are your parents?" Will asked. "Are they alive?"

"No. My mother died when I was little, and my father . . . he followed her two years back."

"I'm sorry," said Will.

"He was a miller. Called me Much because he said I wasn't worth much, but he was just teasing." Much tossed a hunk of peat into the fire. "He was a good man and he loved me."

"So when he died, you set out on your own? Started thieving, pulling knives on people." He'd meant that last part as a joke, but Much wasn't smiling when he looked up.

"No, but I found out pretty quick that a young . . . a young boy on his own needs protection. Learned that lesson the hard way. Met a traveler on the road who offered to share his meal, his campfire. Afterward, though, he tried beating on me. But what he didn't know was I'd pocketed the knife from dinner."

Will didn't say anything. He could only imagine this young boy out in these wilds by himself, trusting in strangers to survive, only to have that trust betrayed so easily.

"I learned that night that I could fight back," said Much softly. "But I'm not big like John. The knife was all I had, so I used it. I gave him a scar to remember me by and made off with the rest of dinner."

"No one can blame you for that," said Will. "You did what you had to do to survive."

"That was up near Carlisle," said Much. "I made my way south after that."

"You're from the North Country?" asked Will. "I thought I knew the accent."

Much nodded. "My mother was a Scot."

"Do you have family up there still?"

"I do, but I don't know them. And another mouth to feed is the last thing they need."

Will, too, had family in a far-off land, and while he barely knew his mother's relatives, his mother herself would be worried sick. She probably feared him dead. The thought of her made his heart ache, and it would be an easy thing to give in to that feeling and make for the coast. It wasn't too late. Across the sea, there was safety and comfort waiting for him. As his mother's son, he wouldn't be heir to foreign lands, but her family would give him a home. Perhaps he could take Much with him—and Rob and John, if they'd be willing to go.

But no. To do that, Will would have to slip into another of those illusions and to turn his back on the reality he'd discovered here. To forget Guy's villainy, and the sheriff's betrayal. He'd made a vow to Osbert not to abandon these lands, and that was a vow he meant to keep.

"Will?" said Much. "Are you still set on killing Sir Guy?"

In part, Will had been expecting this. Much had been acting odd ever since the boy returned from Nottingham. Will would catch him staring when he thought Will wasn't looking.

"I won't put you all in danger, if that's what you're asking," said Will.

"That's not what I'm asking at all," said Much. "I want to know if you still plan on killing Guy. Because I've seen him now, up close."

"And?"

"And you won't be able to do it."

Will started to say something. He opened his mouth to tell him that he was young and foolish and that he had no idea what Will was capable of. But when he saw the look on Much's face, he stopped. The boy wasn't taunting him; he wasn't trying to hurt him. Much was scared. Scared for Will, and when he said that Will wouldn't be able to do it, he was just being honest. And honesty, Will had learned, was something to be treasured among outlaws.

"Maybe," said Will after a moment. "But I have to try."

"Why?" said Much. "I mean, there are other ways—"

The boy stopped suddenly, his eyes going to the door.

"What? You hear something?" Will asked.

The boy nodded. "It's all right. I think Rob and John are back."

Will let out a sigh of relief. And he was thankful not to have to talk about Sir Guy any longer.

"We'll finish our chess game later," he said.

"Not likely," answered Much.

The door swung open and Rob stomped in. He hadn't even bothered to scrape the mud from his boots.

"I need a drink!" he said. "I know Tilley has a bottle of something around here!"

"Nothing, Rob," said John, stepping into the doorway. He had to duck his head to fit inside. "The old man doesn't touch the stuff."

Will had actually seen Tilley with a bottle last night, but one look from John, and Will kept his mouth shut. No one wanted Rob to go back to the wine. But Will did want to know what they'd discovered that had him in such a state.

"What did you find?" he asked.

"The Waltham farm," said John.

"Guy burned it to the ground!" said Rob. "Slaughtered the livestock and left the Walthams to starve."

"What?" said Much. "Why?"

John sighed heavily. "It seems that Waltham decided to

share a bit of his good fortune at the pub in Nottingham. The poor fool bought everyone a round of drinks and told them a tale of the kindhearted outlaw who slept in his barn and filled his pocket with silver."

"And word got back to Guy," said Will. "This is all my fault."

"No!" said Rob, striding over to him. "This is the doing of Sir Guy of Gisborne and his thugs. You tried to help Waltham."

"But he won't stop there," said Will. "He knows we're helping these people with his silver, and he'll keep taking his revenge on them."

"You're right," said Rob. "We're putting Tilley and his sons in danger just being here. They'll be searching every outlying farm and homestead now."

"So what do we do?" asked Much. "Where do we go?"

Rob and John exchanged a look, but Will knew what they were thinking. They'd stayed out here among the farms and villages for too long. But it was no longer just their lives they were putting at risk—it was the life of every single person they helped. Will couldn't put them all in danger.

"We go where any outlaw goes who's on the run," said Will. "We go back to Sherwood."

Rob scratched at his beard thoughtfully for a few minutes.

"I think the lad's right," he said. "No use putting it off any longer. I think it's past time I had a conversation with Gilbert the White Hand."

"And it's about bloody time," added John, smiling.

TWENTY

If Guy wants to keep the respect of the Merry Men,
then he'll have to murder me fairly. Or at least unfairly
but in spectacular fashion.
—ROB

That morning Will awoke to find the sky outside their window still the blue-gray of predawn, and the frenzied chirping of birds told him that the sun was ready to rise. They'd been given beds, while John lay sprawled out in the corner—the floor seemed to be the only thing that could accommodate his massive size. Much slept contentedly in the bed next to Will's, burrowed under the covers like a mole, but Rob's was empty.

Will slipped on his boots, took his coat down from its tack on the wall, and snuck out the door, careful not to let it squeak as it closed. The Tilleys had taken the floor in the front room, and Will had to step carefully so as not to crush exposed fingers or toes.

He found Rob outside near the fence, wrapped in his cloak and staring at the pink glow in the east.

"Well met, Master Will," said Rob.

"Do you mind some company?" asked Will.

"Not at all. Pull up a piece of fence."

Will leaned against the post and looked up at the sky.

"If you wait a bit," said Rob, "you can see bats hunting. You can tell them by the way they fly—not straight like a bird, but more erratic."

Will squinted up where the sky was growing light. After a moment, he did start to pick out dark shapes fluttering about, their flight paths like cracks in a glass.

"I see them," said Will.

"Did you know John's afraid of bats? Hates them. That's why he sleeps with his boots on. Says they go for your toes."

"Do they?"

"Nah. But don't tell him that. The more he keeps those gargantuan feet of his covered, the better it is for the rest of us."

Will watched the bats swoop and dive for their breakfast. Or was this their bedtime snack? Bats were night creatures and would soon hide away to sleep as the sun appeared over the horizon.

"I used to get up at first light to steal sweets from the kitchen," said Will. "The staff would unpack the sweet cream and honey first, and I'd try to grab handfuls while they weren't looking. Nan would examine my fingers at breakfast for any traces of the stuff, but I learned to keep my fingernails short. . . ."

Will trailed off as he realized what he was saying. This was the most he'd spoken about his old life in months, and he'd just come very close to saying too much.

Rob was watching him, those sharp eyes of his hawklike and his face expressionless.

"Well, I was always an early riser, too," Rob said after a moment. "That is, when I wasn't sleeping off a barrel of wine."

Will smiled at this, but even as Rob made light of his drinking, it made Will worry. In spite of himself, Will liked this Rob. He respected him, even. But the drunken braggart he'd met those weeks ago was a frightening, sad creature, and Will now lived his days afraid that he'd look and find that creature had returned.

Maybe he was still foggy-headed from sleep, or maybe experience had made him bold, but somehow that morning Will found the courage to ask a question that had been haunting him for weeks.

"Rob, are you going to go back to drinking?"

Will had been afraid that the question would earn him a tongue-lashing, but Rob just sighed and wrapped his cloak tighter around him.

"Do you mean today?" Rob said. "No, I think not."

"How about tomorrow?"

"Honestly, lad? I don't know. I hope not."

Will nodded. Rob's honesty surprised him, and made him feel good in a way. If Rob had said he'd sworn off wine forever, Will didn't think he would've believed him. But he could take him at his word day by day.

Emboldened, he decided to try another question.

"John said you started drinking because of a girl. Is that true?"

Rob didn't handle this question nearly as well. The man turned around and pointed angrily at the Tilleys' house, his voice rising as he spoke.

"Oh, is that what he said? Well, Little John has a mouth to match his giant, ignorant head!"

Will feared he'd gone too far. "I'm sorry," he said quickly. "He just mentioned her in passing. He didn't even say her name!"

"That's because her name will not be spoken, you hear me?" Rob turned his finger to Will's face.

Will nodded.

"And she's a lady, not a girl," said Rob, looking away. "And I didn't start drinking because of *her.* Not exactly."

"I am sorry, Rob," said Will. "I shouldn't have pried. . . ."

"It's this place, Will," Rob said, gesturing to the fields and trees around them. "It's England. It's this time we live in that makes a man drink himself dumb. It's the simple, spiteful *unfairness* of it all! It's the fact that if I'd been born Robert, Earl of Locksley, say, rather than plain old Rob the yeoman, then I'd have the lady I wanted. I'd have a chance at least. But that's not to be—so, the bottle."

Rob's broken heart, the Walthams' ruined pig farm, even Geoff's murder—they were all a part of William Shackley's England. The England where men were propped up by birth rather than deeds, where the strong took from the weak. It was an England Will Scarlet was beginning to despise.

"It's those same forces that are after us now, you know," Rob said. "Those with power—who said I couldn't dare to love the woman I chose—those are the very same people who are after us now. We've upset the order, and that's not likely to end well, lad."

"You know," said Will, taking a deep breath. "My uncle used to say that the power to rule over another man is like brittle glass. All it takes is a crack to shatter it all to pieces. I don't know if I believed him at the time, but I've grown up a lot since then."

"So what do you believe now?" asked Rob.

"I think no man should starve when another man has so much. And we can show people that. Guy and the sheriff and Prince John himself will hunt us, but if we are clever, we can show people that truth. We can crack their lie to pieces. If we're caught, then maybe we'll be worth a story or two. And maybe someone else will pick up the tale."

At this, Rob broke into a huge grin, that laughing, wild-eyed grin he got, and he clasped his hand on Will's shoulder.

"I may be a good-for-nothing drunkard and a fool, Will Scarlet, but I will say this—that's something worth being sober for! By God it is!

"Come on," he continued. "Let's find some breakfast for these lazy layabouts we call friends! We'll need our strength for the journey into Sherwood, I think. After all, if our luck holds, I fully expect someone will try to kill us today!"

In the short time Will had spent among the outlaws, he'd discovered there was a reason Sherwood Forest was a home to so many scoundrels and brigands. There were really only two decent roads through the forest; the rest was a maze of tangled paths, dark hollows, and impenetrable brush—unless you knew your way around. Many of the so-called criminals who'd fled to the forest were woodsmen and trappers who'd lost too much under Prince John's yoke to make a decent living. It would be a stretch to call them honest men, but they were not without their own sense of honor.

With the exception of Gilbert and Stout, the Merry Men were just such men. Given the choice of robbing or earning an honest living, most of them would take the latter, if an honest living didn't mean being a slave to your lord and master. They were not men deserving of a hangman's noose or the sword, especially if the sword was wielded by the likes of Sir Guy. They needed to be warned about Sir Guy, at the very least.

"Think Gilbert will just have us shot on sight?" asked John as he peered into the thick brush. With only two horses remaining, they'd taken turns riding and walking most of the way, but now the path was getting so tangled that they were all forced to go on foot.

"He would," said Rob. "But the rest of the men love me. I'm a very popular figure among the outlaw type."

Rob either didn't notice or didn't care about the look that John and Much shared with each other.

"If Guy wants to keep the respect of the Merry Men, then he'll have to murder me fairly," he continued. "Or at least unfairly but in spectacular fashion. Something more impressive than an arrow in the back."

"What about an arrow in the front?" asked John.

"Shut up," answered Rob.

"Why would he want you dead at all?" asked Will. "I'm the one Stout tried to kill."

"Oh, he'll kill you, too, don't you worry," said John. "But now you're a small fish. More than anything, Gilbert fears competition. Someone better equipped to lead."

"He's right," said Much. "Now that Rob's sober—"

"Tragedy that may be," said Rob.

"Now that Rob's sober," continued John, "he's the man the rest'll look to. Rob the Drunk was easy to keep in check. Ah, but now Robin—"

"Don't say it," interrupted Rob. "I hate that name and you know it!"

Much and John shared a laugh.

"What name?" asked Will. "What's so funny?"

"Well, my lad," said John. "You know that statue back at the camp? That horned and hooded monstrosity?"

"Yes. Much told me that Wat built it."

"Oh yes!" laughed John. "But he wasn't alone! It takes more than the dim wits of Wat Crabstaff to design such a brilliant engine of banditry! Such a fine, original idea—*Hey, everyone! We don't need to threaten people into giving up their coin. We'll just build a giant hooded monster to do it for us!*"

"All right," said Rob. "That's enough."

"But, Rob," said John. "Surely an act like that is deserving of a name to remember you by? What was it again? Robin—"

"No, I mean shut up!" whispered Rob. "We're being watched!"

No sooner had he spoken than a loud birdcall echoed through the trees. Then the call was taken up by another farther on.

"We've been spotted," said Rob quietly.

"Was that the signal for friend or foe?" asked Will.

"Neither," said Much. "That wasn't one of our calls."

"You think Gilbert's had them changed?" asked John.

"I think we need to be ready for anything," answered Rob. "Will, you still have that longbow?"

"Yes," answered Will. "But I told you I'm no good at it."

"It's not for you," answered Rob. "Hand it over."

Will took the bow off one of the horses and handed it to Rob. As he strung it, Rob ran his hand along its curves, as if testing the wood.

"Good bow. Yew. The best, in fact."

Next he slung a quiver of arrows onto his back.

"Shoddy bunch of arrows, though. Look like they've been fletched by a blind man. If things go badly with Gilbert, if he somehow manages to get the best of me, you and Much make for the trees. Deep in the forest there's a lightning-struck oak with a face like an old crone's. You know it, Much?"

"Yes."

"Good. Meet there if we need to split up. Bring Will with you."

Much started to protest, but Rob cut him off. "Do as I say."

Much looked to John for help, but the big man just shook his head. "You heard him."

Will didn't say anything, though he knew he wouldn't run. If there was fighting to be done, he would be there fighting at their sides.

When the gate came into sight, it was wide open. Men moved about in the camp beyond. A fat fellow walked toward them, waving.

"Stout!" said John. "He made it back after all!"

"Hey there, Rob!" called Stout. "John, Much. Been waiting for you."

"I bet he has," said Much under his breath.

"Where's Gilbert?" said Rob.

Stout swallowed nervously. Will realized the man was scared. Terrified, even.

"He's . . . he's dead," said Stout.

"Dead?" said John.

"It's true," called out a familiar voice. "But he died fighting, I'll give him that."

From one of the tents behind Stout stepped a tall man wearing a broadsword. He was slipping on a most unusual helmet made to look like the head of a corpse stallion. It matched his horsehide armor.

"Stout said if we punished a few peasants, you'd come running home," he said, drawing his sword. "Good boy, Stout."

"Sir Guy!" breathed Will.

"What?" said John. "How did he—"

But Rob didn't wait for him to finish. There was a flash of movement, and then an arrow sang through the air. It landed with a meaty thunk in Sir Guy's right hand. The Horse Knight cried out as he dropped his sword.

"Good shot!" said John.

"I was aiming for his face!" answered Rob. "I'm out of practice!"

Sir Guy shouted an order, and the camp was suddenly alive with soldiers. Some were dressed plainly, disguised as Merry Men, while others came rushing from the tents readied in full armor. A few were even perched in the trees with crossbows. Guy's soldiers had been lying in wait for them to come home.

"Go!" John shouted as he hauled Will up by his shoulders and threw him into the trees to their right. But Will could barely make his legs move. There was Sir Guy of Gisborne, not thirty feet from him. The man who'd killed his uncle and stolen everything from him.

They charged through the trees as crossbow bolts landed around them, John dragging Will and shouting at the boy to run. Soldiers crashed through the brush in pursuit. Rob ran a few feet, let loose an arrow, dropped an opponent, then ran some more. He never missed. Will had lost sight of Much.

Two men with swords suddenly appeared in their path, and John let go of Will as he swung his staff to block their blades.

Sir Guy was shouting orders. He didn't sound very far away. And he was wounded; Rob's arrow had struck him in his sword hand. . . .

John's attention was on the two soldiers in front of him. Will could hear the twang of Rob's bowstring somewhere close by.

His own sword in hand, Will ran toward the sound of Guy's voice. John called out something—it might have been Will's name—but Will didn't stop or look back. He couldn't, not when Guy was this near.

Then he heard another shout. A high-pitched cry that set Will's teeth on edge.

Much.

The call came from the opposite direction of Guy. Down a hill that led into what looked like some kind of ravine or dry creek bed.

Will could make out Sir Guy's words now. He was close and he was calling for his men. Perhaps he'd gotten separated in the chase. Perhaps he was alone. Wounded and alone.

Much called out again, a panicked cry that ended suddenly, as if snuffed out.

With a curse, Will turned and half ran, half stumbled down into the ravine, toward the sound of Much's last cry for help.

The ground leading down was slippery with dead leaves and crumbling soil, and Will was lucky he didn't twist an ankle or spill over headfirst, but quickly enough he reached the bottom.

There he found Much fighting for his life against a soldier. The two of them looked as if they'd tumbled down the slope together. They were scratched and covered with dirt and leaves. They were engaged in a weaponless struggle, a wrestling match in the dirt. The bigger man had a good hold on Much, his hands reaching for the boy's throat. But as Will ran toward them, Much threw a handful of dirt into the soldier's eyes, momentarily blinding him.

Much tried to scramble out from underneath him, but the soldier, grasping blindly, found Much's shirt. The soldier yanked hard and the shirt tore away in his fingers, and Much rolled out of his grasp, backing away from him on all fours.

But the boy's shirt had torn down the front and now hung wide open. At first, Will didn't understand what he was seeing. Around Much's chest was a bandage, a kind of wrapping, which had been pulled loose in the struggle . . .

What Will saw beneath that torn wrapping was hard at first to comprehend. He stood stunned, his mind reeling.

Much was a girl. Much was a *girl*?

Will came to his senses in time to see the soldier, blinking with pain, pull a long knife from his boot.

Much was frantically searching for his own knives—*her* own knives—but they'd gone missing, lost in the fall.

With a snarl, the soldier lunged forward, his knife catching the sunlight as he brought it down toward Much's exposed chest.

It found Will's blade instead.

He reached the soldier just in time to parry the blow, and the sound of steel against steel rang out across the ravine.

Surprised, the soldier stumbled backward a step and turned to face Will.

It was never a good idea to pit a knife against a broadsword, and the soldier eyed Will warily as they circled each other. But in keeping all his attention on Will, he'd taken his eyes off Much.

The soldier never saw the thick tree branch until it cracked against his skull, knocking him, unconscious, to the ground.

Will stared openly at Much, who dropped the branch and wrapped the tatters of her shirt protectively around her. Will opened his mouth to speak, but she held a finger to her lips, shushing him. Then she pointed up toward the top of the ravine.

Soldiers' voices, getting nearer.

She gestured for him to follow as she started to make her way along the ravine floor, away from the sounds of pursuit and deeper into the forest.

Still in shock, it was all Will could do to stay upright.

So he left the unconscious soldier behind and followed this girl, this sudden stranger, to wherever it was she was taking him.

TWENTY-ONE

This is about the life we choose—it's not about you.
—MUCH THE MILLER'S DAUGHTER

Much had always thought the oak's face looked more like an old wrinkled man's than a crone's. An ancient lightning strike had blasted a hole in the center of the trunk, giving it the appearance of a toothless mouth. A broken knob of a branch served as its nose. One only needed one's imagination to find the eyes.

They'd made the journey to the tree together in silence. At first, keeping quiet was a necessity, since Guy's men were still searching the woods. But even after it became obvious that they'd lost their pursuers, they didn't speak. They'd stopped trying to quiet their footsteps, and they marched on, heedless of snapping branches and crunching leaves. Will had handed Much his red coat to cover her own torn shirt, and she accepted it without thanks. And still they said not a word.

They arrived at the tree and waited and rested. When Will finally did break the silence, it was with a question Much wasn't expecting.

"So," he said, struggling for the words, "are you *all* girl or . . ."

"Yes!" snapped Much. "I'm all girl. And you're all idiot."

Will's face flushed a deep red, but whether it was out of anger or embarrassment, Much couldn't have said. Scarlet, indeed.

"It's not a foolish question," said Will. "You hear stories, you know."

Much shook her head in disgust and looked away, searching the trees for any movement. The oak was deep in the wilds of Sherwood, deeper than most had ventured. But a select few knew it. John had been the first one to show it to Much.

"They should've been here by now," she said, hoping to change the subject. But Will wouldn't let it go.

"It's just I'm surprised you kept it a secret all this time. I mean, it had to have been hard."

"Yes, but men are stupid, which made things easier. We've established that just now, haven't we?"

"Does John know? Rob?"

"No and no," said Much, turning on him. "And if you breathe a word, I'll fill you full of knife holes, Will Scarlet, so help me I will!"

Will held up his hands in surrender and said nothing more.

The boy didn't deserve her anger. After all, he'd discovered her secret by accident and in the process of saving her life. It wasn't his fault, but that didn't change the fact that the truth was out now, and though she could make him swear to never tell a soul, once a secret was spoken, it would spread. It was a rule of nature that people couldn't keep their mouths shut. Sooner or later, he'd let the truth slip.

Which meant that Much had to leave. Once they were sure Rob and John were safe, Much would slip away quietly and disappear. But she didn't want to run away from home yet again. Without meaning to, Will had ruined everything.

Bloody Will Scarlet.

"So," said Will. "How old are you? Really?"

Much looked over at him. He just wouldn't let it lie. "How old are you?" she asked.

"Thirteen."

"I've got a year on you, then," she said. "But no one would believe I'm a fourteen-year-old *boy*."

"I would've never known, if I hadn't seen . . . I mean to say . . . you're a very good actor."

His face had turned an even brighter shade of red, if such a thing were possible. She prayed that Rob and John would arrive soon, just to put the boy out of his misery.

But it was getting late in the day. The long afternoon shadows were growing steadily, and Much had no interest in spending the night next to this oak. It was eerie enough in the daylight.

Her mind made up, Much stood and dusted herself off.

"Right," she said. "I'm going to find them."

"What?" said Will. "Are you sure that's a good idea? Rob said to meet here, didn't he?"

"If he'd have been able to meet us here, he would've done it by now. That means they're in trouble."

Will came to stand next to her.

"But we might meet more soldiers out there. And you're weaponless."

"You're right," she said. Then Much walked around to the back of the oak tree, opposite its face. There was a hollow where some of the ground had eroded away from the roots. She reached inside that dark space, wincing at the feel of moist earth and crawling things.

"What are you looking for?" asked Will.

Much ignored him as she scraped away a layer of rotted

leaves. Then she withdrew two bundles wrapped in leather and oilcloth.

"John told me that he put this here in case the camp was ever taken," she said. "Only he and Rob know about it."

She unrolled one bundle to reveal three daggers. The second contained clothes, cloaks, and a small purse of silver.

The clothes smelled vaguely of forest rot, and the blades were rusting in places, but they were sturdy and well-made weapons.

Much pulled a musty old vest over her head and handed Will back his red coat.

"Matches your cheeks today," she said. Then she tucked two of the daggers into her belt and the third away in her boot.

"I should have thanked you," she said. "You saved my life."

Will looked at her.

"I did what anyone would do."

"No, that's not true," said Much. "But if it was, you'd deserve a thank-you all the same."

"You're welcome," said Will. "Shall we go?"

Much turned and began picking her way back through the woods, with Will behind her. While she wasn't really angry anymore, she had still half hoped the boy would insist on waiting for her at the tree. She'd be far quieter on her own. Plus, if his presence had made her uncomfortable back when she was still a boy, it was doubly worse now that she was a girl.

As they walked through the trees, Much heard Rob's voice in her head chiding her for making such a bad decision. A rule of banditry—when you've escaped the enemy, you never return. You cut your losses and run. They'd walked into Sir Guy's trap once; it was a foolish outlaw who would walk into it a second time.

But it was that kind of thinking that Much was counting on. Surely, Sir Guy would abandon the camp once his trap had been sprung. He wouldn't wait around for stragglers to return. Would he?

The stars were up by the time they reached the camp. If they did have to make another sudden escape, at least the dark would work to their advantage.

The woods were alive with the sounds of creatures waking, but empty of the sounds of men. The hum of insects disturbed the otherwise peaceful silence. Although patches of upturned earth spoke of fighting, no bodies remained. Guy's soldiers must've taken their own with them.

As for the missing Merry Men, Much and Will found them lying in a shallow open grave dug just on the outskirts of the camp. The bodies of five or six men were heaped together in a tangle of bloody limbs. The bodies on top were at least several days old and already smelled. Despite the bloated purple faces, she recognized Gilbert the White Hand among the corpses, his eyes open and staring at nothing.

Will stood gazing at the pit for a long, long time.

"All these people," he said at last. "I tricked you all into robbing Guy in the first place."

"Will, you can't blame yourself for what Sir Guy did here. The Merry Men are bandits. We steal, and we do it at the risk of our own lives. Every day. This is about the life we choose—it's not about you."

She'd been about to suggest searching the rest of the camp for signs of Rob or John when she heard a moan coming from the far side. Will readied his sword, and the two of them crept cautiously toward the source of the sound.

A figure lay at the foot of the Horned and Hooded God.

A trail of blood led from where he'd fallen to the base of the Merry Men's statue. Their good-luck charm. But Stout lay prostrate beneath it, as if praying.

His shirtfront was soaked through with blood. It looked almost black in the dim moonlight. As Much and Will approached, his eyes fluttered open.

"You . . . you made it," he whispered. Much hadn't realized a man could bleed that way and still live.

"Where's John?" she said. "Where's Rob?"

Stout looked around, as if momentarily surprised at his whereabouts.

"Guy took them," he said. "Wants to hang them proper and in public . . . he said."

Much let out a breath she didn't realize she had been holding in.

"They're alive at least," said Will.

"Huh? That you, Scarlet?" said Stout.

"Where are the others?" said Much. "We found bodies, but not everyone's."

"Gilbert fought back. Got himself killed. Wat and the others . . . got put in irons."

"They'll be hanged, too," said Will.

"Please," said Stout. "Give me a drink of water. Thirsty."

Much leaned in close and grabbed the man by the collar. "You might as well beg the Horned God! You'd have a better chance of mercy from this statue than from me, you traitorous filth!"

Stout cried out in pain as she shook him, and then Will's hands were on hers. Slowly, he pried her fingers from Stout's collar.

Stout was weeping.

"Guy caught me out on the moors! Tortured me!" he was

saying. "Couldn't . . . had to do as he said. He set Crooked's Men loose on the farms. He's . . . he's mad."

Will went to one of the tents and came back with a waterskin.

"Here," he said, putting it to Stout's lips. "Have a drink."

More water spilled down the man's chin than made it into his mouth, but it seemed to calm him.

"What now?" said Will.

Much looked up at the sky. Stars blinked back at her from the heavens.

"In the morning, we finish burying the rest. We can't leave them to the animals in the forest."

She looked down at Stout's pallid face. His eyes were closed, and his breath came in shallow gasps. "And we'll make room for one more."

Will stayed up with Stout through the night, giving the man water when he asked for it and covering him with blankets when the air turned chill. Stout died in the early morning, just a few hours before dawn.

At one point, when Stout's cries had quieted and he'd finally drifted into unconsciousness, Much asked Will why.

"Why are you helping him?" she'd asked. "What do you owe Stout?"

"This isn't about Stout," Will had answered.

By the time dawn arrived, Much saw Will Scarlet as if for the first time. Before, he'd infuriated her and even fascinated her at times. *Scarlet.* She'd thought it such a childish name, a name chosen out of a desire for revenge. A reckless name for a boy on a dangerous quest.

But now she saw the name differently. It wasn't about the

blood he planned on spilling; it was about the blood that had already been spilled. All the deaths he felt responsible for. His name was his guilt.

She understood Will Scarlet at last, and in understanding, he broke her heart. Straight down the middle, cleaved in two.

TWENTY-TWO

Why do our plans always make my stomach hurt?
—MUCH THE MILLER'S DAUGHTER

The road out of Sherwood was a lonely trek today, and empty of even a passing farmer and his mule. But Will and Much found Bellwether just as they neared the edge of the forest. A true coward to her core, the mare had escaped the fighting back at the camp and fled along the South Road until she'd found a nice patch of thistles to munch.

Will was as happy to see her as he'd ever been. In many ways, she was all that was left of his old life, of the boy he used to be. As he scratched her neck and fed her thistles, he hid his face in her mane so that Much wouldn't see the tears that'd welled up in his eyes.

They rode Bellwether the rest of the way out of Sherwood and into Nottinghamshire. For fear of being recognized, they covered themselves with the cloaks from the old crone oak, and Will assured Much that at the first sign of trouble they could count on the mare to get them out of there, and fast. Whether they liked it or not.

When they got closer to civilization, they learned exactly why the road felt so barren.

They finally came across a peddler hurrying out of Nottingham, and he told a story that farmers had become refugees on their own land. Crooked's Men had turned marauders, and they'd done it with Sir Guy's blessing. They targeted any home that might have benefited from Guy's stolen silver and razed it to the ground. In just a few days, they'd cut a swath of carnage across Nottinghamshire. The sheriff was furious with Sir Guy, and the Horse Knight's actions had opened a deep rift between the two men. The sheriff set his soldiers after them, and they'd caught Guy and his bandit-mercenaries as they were marching out of Sherwood Forest, not a day back. The sheriff chased them all the way to Shackley Castle and was camped outside the castle walls even now, threatening a siege and demanding justice.

But the damage was done, and the lives of many people that Will and his companions had tried to help had been ruined.

Much and Will decided to stop along the side of the road and make camp on the far side of a hill, where their fire wouldn't be spotted. Much had managed to bag a hare on their way out of Sherwood, and that night they dined on roast rabbit as they pondered the enormous task ahead of them—how to save Rob and John.

"Rob would want us to escape," said Much. "Make for the North Country, maybe, and start fresh."

"Is that what he would do for you?" asked Will. "Would Rob leave you to hang?"

"No," said Much. "Not sober, he wouldn't. Even blind drunk he'd try a rescue, I think, but he'd surely get himself caught."

Will laughed. "Probably knock on the front door and challenge the whole castle to a duel."

"But he'd forget to wear pants!" Much joined in the laughter. Will had never noticed it before, but Much covered her mouth when she laughed, almost as if she were self-conscious of her smile. He didn't know why, but it charmed him.

It was strange, but now that he knew she was a girl, he noticed things about her that he hadn't before. Giveaways. Her eyes, for one. They were almond-shaped and pretty when she actually brushed her hair away so that you could see them. Her disguise, which had been so perfect up until yesterday, now seemed full of holes. Of course Much was a girl; it should have been obvious from the start.

"So," she said after they'd had a chance to recover from the image of a drunken Rob bellowing outside Guy's gate. "We won't abandon Rob and John. But what can we do? Can we use your secret passage to smuggle them out?"

"I wouldn't trust that way a second time," said Will. "Stout spent too long in Guy's custody. I'm sure he told them how we used it to get inside."

He pulled another piece of rabbit off the skewer. The grease dripped down his fingers, and the charred meat was overdone and tough to chew, but he was so hungry nothing had ever tasted so good.

"If we can get close enough, we might be able to get in the way we left," he said.

"The slop gate?"

Will nodded. "And that would put us near the cells. We're both small enough to fit, but the trouble would then be getting Rob and John out. They're too big to use the gate."

"And that's if we can get to the castle," said Much. "They say the sheriff's camped outside. We'll have to cross his lines unseen just to get close enough."

The Sheriff of Nottingham. Will wondered if he would find the opportunity to ask him why he'd thrown his lot in with men like Prince John and Sir Guy. Why he'd betrayed his best friend in the world, and if it was all worth it. But if he wasn't careful, Will would be asking as a hangman fitted a noose over his own head. This plan of theirs, such as it was, was foolhardy. But what choice was there?

"And that's it, then?" said Much. "We just march in and see what happens?"

"That's it," said Will. "And hope that we're small enough that no one pays us any mind."

Much stretched herself out on the other side of the fire and closed her eyes.

"Why do our plans always make my stomach hurt?" she said. "I think we'd have better odds with a drunken Rob at the door."

As they crossed Nottinghamshire the next morning, they saw firsthand the devastation wrought by Tom Crooked and his band of raiders. They followed a plume of smoke to a farmhouse on the outskirts of the county. Dead livestock littered the fields, needlessly slaughtered and left to rot out in the sun. From the road, they could see the charred remains of a farmhouse, little more than a pile of smoking timbers now. A man and his weeping wife were picking through the blackened embers, but there was little left to pick through. A young girl with soot-streaked cheeks stood watching, her face expressionless. The couple looked startled at first when they spotted Will and Much riding by on Bellwether, but they relaxed when they saw they were not marauders and went back to their fruitless search.

"Do you know them?" asked Will as they rode by.

"No," said Much. "They aren't anyone we helped."

Will shook his head. "These poor people probably never even heard of Rob and his Merry Men."

As they rode the rest of the day, the signs of ruin increased. Some homes had been spared, while others were utterly destroyed. This path of brutality might have started out as targeted retribution, but it had turned into a random, senseless rampage. But only homes on the farthest outreaches of the territory had been attacked, those farthest from the village of Nottingham and the law. Perhaps Sir Guy feared the sheriff after all.

As Shackley Castle came into view, they got a glimpse of why.

The road led up a small rise, and at the top you could look down on the wood and stone castle and its surrounding countryside. The Sheriff of Nottingham had camped his men in a ring around the fortress. The open green fields that in better times were used to host tourneys and festivals were now littered with tents and campfires. They'd blockaded the roads, and scores of armed men marched in drills within full view of the castle. The sheriff had isolated Sir Guy inside his stolen castle, and now he was letting him see his force. A clear message to surrender—or else.

That message had so far fallen upon deaf ears. The castle drawbridge remained shut up tight, the windows barred. The parapets smoked with cauldrons of burning pitch just waiting to be poured on those foolish enough to try to scale the walls. Archers lined the battlements. And above it all, the Horse Knight's silver and black stallion banner fluttered in the breeze.

Will had never seen Shackley House under siege, and never thought he would. Not since the Norman invasions of his great-grandfathers' times had war come to Shackley Castle, but Will couldn't help feeling some spark of satisfaction at seeing these two villains at each other's throats. His father had always said that ex-allies made the most dangerous enemies, and therefore you never joined with someone you couldn't trust with your whole heart. Will suspected that Guy and the sheriff were about to learn that lesson for themselves.

If not for Rob and John, Will would've been content to sit back and watch as Guy and the sheriff murdered each other. But his friends wouldn't be likely to last the night, much less a long siege. Guy wanted them dead for stealing his silver, and the sheriff had come here to hang bandits. He wouldn't discriminate between Merry Men and Crooked's Men. There were a few hundred people down there who wanted them dead, and only two up here who wanted them alive.

"What do we do now?" asked Much as she looked out over the throngs of armored men. "Ask if we can walk up and knock?"

"That depends on the sheriff's plans," said Will. "If we wait for the cover of night, we might be able to sneak across the lines. They won't be looking for people trying to get *into* the castle."

Will squinted at the formations of soldiers below.

"But I'd hate to be between that army and the castle walls when the sheriff decides to attack," he said. "They look like they're waiting for something."

"How can you tell?"

"Military strategy was one of my required lessons," he told her. "And the sheriff won't attack Shackley without siege weapons." He pointed to a line near the back of the camp, where men were hammering away, building wooden catapults, battering rams, and siege towers. "When he begins bringing those to the front, we know the attack's coming."

"Then we'd better move before that happens," said Much. "As soon as night falls. But just one thing."

"What is it?" Will asked.

"I need you to make me a promise. I need you to promise that we're going in there to rescue John and Rob. Not to kill Guy."

"Much, I—"

"Promise me, Will Scarlet, or I'll go in there alone!"

Will poked a stick into the fire, causing the coals to flame a bright orange. In the sparks and smoke, he saw Guy's face. The Horse Knight was sitting in his father's chair, laughing at him.

"You don't know your way around," Will said. "You'd walk in circles till dawn."

"Then you'd better make the promise."

Will looked at her for a long, hard moment. She meant it. She'd leave him right here and march in alone. The last time they'd been in that castle together, Will had risked all their lives to try to get his chance at Sir Guy. But some things had changed since then. Not his desire for revenge; that still burned, just not as hotly as before. What had changed was friendship. Those were his friends in there now, and he was done with seeing his friends die.

"I promise," he said. "This is a rescue mission only."

"Good," she said. "Then you can come with me."

"And Much?"

"Yes?"

"We'll get them out. I promise that, too."

TWENTY-THREE

No doubt Sir Guy wants them to stare at the hangman's noose for a while before being fitted for it.
—WILL SCARLET

The moon was little more than a fingernail sliver in the sky, and so their trip past the sheriff's camp was easier than expected. The night hid them well, and the soldiers were too busy hauling the siege equipment to the front of the line to be on the lookout for a pair of children sneaking toward Shackley Castle. The sheriff looked to be planning for a siege at dawn.

Will untied Bellwether, and they set out on foot across the plain. If they didn't return, at least she'd be free to roam. Will hoped she'd find a nice farmer somewhere who was averse to hunting, for both their sakes.

Once Will and Much had circled past the bustle of the sheriff's lines, they had to be more cautious. Sir Guy was bound to have men on the lookout for intruders. Watch fires burned brightly all along the wall, and so Will and Much had to trust in luck as they made their approach. The shadows had covered them well thus far, but the final few feet to the wall would be a dash, and they had to pray that the soldiers there were looking the other way, busy staring at the sheriff's army lining up against them.

Will held his breath until they reached the rocky incline that led up to the slop gate. But no alarm was raised; there were no cries in the night. As should have been expected, the climb up the slope was far harder than the climb down had been. The rocks were slick with the daily garbage, and Will thought it best not to imagine exactly what it was they were climbing through. The smell alone brought terrible pictures to mind.

They managed to scale the slope without incident, but once there they were still well out of reach of the gate. *Gate* was a generous word for the little wooden hatch some ten feet up the wall. It was purposefully out of reach of any man outside, and too small for most. That was where Much came in. She hiked herself on top of Will's shoulders until she could just reach the gate. With her knife, she pried open the hatch, which swung outward. Then, in a feat of remarkable balance, she tied her knife to the rope, turning it into an improvised grappling hook. She used her free hand to swing the hook over the gate's edge.

Again, luck played no small part in their adventure—the hall next to the slop gate was empty. Much pulled herself through the open hatch. Will followed, and after some grunting and groaning, he managed to squeeze his body through, though he landed with a rougher thud than she had. There was certainly no way that Rob, and especially John, would fit through there. They'd have to work out another means of escape.

But first things first—they needed to find their friends.

The slop gate deposited them near where they wanted to be, at the far end of a T-juncture that led upstairs at one end, down to the cells at the other. The last time, they'd been able to sneak into the cells unnoticed. Tonight, however, there was no alarm to lure the jailer away from his post, and they could already hear him down the hall, humming to himself.

Fortunately, they had devised an inspired plan for dealing with him. Much stepped into the hallway and shouted, "Hey, lard bottom!"

When the jailer came running, Will hit him with a stool. Then a crate. It took the pommel of his sword to finally knock the man unconscious. It seemed being thickheaded was a qualification for being a jailer in Guy's castle.

There was no need for Much's lockpicks as they now had the jailer's keys, so they dragged him into an empty cell and locked him in there. Then they started searching for John and Rob, beginning with the next cell over. One after another, they opened the doors, only to find each as empty as the last. When they reached the last door, Will felt a keen pang of disappointment. In his heart, he'd hoped they'd find Osbert still alive, but there was nothing but an empty straw mat. Their jailer had been guarding an empty dungeon.

Will said a prayer that old Osbert's soul was at peace.

"Where are they?" asked Will after a moment.

"We could ask the jailer when he wakes up in an hour or so," said Much.

"We can't wait that long."

Will tried to brush away the fear that they were too late. What if their friends had already been hanged? From the look on Much's face, she feared the same thing. Will had been forced to leave one friend to die in Sir Guy's custody; there was no way he was leaving two more.

Will examined the jailer's station for any clue as to their missing prisoners. The table was filthy with chicken scraps and dried puddles of spilled wine. But among the refuse was a piece of fresh parchment.

"Give me some light, will you?"

Much took a torch from its sconce and held it over the paper.

"What's it say?" she asked. Will didn't suppose she'd ever been taught to read. He made a note to himself to correct that if they both survived the night.

The paper was an official order stamped with Sir Guy's own signet ring. In lieu of a court trial, the Horse Knight had proclaimed the following criminals guilty of theft. Below the list, the jailer had made his own mark, a thick black X.

Will read on. After all the flowery legal wording was done, it came to the final, crushing judgment.

"The prisoners were moved into the courtyard stockades today, where they were to be given twenty lashes," he said. "They'll remain there tonight, and they'll be hanged at dawn. No doubt Sir Guy wants them to stare at the hangman's noose for a while before being fitted for it."

"How are we going to save them now?" asked Much.

Will crumpled up the paper and tossed it away. Rob and John had been whipped and beaten, but, worse, they were being kept in the courtyard, out in the open, under lock and key. It would take more than stealth to rescue them now.

They'd all been through too many struggles in such a short time to give up. And now Much was looking to Will for the next move. She had the same look in her eyes that Will had seen in Osbert's, the same look he sometimes saw in Rob's—like they were expecting something of him. She'd come all this way with him, and now she was waiting for him to devise something brilliant, as if he were the clever one of the pair. This orphan, a lost girl who'd so cleverly disguised herself all along . . .

A lost *girl.*

He had an idea, but it was one that relied heavily on luck and sheer bravado. Rob would love it, but he'd be the only one.

Will turned to Much. "We're going to save them, Much, and I know how. So here's what we are going to do, but I want to warn you, you're going to hate it. You're really going to hate it. . . ."

PART IV

FINALE

TWENTY-FOUR

One hanged man looks as good as another.
—Sir Guy of Gisborne

The easiest way to go unnoticed, Much had learned, was to act like you belonged. It took guts to look a courtyard guard in the eye and tell him that you were there to empty the prisoners' chamber pots. It took more than guts to tell him he could do the job himself if he didn't believe you. But perhaps unsurprisingly, this part of the plan didn't worry Much. She'd faced worse, and she had guts aplenty.

What was harder, more frightening, and, yes, *infuriating* was the dress.

Boys created suspicion, Will had said. Even serving boys, if they were caught skulking around the castle at night, would be detained and questioned. But a serving *girl*—a young kitchen maid, say, who'd drawn the unlucky straw of having to clean the privies late at night—well, she'd be allowed to pass without so much as a second thought.

Bloody Will Scarlet.

They'd found some dresses in a servants' closet just off the kitchen. Will said they kept them there in case one of the girls made a mess of herself during the dinner service. Can't have filthy servants at a royal feast. Finding one that fit her skinny little frame was more difficult, but in time they found one that wasn't too baggy, and they belted her in tight. A kerchief to cover her short-cut hair, and as they wiped the grime from her face, they revealed a fetching sprinkle of freckles across her cheeks and nose. Much the Miller's Son was suddenly transformed into a pretty young manor girl.

If anything, Will mused, he was worried that she might be a touch too pretty, and he hoped she didn't attract unwanted attention.

Too pretty? Much thought. Bloody stupid Will Scarlet.

But in the end, he'd been right. They borrowed the jailer's chamber pot (a particularly nasty piece of work), and with it Much strode defiantly into the courtyard, past the castle guards. An advantage of Guy using mercenaries as his guard was that there were always new men about, and they didn't have time to learn the faces of all the household staff. Another stroke of luck.

Much took a deep breath as she walked, and she took a moment to smooth down her skirt before she nearly tripped over it into the mud. Much the miller's daughter was so long forgotten she barely remembered how to even walk in these garments. Across the courtyard, Guy had erected a hangman's gallows, and in front of that was the stockade. John's and Rob's hands and heads were locked in tight, and their faces looked misshapen in the torchlight. At least, Much hoped it was just the torchlight. She knew they'd been whipped and beaten, but she was counting on them being well enough to still walk out of here. There would be no carrying Little John.

Chained against the wall behind them were the rest of the Merry Men—Wat and those who'd surrendered rather than fight. Not that Much blamed them. If they'd chosen to discover a bit of bravery during Guy's attack, they'd have ended up in that pit with Gilbert. Though doubtless they'd seen what Much now saw—there were enough nooses on those gallows for them all.

Much took a deep, calming breath. If she and Will succeeded, if they managed by this foolhardy plan of Will's to free the Merry Men and make it out of here alive, then her secret would be ruined forever. No one could look at Much in this dress and ever believe again that she was just a boy. It was nearly as terrifying a thought as facing Sir Guy himself, and walking through the courtyard dressed like that, she might as well have been naked.

But it was worth it if they could save John and Rob.

She'd just stepped out into the open when a horn sounded.

Much looked to the walls. Was that Will? Was that his signal? He'd said that he'd find a way to distract the guards so that Much could free the prisoners, but if that was him, then he'd timed it too soon.

But it wasn't Will. Someone was at the gate. There was a great groaning squeal as the giant wooden doors were pulled open. Beyond, Much could see a small company of mounted men, and at their head was the sheriff himself.

Much froze on the spot as another figure strode up behind her. Sir Guy was flanked by a small guard of his own, including Tom Crooked. They were all armored to their teeth, but their weapons were still sheathed. As Sir Guy passed her, he gave her a curious little nod. Perhaps he was trying to appear regal in front of the wide-eyed young kitchen maid. She would've liked to spit in his face, but instead she did her best bow and curtsy. It was an awkward and rather sad show.

Unfortunately, Sir Guy and his men crossed right between

her and the prisoners. Not that she could do anything to help them now, not with Guy and the sheriff right there. She was frozen, not sure where to go or what to do. She'd suddenly found herself standing mere feet from Sir Guy and the sheriff.

If Will was going to create a diversion, this was a good time.

"You wanted to see me?" asked the sheriff.

"Knock it off," said Guy. "You've got half of Nottingham sitting out there waiting to bury me! It's a hell of a way to treat a friend."

"It doesn't have to be this way," said the sheriff. "Hand over the bandits. Agree to pay restitution for the homes you destroyed. Then I'll take my half of Nottingham and go home."

"I'm not some poacher or pickpocket!" said Guy. "You don't have the authority to arrest me!"

The sheriff pulled a scroll from his belt.

"I've been given the authority. This is a decree signed by Prince John himself. I warned you that you would go too far, burning down homes and harboring fugitives."

The sheriff leaned in on his saddle and lowered his voice, but it was still loud enough for Much to hear.

"You're making him look bad," he said, smiling.

"Fine. Here are your bandits," said Guy, pointing to Rob and the rest. "They'll hang at dawn."

"Those are not the men I'm after, Guy," said the sheriff, pointing at Tom Crooked. "You let that lunatic and his thugs loose on my lands! The peasants are ready to revolt!"

"One hanged man looks as good as another," said Guy, with a smirk. "Good enough for the peasants, I should think."

"But not good enough for me," said the sheriff. "My terms

are simple, Sir Guy. I ride back to Nottingham with Tom Crooked and his men in chains and you pay for the damage you've wrought, or I will take this castle by force. You're outnumbered, and the walls of Shackley House won't save you. And no one will come to your aid. You've made too public a mess of things. I'm offering you a way to save your head."

Sir Guy smiled as he seemed to be considering this. Much began to wonder if the knight had truly and finally lost his mind.

"I'll await your answer before dawn," the sheriff said.

"You can have it now—" said Guy, stepping forward.

But he was cut off by a sudden shout from the wall. Two shapes were fighting up top. They struggled for a moment, then one fell screaming from the edge. As he did so, he grabbed hold of a large watch fire cauldron, pulling it over and raining fire down upon the stable beneath. At once, the stacks of straw took up the flame, spreading it to the wooden timbers.

Guy spun back around to the sheriff, his hand going for his sword.

"You rode in here under a banner of truce!" he shouted. "So you could send a sneak attack over the wall!"

With a shout, Guy charged toward the sheriff. Tom and the rest surged forward as well. The sheriff, looking totally bewildered, drew his own sword to defend himself.

Much understood what they didn't—there wasn't any sneak attack, at least not from the sheriff. Will had promised a distraction, and as the courtyard erupted into fighting, that was exactly what he'd delivered.

Then the sheriff's soldiers and Guy's mercenaries rushed toward each other with weapons drawn. Someone was shouting to close the gate, while another was shouting for water to douse the spreading fire. But smoke from the burning barn was already filling the air as the flames quickly spread. The courtyard was in chaos, and Much was standing in the middle of it. In a dress.

TWENTY-FIVE

Archers! Kill him!
—Sir Guy of Gisborne

There were ways to move around Shackley Castle without being seen, and in his years spent running from Nan and her paddle, Will had learned them all. One of his favorite places to hide had been the wall itself. Out the hallway window just past the kitchens there was a grinning gargoyle that one could use to climb to the drainage gutter. The gutter made the perfect makeshift ladder to take a nimble person all the way to the wall. Best of all, the gutter ran along the edge where the wall met the castle keep, and at night the shadows were so thick that anyone climbing it would be mostly invisible from prying eyes below.

Atop the wall, the watch fires still burned; few were manned. Everyone's attention was on the sheriff and his men at the gate. The archers were the problem. Will needed to get everyone's attention off the prisoners down there and onto him up here. But he needed to do so without getting stuck full of arrows.

Odds were he wouldn't make it out of here tonight, but if he could create an opening for Much, she just might be able to free Rob and John, and with a bit of luck, the three of them could escape in the confusion.

The gates were open; the sheriff sat mounted on his stallion as he faced off against Guy and his bandit-mercenaries. There wouldn't be a better opportunity.

Will had just reached the first watch fire when he heard a board squeak behind him. He turned in time to see a guard not two steps away, ax in hand. Not everyone, it seemed, was interested in the sheriff.

Will was outmatched in size, but he had one advantage the big fighter didn't—Will knew this castle. Milo and he would run laps around the battlements, earning curses from the watch guards. And it was dark up here despite the fires, and the guard was on uncertain footing.

Will pivoted away so that the watch fire was between him and the guard, making the man come to him. As the guard crossed in front of the burning brazier, he took a swing at Will, but Will parried it easily. The man wasn't balanced well enough to put much power into his blows, and Will leaped to the side and stuck out his boot, tripping the man as he took a follow-through step.

The ax slipped from the man's fingers, and he shouted in pain as his arm went into the fiery brazier. Instinctively, he jumped backward from the flame and right off the edge of the wall. But in his panic, he'd upended the brazier as well, and it toppled and then rolled off the ledge with him.

Will heard a crash below him, followed by a sharp whispering sound. He peered over the edge and saw that the whispers belonged to the greedy flames spreading over a heap of straw piled up against the stable. Milo's stable.

Already he could hear the whinnies of panic from within.

In minutes, the barn itself would catch and everything inside would burn.

Will had begun searching for a ladder down when he heard a voice call out from below.

"Archers! Kill him!" shouted Sir Guy as he pointed up at the wall. Will knew the Horse Knight wouldn't be able to identify him up here in the dark. But then, he didn't need an excuse to have him killed. An arrow landed in the wood just inches from his foot. Below him, the rest of Sir Guy's men were drawing their weapons and squaring off with the sheriff.

Will sheathed his sword before dropping to his stomach and crawling toward the edge overlooking the courtyard. Milo and he had once devised a dangerous game, wherein you would hang from the edge of the battlements and drop to roofs of various buildings below. It was quite a drop from the wall to the buildings, so you had to be careful when you landed that you didn't twist an ankle or, worse, tumble off entirely. But back when he and Milo had made a sport of it, the rooftops hadn't been on fire.

As he dangled his legs over the stable, he prayed that the same rising smoke that stung his eyes would make him a more difficult target for the archers. Below, the flames had crawled up the side of the stable and had begun licking the thatch roof. Once that caught, the rest would go up like tinder. Will kicked his legs as best as he could away from the flames and dropped.

He landed on the roof without slipping and quickly scrambled to the far side of the stable, the one that wasn't on fire. From there, it was a small jump to the ground below. The courtyard was in turmoil as the sheriff's men on horseback fought with Sir Guy's foot soldiers. There were a couple of riderless horses wandering about and several bodies lying on the ground riddled with arrows.

No one else seemed to have noticed him yet, so Will unlatched the door to the stable and, covering his mouth and nose against the growing smoke, ran inside. One by one he threw open the stalls, just barely dodging the panicked horses as they kicked their way free. By the time he'd freed them all, the stable was so thick with smoke that he couldn't see the exit. He ran blindly, following the horse stampede out to safety.

After taking a few moments to clear his lungs, Will saw what he'd wrought. What had been a chaotic battle a few minutes ago had been transformed into pure pandemonium. The courtyard was filling with smoke as spooked horses ran everywhere. Servants had given up on putting out the fire and were abandoning the castle and running for the gates, while Sir Guy's guards and the sheriff's soldiers still hacked away at each other. And somewhere, in all of that panic, was Much.

TWENTY-SIX

Robin Hood dares!
—ROBIN HOOD

All pretense of this being a sneaky rescue was gone. Much's only goal as she weaved her way through the courtyard was not to get trampled. If Will's aim had been to create a distraction, he'd succeeded. If his aim had also been to bring the castle down around their ears, he might well succeed at that, too.

With the smoke, the stampede, and the fighting soldiers, no one paid her any mind. By the time she reached the prisoners, the Merry Men were crying out for help even as they tried to cover their mouths against the smoke. But Wat and the rest of those scoundrels could wait. Much set about working on the locks to the stockade to free Rob and John.

"Who's it?" croaked John, squinting up at her. "Who're you, girl?"

"Stop talking, you giant oaf," said Much. "Save your strength."

"Eh?" said Rob, craning his neck to see. "Is that . . . Much?"

"You drunk, Rob?" said John. "This is a girl. Much is a boy!"

"Will you both shut up?" Much said. She couldn't focus on the lock with the two of them arguing.

"My Lord," gasped John. "It is Much! Why are you in a dress?"

"Much? Really?" another voice called, and she looked up to see Wat holding out his shackled wrists. "Throw us a pick there, boy! Er, girl . . ."

She bit back the choicest insults that sprang to mind and chose the best tool for her own job. Then she tossed the bag to the toothless outlaw. She felt the click of the tumblers moving, but the lock slipped and she had to take another breath to calm herself—her hands were shaking with excitement and fear and more than a little bit of anger. It was hard to focus on something as tiny as a lock when the world was literally burning down around you.

On the second try, it gave way, and she lifted the top of the stock, which was surprisingly heavy. But not for John Little. He threw off the wooden cuffs and let out a load moan as he straightened himself. His face was bloody, lips swollen and cracked.

"Much," he said. "You haven't got a sip of water, have you?"

She did. As John sucked gratefully on a waterskin, she freed Rob. He looked no better than John. Worse perhaps.

As Rob worked life back into his raw, chafed wrists, John handed him the drink.

"Wine?" asked Rob.

John shook his head.

"What kind of rescue is this?" asked Rob, but he drank anyway.

In the time it took Much to free John and Rob, Wat had picked the lock of every surviving Merry Man. Six in all. The man really had a talent for skulduggery.

But they weren't free yet. There was still an entire courtyard of men with swords between them and freedom. And the fire was spreading. If they didn't get out soon, they'd burn right along with the castle.

But the men didn't seem too concerned with that. They were all staring at her.

"So . . . are you . . . ," said Wat, his face in obvious pain from the mental acrobatics his brain was being forced to do just to comprehend what he was seeing. "Why are you wearing a dress?"

"I knew it all along!" said John.

"No, you didn't," said Rob. "But we'll discuss the dress later. Though it is a fetching color, Much—"

"Shut up," she said.

"But right now we need to clear a path out of here," Rob said, ignoring her.

At that moment, they spied a man on a white stallion. He was making for the gate, and Much recognized the shining gold badge across his chest.

"The sheriff!" she shouted, pointing.

"He'll do," said Rob, and he began climbing the gallows.

As the sheriff rode by, Rob swung from the gallows on a loose stretch of rope, his hands gripping the noose. He landed atop the horse, knocking the sheriff from his saddle.

The sheriff rolled to his knees and reached for his dagger.

"Who dares?" he asked as he struggled to stand.

"Robin Hood dares!" cried Rob. "Remember the name!"

Then he reared the charger up on its hind legs, and as the sheriff made a grab for him, one of the hooves caught him in the head. The sheriff fell back, knocked unconscious.

"Robin Hood!" Rob said, laughing. "Look at that, John. I'm beginning to like the sound of it!"

But Rob didn't see the large shape emerging from the smoke behind him, a man Much recognized at once—Tom Crooked himself.

Even with Rob on horseback, Crooked still had the reach he needed. He'd run Rob through before the man could blink. Much shouted a warning, but she was too far away to do anything about it.

John moved with a speed that belied his great bulk. As Crooked's sword swung, John's hand reached out and grabbed hold of Crooked's wrist. The murderous bandit snarled, the veins in his neck bulging as he fought to free his arm, but John had him now. With his other hand, John grabbed Crooked's shirtfront and lifted.

Tom Crooked screamed as he was hoisted high over John's head and then thrown, headfirst, into the wall.

"Eh?" said Rob, turning to see Crooked lying in a crumpled heap on the ground. "What're you all shouting about?"

"Tom . . . Crooked," breathed John.

"So?" said Rob. "Look at him. He's out cold. You really do worry like an old woman, Little John."

John gritted his teeth and muttered something awful about Rob's parentage; then the lot of them began making their way toward the gate.

Rob led the escape on his stolen charger, dodging fighting men and fleeing horses, while Much searched desperately for any sign of Will. Her stomach turned whenever they came across a new body on the ground, but John wouldn't let her stop long enough to check the dead. The inner buildings were already engulfed in flame, and the fire would soon spread to the main keep. Shackley Castle was going to burn to the ground. John wrapped one strong arm around Much and dragged her away from what would soon become an inferno.

By the time they reached the gate, most of the soldiers had given up the fight and were fleeing, too.

Outside, the servants who'd pulled themselves clear sat on the grass, coughing and gasping for breath or tending to their fellow wounded.

Much and John searched the faces of the survivors for Will, but he was nowhere to be found. If he wasn't here, then that meant he was still in there. Somewhere.

John grabbed Much just as she turned to run back to the gate.

"Where do you think you're going?" he asked.

"Will's still in there," she said. "I've got to find him!"

She saw the worry on his face as he looked past her to the castle. The entire night sky was aglow with flickering amber light. It looked like the end of the world.

Rob rode up on his big white horse, grinning from ear to ear.

"Now *that* is what I call a rescue!" he said.

"Will's gone missing," said John.

"Scarlet?" asked Rob, the smile slipping from his face.

"He's still in there somewhere, and John won't let me go!" Much hit the big man with her fists, but he didn't loosen his grip on her.

"I'll go," said Rob. "John, take the rest and make for the old crone oak in Sherwood. We don't want to stay here long enough for the sheriff's men to start asking questions."

"Rob, that thing's going to come down any moment!" said John, but Rob had already turned his horse around and started galloping toward the castle. He didn't make it twenty yards before there was a terrific cracking, the snapping of timber and the creaking of stone, and the front gate came crashing down in a hail of ash and smoke.

Even as far away as she was, Much could feel the wave of heat roll out from the collapse as a hot wind blew across her face.

Rob stopped his horse and stared. With the gate, a part of the stone wall had collapsed, creating a barricade of fire and stone. There was no way in now. And no way out.

John slung Much over his shoulder as she began screaming Will's name.

TWENTY-SEVEN

Wolfslayer.
—Sir Guy of Gisborne

Will's father often compared being in a battle to being lost in a heavy fog. It was why it was so important to have well-trained soldiers, because once on the battlefield, an undisciplined army would break down. Wars were unpredictable and battles were confusing, and in the end only discipline kept a force together.

Will had thought he understood what his father meant—until now. Lord Rodric hadn't been speaking in metaphor; he was being literal. In war, horses' hooves kicked up dirt, smoke billowed, and the air hung heavy with sweat and blood. The fog was a real, palpable thing that blinded you, and Guy's hired swords quickly lost their zeal for the fight and began fleeing.

He'd meant to create a distraction, but in doing so, he'd set fire to his father's house. Shackley burned around him as men fought and died.

For the briefest of moments, Will spotted Much in the fighting. John was pulling her toward the gate, but then Will's view was blocked by a wave of fighting men. They'd sensed what he already knew—if they stayed here much longer, they would all end up buried beneath the ruins of a burning castle.

The real battle had moved to the gate, where men pushed and shoved and battled their way to safety.

Will had just started to follow when a pained groan caught his attention. It came from a man lying several feet away, whom Will would have taken for dead if not for the pitiful moaning. His white cloak was stained with soot and mud, and the gold badge of his office lay broken at his side. Mark Brewer, the Sheriff of Nottingham, had a nasty bump on his forehead and seemed to be drifting in and out of consciousness.

It would be fitting, thought Will, for the sheriff to burn along with the house he betrayed.

The shouts were barely audible all around him, and the roar of the flames became a distant rumble as he stood over his onetime friend. The sheriff's eyes fluttered but did not open. Will bent down and scooped up the gold badge. The chain had snapped, and it was filthy with mud. In the end, this badge had been all Mark wanted.

Will tucked the badge away in his belt and hooked his arms underneath the sheriff's. The man was deadweight, and it took every bit of Will's remaining strength to drag him toward the gate. He'd crossed half the courtyard before he stumbled and fell. He was just pulling himself up again when he heard the sound of snapping timber and turned in time to see the gate come tumbling down in front of him. A shower of sparks and coals crashed over Will like a wave, singeing his hair and stinging his cheeks.

When the dust settled, Will found himself trapped inside the courtyard behind a wall of flame. The heat was nearly unbearable, and the smoke would soon choke out what little fresh air hadn't already been consumed by the fire. With a heave, Will took the sheriff once more in his arms and began dragging him back toward the main castle keep. Pieces of burning wood were falling off the battlements all around him, and more than once Will found his path blocked by flaming debris.

Eventually, he made it into the keep, where he slammed the door shut against the inferno outside.

It was mercifully cooler inside, and for a moment Will lay against the hard floor feeling the cold of the stone against his hot cheeks. He gasped for air like a fish on the shore, but he couldn't rest for long, because smoke was already billowing in through the windows, and down one hall he could see the flicker of orange light as the fire spread to the castle's interior. The main keep might have a solid stone foundation, but the wooden upper floors would burn just as easily as the outside walls did, and soon they'd come crashing down on his head. He needed to act before it was too late.

The sheriff was still only semiconscious, and for a second Will had actually feared for his life. But his chest was still moving, and he began to stir. Will didn't want to have come all this way only to have the man die now.

It was easier to drag the sheriff's weight along the castle floors than the courtyard mud, and Will found a way of supporting him on his shoulder that made the going a bit easier. Around to the rear of the castle he went, searching for the hidden storage room passage and, from there, the tunnel to safety.

The closet was undisturbed. And the tunnel disappeared into the damp blackness below. His plan was to drag the sheriff down into the tunnel and leave him there. If waking up alone in the dark caused him a few minutes of panic, then all the better. It was the least he deserved. But first he had to get him there without dropping the man on his head.

He left the sheriff moaning on the floor of the storage room as he searched for a length of rope. If he couldn't manage the ladder, Will would need something to lower him down with. It took him longer than he would have liked to find a bundle of rope long enough for the job. He was on his way back when the castle tower suddenly shook. A large section of burning wall had collapsed near enough for him to panic. Very soon now he'd be overtaken by heat and smoke.

As Will ran back down the hallway, a figure suddenly appeared in his path. His horsehide armor was scorched and blackened in places, and he had a long, wet cut across his jaw, but he still grinned when he saw Will.

"Wolfslayer," he said. "When I spotted you down there in the courtyard, dragging this miserable wretch away from the flames, I didn't believe it."

He gestured to the sheriff lying on the floor.

"I'd long suspected that you were out there somewhere, plotting against me, but I didn't expect to see you again like this—saving the man who betrayed you. How very Christian of you!"

"Not entirely," said Will. "I would have happily let *you* burn."

Guy let out a laugh. "Indeed! And I'll gladly do the same for you, but I think I'll run you through first!"

Will drew his sword as Guy moved toward him. This was the moment he'd waited for, but he was dead tired from dragging the sheriff's body through the halls and sick from inhaling all the smoke, and on his best day he was half the swordsman that the Horse Knight was said to be.

Sir Guy opened with a feint, which Will, exhausted as he was, fell for. He brought his sword up to block the blow that never came, leaving his side exposed. Guy's blade slashed along his back and shoulder, not cutting deeply, but still drawing blood.

Will, however, managed to get his sword around to block

Guy's next attack, a slash aimed at his head. Behind him, he could feel the heat of the flames as they consumed the hall. Smoke drifted up from between the floorboards. How long, Will wondered, before the whole thing gave way?

Once, Will would have been content to have the whole castle come down on both their heads. When his grief had been at its worst, he'd viewed his own life as a small price to pay for revenge. But that was before he'd come to know Rob and John. And Much, most of all.

Today Will Scarlet stood for the bright red fullness of life. Today he wanted to live.

He parried another of Guy's thrusts and managed to knock the big knight back a few steps with a slash of his own. But Guy was stronger and faster. Unless he made a mistake, it was just a matter of time.

The Horse Knight retreated as he regained his footing, and when he brought his sword up for another advance, a second figure stepped into the fray.

The sheriff was holding his head with one hand as he stumbled, groggily, into the hallway, blocking Sir Guy's path.

Sir Guy shouted a curse at the half-conscious sheriff and swung at him instead. The sword connected with a slash against the man's chest, but the sheriff's armor turned away the blade.

The sheriff cried out as he stumbled backward, and Will found his opening. The sheriff's fall brushed Guy's sword aside, and Will lunged. It was a move that went against all his training, a full-force stab that would leave him defenseless if he missed.

He didn't miss, but Guy swerved at the last instant, and Will's blade scraped along the Horse Knight's ribs instead of finding his heart.

Sir Guy cursed in pain, and Will fell onto his knees. Both lost their swords.

For a moment, their eyes met. There was an ominous creaking of wood as the floor shifted beneath their feet. Each of them had a split second to act—to decide. Will leaped toward the open passage door while Guy tried for the fallen blade.

Will landed hard on his stomach—he'd made it inside the passage, but in doing so, he'd had the air knocked out of him. He could barely roll over in time to see Guy standing in the hallway outside the door, his sword raised, the flames behind him lighting his grinning face like a demon.

The hallway floor gave way and Sir Guy disappeared, falling into the raging fire. Will heard a scream beneath the rumble of the falling wood, then nothing but the roar of the flames.

Wasting no time, Will shoved the sheriff into the open passageway. The man practically fell down the ladder, but Will didn't let up. Together they ran from the collapsing building, fleeing into the underground blackness of the dirt tunnel.

Down there the air was cooler, and the smell of burning wood was replaced with the sweet smell of earth. It was dark, and so they stumbled on blindly through the tunnel, eventually relying on their hands and knees to travel.

Once they were far enough from the blaze to feel safe, the two of them collapsed in exhaustion. There was nothing to hear down there but the sound of their own breathing.

Will had played this meeting out in his head a hundred times since the day Geoff was murdered. What would he say to the man who'd been a friend to his family for years, only to betray them in the end? In his fantasies, his daydreams, Will delivered such a speech as to make the sheriff burst into tears and beg for forgiveness. In others, he'd done away with words and used a sword. But if he'd really wanted the sheriff dead, he could've left him back in the burning castle. And as for the power of his wounding words, well, he really couldn't think of anything to say.

The sheriff prided himself on being practical, a survivor. But what the last few months had revealed about him was this—he was weak. Too weak to stand up to Prince John. Too weak to control Sir Guy, until he was forced to by the threat of a peasant revolt on his own lands. He might not have meant for Geoff to die, but by bringing Guy's mercenaries into the castle, he'd been responsible. Let him live with that for the rest of his life. Let him try to control Nottinghamshire now that the people saw him for the puppet he really was. Let him wonder at the boy who saved his life this day, and what a small, cowardly man such as him could have possibly done to deserve it.

Finally, the sheriff spoke.

"Who are you?" he asked, his voice hoarse and full of pain.

"A ghost," answered Will. Then he stood and began walking again, feeling his way through the dark.

"Wait," called the sheriff. "My leg's hurt. I can't go as fast as you!"

Will didn't answer, and he didn't slow down. He stumbled out of the underworld and left the sheriff alone in the dark behind him.

TWENTY-EIGHT

We've all got pasts. It's what you are now that counts.
And what you do.
—Robin Hood

John had carried Much throughout most of the journey to Sherwood. She was ashamed, looking back on it. John had spent days locked up in the stocks, he'd been beaten and whipped, and yet there he was, carrying her like she was some infant girl. Even after she'd stopped fighting him, after she'd given up the thought of running into the burning castle, he still carried her. When she'd buried her head into his big chest and cried so softly that only he could hear, he carried her.

When they reached the boundary of Sherwood Forest, John finally let Much walk on her own, but he kept his eyes on her. Nine Merry Men made it out of Shackley Castle; only one had been left behind.

Will Scarlet, bloody stupid Will Scarlet, was dead.

The old camp was no longer safe, so they made their way deeper into the forest, to the old crone oak. By the time they reached it, the men were asleep on their feet, and they collapsed at the foot of the tall tree, exhausted. After a rest, Wat and a couple of the others went to fetch water while Rob and John set about making plans. They needed weapons, money, and food. Will had been carrying the coin purse they'd taken from the hidden cache, but if Rob was angry about their secret stash being looted, he didn't say anything.

Much craved solitude, but John wouldn't let her wander far from his sight. He worried that some of Crooked's Men might have fled back to Sherwood after the fighting had turned against them, and he didn't want anyone walking these woods alone. Much was too tired to argue.

She found a tree to climb instead. Despite the stupidly awkward dress, she climbed one she'd been up in before, when John had first shown her the old crone oak. It was a tall fir with enough cover to hide one from below but a good view of the forest floor in all directions. She'd spotted it almost immediately. Near the top, she found her old perch. Carved into the trunk was a sun and a moon, for father and daughter. She would've added a third, a star, but she'd lost all her knives.

She stayed up there the rest of the day, until the smell of cooking meat and a rumbling stomach lured her back down.

Wat had caught a brace of squirrels and was roasting them over a crackling fire. The men were drinking fresh water they'd hauled back in their caps—not a pleasant thought to touch Wat Crabstaff's cap, much less drink from it, but she was thirsty.

John and Rob were still bickering over their next course of action.

"We need weapons," John was saying. "What are we going to do if we run into Crooked's Men? Wave?"

"You'll just uproot a tree and swat them with it," said Rob. "Isn't that what you're used to fighting with anyway?"

John threw up his hands.

"We'll find weapons," said Rob. "But let's take a day or two to rest first. If Wat can do a little more hunting—"

"I almost had a rabbit, but he nipped me on the thumb," said Wat, showing everyone the swollen bite. "Might turn rabid now."

"If Wat can find us food before he turns rabid," Rob continued, "we can get our strength back, and then, in a day or two, we hit the South Road. See if we can't convince some kindly travelers to part with their silver."

"And how do we do that without weapons?" asked John.

"That's how we get the weapons!" shouted Rob, his patience gone at long last. "It's not like Herne the Hunter or some woodland spirit is going to appear with a box of money! We have to steal it! That's what we do—we steal things!"

Rob took a breath as John mumbled something too quietly to hear.

"In the meantime, we'll have to make do with clubs and throwing stones," said Rob. "You can handle that, can't you, John?"

The men's bickering eventually faded into a low roar in the back of her brain, and Much stared at the fire and remembered something Will had said to her. He'd told her that there was a time when it was necessary to become someone else, as he had. As she had. She'd been Much the miller's son to protect Marianna the miller's daughter, but what use was protecting yourself when you were already wounded near to dying? Who was she hiding from now?

"John," she said, but the big man was too busy arguing with Rob to hear her.

"John!" She shouted this time. Her voice echoed out among the trees.

"God's blood, what is it?" he asked. "You're bound to wake the dead!"

Everyone else had gone quiet. Rob looked at her, his eyes curious.

"Yes?" said Rob. "You have something to say, Much?"

"I need to tell you something," she said. "About who I really am."

"You are Much," said Rob. "You are a thief and a ne'er-do-well and a proud member of the Merry Men. Who you were before doesn't matter. Whether you are Much the boy or Much the girl, it doesn't matter. Not to us."

"Matters a bit to me," said Wat.

"Shut up, Wat," said John. "What Rob's saying, lad—er, girl—is that we all of us were once something different than we are now. You think Rob was christened Rob the Drunk? Or Robin Hood, for that matter?"

"We've all got pasts," said Rob. "It's what you are now that counts. And what you do."

Much nodded. She'd been afraid of her secret so long that it was hard to let go of that fear. Especially when her heart was already pained with grief.

"Besides," said John, "I always knew you were really a girl."

"No you didn't," said Rob.

"Hey," interrupted Wat, sitting suddenly upright. "You hear something? Something out there, I mean?"

Rob gestured for quiet as they listened for something amiss in the night sounds, but all Much could hear was the buzz of insects and the crackle of their fire. She squinted against the blackness, but the wall of trees was impenetrable.

"Sounded like someone calling," whispered Wat. "I swear."

They were at a disadvantage. It was night already, and in the dark the glow of their fire would be visible to anyone approaching. Much and her companions wouldn't be able to see farther than twenty yards into the trees. They'd been too tired to set up a lookout, and anyone could be out there now.

"There," said Wat. "There it was again!"

That time Much heard it, too. A voice calling out.

"Crooked's Men?" asked John.

"They wouldn't let us know they were coming," said Rob. "They'd just come. With swords."

The voice called out again. This time Much could make out names. *Rob, John . . . Much.*

Much bolted to her feet and ran for the trees, ignoring Rob's orders to wait. She burst through the stinging branches and tripped over roots hidden in the dark, nearly breaking her ankle in the process, but she got back up and kept running. The voice was getting closer, and soon she could see a shape stumbling through the trees, heading for the glow of their campfire.

She called his name and he answered her, and when she bounded out of the brush, he wrapped her in a great hug.

"I thought you were dead," she whispered.

"Nearly," he answered.

Then he loosened his hold on her, and she looked up into his soot-stained face. His eyes caught the firelight. Two tiny orange specks in the dark.

"I thought I wouldn't see you again," he said.

"Will . . . ," Much began.

He leaned close.

"Hey!" a voice called out from behind them suddenly.

Wat appeared out of the trees, pointing. "Will Scarlet's alive!" he shouted. "And he's filthy!"

TWENTY-NINE

We'll never be slaves or masters again. Merry Men all!
—WILL SCARLET

"Up before me? That's a break in tradition," said Rob, yawning and stretching as he stumbled over to the edge of camp.

Will was seated on a fallen log, watching the sun come up between the trees. He made room for the bandit leader—for that's what he was now—and tried to take a deep breath of morning air. It ended in a painful cough.

Rob gave him a light pat on the back. "You all right?"

Will nodded as he rubbed at his sore chest.

"You swallowed a good deal of smoke in the fire yesterday, I'd imagine. Your lungs will hurt for a couple of days, but you'll feel better."

"I'm not up before you," said Will, clearing his throat.

"What's that?"

"I'm not up before you. I just never went to sleep."

Will had spent part of the night tossing and turning on the hard ground. Long after the rest of the band had given over to exhaustion, Will found himself unable to sleep. At first he was frustrated, but soon he just accepted it and lay there staring up at the stars. Once the fire had burned low, he found a fallen log and spent the night there, alone with his thoughts.

Rob scratched at his beard. "Was it John's snoring that kept you awake? Some nights I want to plug his mouth with his socks, I swear."

"No, I was just thinking about everything that happened," said Will. "You know, when I lived back at the castle, I used to begin every morning the same. Same breakfast, my clothes laid out the same way. Ever since I came to Sherwood, I don't think I've woken up in the same place twice."

Rob looked at him. "They make it a habit of setting out clothes for steward's sons back at Shackley?"

Will shook his head. "I'm not a steward's son. I'm—"

"I know who you are," said Rob. "I've known all along."

Will looked up at Rob. In the morning light, his eyes almost shone. So unlike the bloodshot eyes he'd first seen in that tent these many weeks ago.

"Word travels, and I caught wind of a story that Lady Katherine and her son were on the run and that they might be traveling separately for the coast. I think Gilbert had it guessed correctly, too."

"Gilbert knew?" asked Will. He had been so careful in his story, and here these men knew all along.

"You were trouble from the start, and your story about the treasure was the only thing that kept you alive."

Will still couldn't believe that the secret he'd been so careful in keeping had been so useless. He felt foolish. Childish.

Rob must've seen the look on his face. "Don't go berating yourself because a few of us sussed out your secret. Truth is, in the end, it doesn't matter. It's not about who you were, it's about who you proved yourself to be, Will Scarlet."

But that was just the problem. Will didn't have any idea

who that person was. Geoff had talked about Will someday proving his mettle, but what had he proven to be?

"Last night, every time I closed my eyes, I just kept seeing the things I did these last few weeks. Over and over again. Decisions I've made. People that are gone. I feel . . . lost, Rob."

"Aren't we all?" said Rob with a sigh. "Look around you. Much the Miller's Son, who's really, it turns out, a girl—and before you ask, no, I didn't see that coming—Wat the fool, John, who's determined to be father to the whole world, and Rob the Drunk with illusions of greatness! Aren't we all a little lost, Will? But isn't that why we're all together?"

He put a hand on Will's shoulder. "Tell me true—do you want to go back to your old life? Do you want to go across the sea and rejoin your family there? Wait for King Richard and your father to return so that you all can rebuild? Because I can help you get there, if that's your wish."

Will thought about it. But for so long he'd had one thought only—to get revenge on Sir Guy. He hadn't seen clearly beyond that bright red revenge. He understood now just what a dangerous path he'd been on, and how close he'd come to burning away what was good in him just to get vengeance on Guy. But little by little, something else had taken the place of all that hate. Something that lived right here with these people.

His heart ached when he thought of his mother worrying about him. And he longed to see his father free again. But though they were his family, this was his home now. He'd burned his old one to the ground long before he'd set fire to Shackley Castle.

"No," he said, at last. "I don't want to go back. But I'd like to get a message to my mother, if such a thing could be arranged."

Rob nodded. "I know a man who could deliver a message.

A pirate and scoundrel, but he makes regular trips to the Continent, and he owes me a favor or two. And he's as illiterate as a stump, so your letter would be safe with him."

Rob extended his hand. "Since you'll be staying awhile, let me, officially, welcome you, Will Scarlet, to our merry band!"

Will took Rob's hand. "We'll never be slaves or masters again. Merry Men all!"

Then Rob stood and dusted off his pants. It was a useless gesture, as one layer of grime only had another beneath it.

"Wat was right—we really are a filthy bunch," he said, waving away the cloud of dust. "Let's go wake the rest of those good-for-nothing outlaws. There's work to be done, and I don't doubt someone will try and kill us before the day is through!"

EPILOGUE

The sheriff stared at the stack of notices before him. How long had Leopold been waiting for his signature on these? His manservant had been hovering outside his door all morning, and if the sheriff tried to leave his office with the papers unsigned, Leopold would follow him to his rooms, quill and ink in hand. His persistence was infuriating.

"How are the preparations coming for the new keep?" the sheriff called out.

Leopold stepped into the room. "The stonemason's waiting to be paid. All the labor's in place."

"Why haven't we paid the stonemason yet?"

"Don't have any money."

The sheriff looked up from the unsigned stack. "I'm bleeding Nottingham dry as it is. How can we not have any money?"

"That's just it," said Leopold. "Those taxes are all going to Prince John's war chest. Our coffers are near empty."

The sheriff rubbed his temple where a spike of pain threatened to split his skull in two. "Lackland's taxes . . . Fine. Effective immediately, a new local surcharge on all goods and services produced within Nottinghamshire for purposes of maintaining security of the realm."

Leopold nodded. "How much of a surcharge?"

"Whatever it takes to build the bloody keep! I'll be Prince John's enforcer, if that's what it takes, but I won't do it sitting inside a wooden tinderbox. I want stone walls between me and the . . . unsavory elements that have cropped up as of late."

"The people won't love you for this."

"I don't need them to love me. I need a stone castle."

Leopold walked over to the edge of the sheriff's desk. He said nothing, but he drummed his hand on the table.

"What?" asked the sheriff.

"The notices, my lord," answered Leopold. "They need to go out today."

The sheriff gestured to the papers. "You have a real interest in this one, don't you?"

"As should you, my lord. The people are talking. Makes you look weak."

With a curse, the sheriff snatched up the quill on his desk and stabbed it into the inkpot. Then he began scrawling his name across each paper, careless of the splatters and smudges he was leaving behind.

"One hundred silver?" said the sheriff as he signed. "Where are we going to get one hundred silver?"

"Surcharge for the security of the shire," Leopold answered, with a wry grin.

"*Reward,*" said the sheriff, reading the last paper aloud. "*For information leading to the capture or killing of the outlaw Robin Hood.*"

"We'll have his head by the end of the week," said Leopold, taking up the signed notices.

"We'll see," answered the sheriff.

"Are you sure you don't want to post rewards for the rest of his band? That Little John fellow. And the boy . . ."

"Robin Hood only," said the sheriff quickly. "We get the leader, and the rest will disappear into Sherwood with the other vermin."

Leopold appeared ready to argue, but a look changed his mind. The sheriff had taught him the limits of his patience, and he had reached them today.

Leopold left with the reward notices tucked under his arm, and the sheriff sighed and sat back in his chair. Such a nice chair. It was once his favorite thing about his chamber. He'd gotten it from a true craftsman, an Italian woodworker who'd tried to set up shop in Nottingham. Fine cherrywood base, a supple leather cushion and headrest. The man had worked olive oil into the leather to make it as soft as cloth. In the end, he'd been forced to move on from Nottingham because the locals couldn't afford his goods. He'd traveled south to sell his kingly wares to more kingly folk.

The sheriff doubted that even the most well-born lords had such an exquisite piece of furniture. But what once had been a symbol of luxury and achievement now felt like a prison bench.

When he was sure Leopold was gone, the sheriff opened his desk drawer and removed two items. The first was a piece of paper, sealed with Sir Guy's own signet ring. It was a confession, made by a prisoner called Stout. In it, he named the names of his band of outlaws, the ones who'd stolen into Shackley Castle and made off with Guy's silver. The sheriff began reading the names to himself.

Robin Hood and his Merry Men . . .

The second item had arrived only yesterday. It was a plainly wrapped package, and there was no note or mark of any sort. The man who'd delivered it had been paid a halfpenny by a stranger to see it safely to the sheriff himself.

Intrigued, the sheriff had opened it, but seeing the contents, he'd put it in his drawer. He hadn't touched it since.

Little John . . . Much the Miller's Son . . .

He opened the package and looked down at it. A golden sheriff's badge of office, mud-covered and broken. It stank of charred wood.

. . . and Will Scarlet.

A grand royal carriage rolled through Sherwood on a fine spring day. The sun baked the earth by midday, as summer was near, but the cool shade of the tall poplar trees spared travelers from the worst of it. It was an odd sight for these times, such a lavish carriage using these dangerous roads. The ivory lace curtains drawn across the windows would fetch a tidy sum by themselves. And the ornate door handles (could they be real silver?) were freshly polished. With such ostentatious wealth on the outside, one could only imagine what riches were hidden within.

All the stranger to see such a carriage with only a pair of guards riding up top for protection.

As they passed beneath an overhang of leafy branches, the quiet stillness of the forest was broken by a shrill birdcall echoing from the trees above. Within a few seconds, another call seemed to answer it. But the second birdcall sounded, if such a thing were possible, to be in the form of a question. Then the first call repeated itself, only it sounded louder and even sterner than before.

As the guards riding on the carriage listened to this curious exchange of bird argument, they tightened their grips on their weapons and scanned the trees. One of them knocked lightly on the carriage door and was answered by the sounds of rustling and whispered voices within.

By the fourth birdcall, the outlaws appeared. Two men stepped out of the trees several yards ahead of the carriage. One was tall, taller than most, and hefted a long quarterstaff in his hands. The black-bearded other fellow had a sturdy English longbow at the ready.

"Good afternoon!" called the bowman. "I don't suppose you gentlemen have seen the notorious outlaw Robin Hood on your travels? I hear there's quite a reward for the man's capture."

The carriage slowed to a stop. The older of the two guards drew his broadsword.

"Aye, I've heard that, too," he said, grinning. "And I'm looking forward to my share!"

With that, the guard knocked once more on the carriage, and the sounds of movement increased. But they quickly gave way to curses, and when the guard glanced back at the doors, he saw that someone had slid two wooden poles through the handles, barring them closed from the outside. Whoever was within the carriage was trapped.

The guard quickly spotted the culprits, a short-haired girl and a boy in a scarlet coat. The young man's coat of red seemed particularly out of place among the greens and browns of these bandits, but he wore it with pride. In one hand, he held a sword; in the other, an unlit torch. While the guards' attention had been on the men, he and his companion had snuck up from behind, barring the doors tight.

"It would've been awfully disappointing to open up that carriage and find five or six armed men waiting for us inside," said the boy in scarlet.

The guard spat at the ground, but he lowered his sword and

motioned for his companion to do the same. The men inside began hacking away at the doors, trying in vain to free themselves.

"I wouldn't do that if I were you," called the girl. She produced a flint from her pocket and struck it next to her companion's oil-soaked torch. It flared to life at once.

"Tell the men inside to stop their fussing or we'll set fire to the carriage," said the bowman. "Cook them alive."

The guard eyed them suspiciously. "If you are Robin Hood, there are tales about him. They say he treats men mercifully. He wouldn't do such a thing."

"Who's to say I'm the real Robin Hood?" asked the bowman as he nocked an arrow. "And who's to say all the tales are true?"

The guard banged once more on the carriage. "Hey, knock it off in there!" he shouted.

The sounds of struggle quieted down.

"That's better," the bowman began, but before he could finish, the guard grabbed the reins and gave the horses the lash. The carriage suddenly lurched forward and began barreling toward the bowman and his big companion. The two managed to jump out of the path and narrowly escaped the hooves of the charging horses.

As the carriage careened down the road, the bowman turned to his two young companions.

"I told you to block the wheels!" he shouted.

"No you didn't," answered the girl.

"Yes I did! I whistled the call for *Block their wheels!*"

"No," answered the girl, folding her arms across her chest. "You gave the call for *Let's call it a day and eat lunch.*"

"What?" asked the bowman.

"You really need to learn the calls, Rob," said the boy in scarlet.

The bowman looked to his big companion for help, but the man only shook his head.

"Learn the calls." The big man shrugged.

"Bah," answered the bowman. "I know the calls. It's all of you that need to practice—"

The bowman was interrupted once again, this time by the sound of something large crashing.

They looked up to see that the fleeing carriage had come loose from the buckboard and turned over in the dirt road. The two guards glanced over their shoulders but didn't stop. They kept whipping their horses and disappeared down the road in their newly converted two-wheel wagon.

Moans and groans of pain came from within the wrecked carriage.

The bowman gave the two young outlaws a curious look.

"We did pull the carriage pin," the boy in scarlet said as the girl held up a long wooden pin.

The bowman grinned, and the big man laughed.

"Well, then," said the bowman. "Let's go relieve some of the sheriff's finest of their coin purses!"

Then the four of them walked over to the ruined carriage. One began singing a raucous song, and the other three quickly joined in. The lyrics were coarse and not fit for proper ears, but mostly they had to do with the Sheriff of Nottingham being kin to a braying ass.

By the end of the afternoon, they'd taught the captured guards every verse.

ACKNOWLEDGMENTS

A finished book is always the work of a team, a group of Merry Persons, if you will. Despite the fear that I will leave out far too many, the following thank-yous are due:

To my amazing editor, Michele Burke, for all of her insights, her patience, and her constant support.

To assistant editor Jeremy Medina, who helped us immensely before heading off on adventures of his own (good luck, sir!).

To my longtime friend and agent, Kate Schafer Testerman, who's always there to talk it out, no matter how neurotic and writerly the question is.

To publicists Mary Van Akin and Dominique Cimina, who work tirelessly to get good books into the hands of good people, and to all the folks at Knopf who've made me feel at home for the last six years.

To the terrific Random House sales-rep team for having such faith in Will and his dastardly compatriots.

To my son, Willem, the real Will in my life and the reason I do all this.

And lastly to my first-reader and wife, Alisha, who didn't know she was getting an author when she married me but, I think, has adjusted nicely regardless.

AUTHOR'S NOTE
THE REAL ROBIN HOOD

A question that some of you may be asking yourselves at the end of this tale is "But is this the *real* Robin Hood story?"

Well, as it reads on the copyright page, this is a work of fiction. What's more, this is a work of fiction based upon a legend, which is itself a work of fiction. And while there is some evidence that there may have indeed once been a bandit named Robin Hood, I'm just not all that interested in that guy. I'm interested in Robin Hood the legend. So much so that I decided to write a book about him.

I will admit I was intimidated at first. Tackling such an iconic figure as Robin Hood invites comparison. What if I got him wrong? But I quickly discovered in my research that the character of Robin Hood had changed drastically over the centuries. The more I looked, the more Robins I found scattered throughout history.

Some of the earliest versions of Robin were nothing like the good-natured, green-tights-wearing hero that exists in popular culture today. Robin Hood tales from the fourteenth century portrayed the bandit as a freeman who robbed from the rich—and gave to himself! Later versions introduced the idea of Robin as more of a revolutionary hero, fighting a corrupt and tyrannical government. But it wasn't until the sixteenth century, when certain people were less comfortable with the idea of such an antiestablishment hero, that Robin was recast as a displaced nobleman, a bandit by necessity, yet still loyal to good King Richard.

All this research filled me with a Robin-like sense of bravado—a swashbuckling derring-do. I was free to do whatever I wanted! I could add my voice to the tale without worrying about tarnishing the definitive version *because there was no definitive version*.

There was only one problem: The more I read about Robin, the less I saw him as my hero. The quality that I connected to in so many of the stories was the world-weariness of the outlaw leader, and world-weariness is just not a strong selling point in the world of middle-grade fiction.

But I still had a story I wanted to tell. My research had given me permission (or so I felt) to tell it as I saw fit, but who would tell it for me? If not Robin, then who?

Enter Will Scarlet. He was one of Robin's core Merry Men, and yet I'd never really had a strong sense of the character other than liking the name. And just as history had given us multiple Robins, there were half again as many different Wills. Scarlet-clad dandy, vengeance-driven widower, even Robin's young cousin—these have all been Will Scarlet at one time or another. Unlike, say, Little John, whose very name conjures up a specific and archetypal image of the gentle giant, the character of Will Scarlet has always been something of a blank slate. He shifted and molded himself to fit the needs of the particular Robin of the day, without much of a story himself. Poor guy.

Which is where it all clicked for me, where my mind started to race with possibilities. My Will could be young. There would be no world-weariness about him—in fact, he would just now be discovering his world. His journey from sheltered innocent to fighter for social justice would be the catalyst that started a legend. He could turn a drunken outlaw into a hero, by finding the hero in himself.

In the end, it's up to you to decide if I succeeded, but I am happy that I found my Will. And I'm pleased that I could, with my little book, contribute to a legend that has been in the telling for seven hundred years or more. I got to add another Robin, another Much, another Little John, another Sheriff and, best of all, another Will Scarlet to the mix.

So back to our original question: Is this the real Robin Hood? Maybe. I doubt it. But I guess he could be. I think the mysterious longbowman of the book's epilogue puts it best:

"Who's to say I'm the real Robin Hood? . . . . And who's to say all the tales are true?"

Matthew Cody
New York City,
October 8, 2013